continued . . .

MAR 2012

OTHER NOVELS BY LYNN VIEHL

The Kyndred Series

Shadowlight
Dreamveil
Frostfire
Nightshine

The Darkyn Series

If Angels Burn
Private Demon
Dark Need
Night Lost
Evermore
Twilight Fall
Stay the Night

NIGHTBORN

LORDS OF THE DARKYN

Lynn Viehl

A SIGNET SELECT BOOK

SIGNET SELECT
Published by New American Library, a division of
Penguin Group (USA) Inc., 375 Hudson Street,
New York, New York 10014, USA
Penguin Group (Canada), 90 Eglinton Avenue East, Suite 700, Toronto,
Ontario M4P 2Y3, Canada (a division of Pearson Penguin Canada Inc.)
Penguin Books Ltd., 80 Strand, London WC2R 0RL, England
Penguin Ireland, 25 St. Stephen's Green, Dublin 2,
Ireland (a division of Penguin Books Ltd.)
Penguin Group (Australia), 250 Camberwell Road, Camberwell, Victoria 3124,
Australia (a division of Pearson Australia Group Pty. Ltd.)
Penguin Books India Pvt. Ltd., 11 Community Centre, Panchsheel Park,
New Delhi - 110 017, India
Penguin Group (NZ), 67 Apollo Drive, Rosedale, Auckland 0632,
New Zealand (a division of Pearson New Zealand Ltd.)
Penguin Books (South Africa) (Pty.) Ltd., 24 Sturdee Avenue,
Rosebank, Johannesburg 2196, South Africa

Penguin Books Ltd., Registered Offices:
80 Strand, London WC2R 0RL, England

First published by Signet Select, an imprint of New American Library,
a division of Penguin Group (USA) Inc.

First Printing, March 2012
10   9   8   7   6   5   4   3   2   1

PUBLISHER'S NOTE
This is a work of fiction. Names, characters, places, and incidents either are the
product of the author's imagination or are used fictitiously, and any resemblance
to actual persons, living or dead, business establishments, events, or locales is
entirely coincidental.

    The publisher does not have any control over and does not assume any re-
sponsibility for author or third-party Web sites or their content.

For Marshall Mathers,
with respect and thanks
for the music
and the hand.

Every night and every morn
Some to misery are born,
Every morn and every night
Some are born to sweet delight.
Some are born to sweet delight,
Some are born to endless night.

—William Blake, "Auguries of Innocence"

October 12, 1307
Castillo de Loarre
Aragon, Spain

A shout outside the barbican tower jerked Brother Frémis from his contemplation of the insides of his eyelids. He fumbled for the candle, finding only a cold stub, and entreated Saint Ambrose for patience as he stretched his stiff arm to take down the only torch left burning. The sputtering flame provided just enough light for him to see his way down the narrow stone steps to the portcullis. There he peered through the oilette of an old arrow loop in the stone.

Seven men on horseback waited just outside the iron gate. All had dressed in dark hoods and plain, rough garb, and appeared at first glance to be nothing more than a group of pilgrims. Yet each man's cloak only partially concealed the two-handed sword he carried, and did nothing in the slightest to disguise his mount. Frémis, who in his misbegotten youth had been a stable boy, knew horses.

Pilgrims did not travel by means of battle destriers. Killers did.

"Who are you?" he called out in Spanish. "Why do you come here?" When they didn't answer, he repeated himself in French.

"God's work," an amused voice replied in the same. "Raise the gate, brother."

No canny siege master would attack the *castillo*; all knew that King Sancho had given it to the Church only after everything of value had been removed from its walls. Nor would a band of Moorish raiders attempt to take refuge here or anywhere in Aragon; once sighted they would have been pursued by the road patrols until their mounts dropped dead of exhaustion.

Besides that, what manner of God's work had to be attended to after midnight? Even by the French?

"Brother?"

"Come back at dawn," Frémis blurted out. "You may apply to the abbot after matins."

One of the men dismounted and strode up to the gate. He did not snarl threats or brandish his sword, but simply stood there.

"There is no time for niceties." His voice changed. "Raise the gate."

Pain jabbed inside Frémis's head, and he cringed. "Our order follows the path of Christ. We have nothing of value but the purity of our souls."

A harsh laugh rang out. "Then you are infinitely wealthy, little monk."

As the man pushed back his hood from his dark, handsome face, the scent of warm black cherries teased Frémis's quivering nose.

"My lords," he heard himself whine, "do not trespass here. I beg you. Nothing awaits you behind these walls but disgrace and damnation."

"Of those, we have an abundance," the knight assured him. "Let us in, brother."

Frémis marveled at the air drifting through the slot, which had become as warm and luscious as a *clafoutis* delivered straight from the kitchen. Such was his preoccupation with the delicious scent that he ignored his feet, which moved of their own accord back to the steps and climbed up to where the counterweights hung. Rust from the old chains flaked from his fists as he yanked on them before he hurried back down to secure the ropes.

By the time the gate had been raised and secured, Frémis felt so weak and exhausted that falling to his knees seemed a blessing. "I beg forgiveness, my lord."

A worn, scarred gauntlet landed on his shoulder. "We must see to the horses."

As Frémis struggled to stand, the huge hand encased in the blackened glove provided assistance. "May I do this for you, my lord? I was born in a stable, you know. Just as the son of God was."

"And every other poor nameless bastard whelped by a homeless whore," one of the other men muttered.

The dark knight said something in English, which Frémis did not understand, but it served to silence his foulmouthed companion.

"This way, my lord." Frémis stumbled over his own feet, such was his haste to lead the men to the stables.

Once more the knight's gauntlet descended, this time to catch the back of his robe and steady him. A fold of his cloak fell away from a snowy white tunic, upon which the passion cross blazed in all its scarlet glory.

"Saint Ambrose protect us. You are God's warriors." Frémis, who had only heard stories of the Knights Templar, thought his eyes might pop out of their sockets.

"Why did you not say, my lord? I shall summon the abbot at once—"

"Our business here is with your smith," the knight said. "Brother Noir. Where does he keep the forge?"

Frémis blinked. "We have no forge of our own, and Brother Noir is not a smith. He works the stone."

"Indeed." The knight sounded exasperated. "Where is he to be found hammering rocks, then?"

"Our brother has given himself over to God, my lord," the monk said. "He retreated to the crypts during harvest so that he might devote himself to prayer."

"Or the rats." The foulmouthed knight swore again. "Richard, he will refuse us."

The dark knight eyed his companion, who ducked his head. "Have faith, Hugh. I believe our brother may be persuaded to once more take up his hammer."

Frémis helped the knights see to their mounts before leading them across the bailey to the old chapel. "There are other ways to reach the crypts, my lord," he told the dark knight, "but this passage leads directly to the tombs. That is where Brother Noir has sought solace."

"You will show us the way," the knight urged.

Frémis took them to the door hidden in the panels behind the altar, and led them along the twisting steps, brushing aside cobwebs as he went. The air grew cool against his sweat-glazed cheeks, while puddles of water dragged at the rough hem of his robe and chilled his sandaled feet.

Another, faint light met that of the monk's torch, and guided him the rest of the way to the penitent's cell. The abbot had forbidden all contact with Brother Noir, promising severe punishment to whoever dared defy him. At the wooden door to the cell Frémis hesitated, not wishing to defy the rule of order, but the dark knight brushed past him.

Inside the room sat Brother Noir, his head completely shaved, his body shockingly naked but for a length of threadbare rag wound about his loins. In one hand he held the Agpia, the book of prayers for each of the canonical hours. His other hand gripped a gleaming dagger of reddish metal.

The other knights filed in behind the dark man, taking up positions around him. The silence stretched out from there, thick with words unsaid. The air became unbearably sweet, until Frémis's head spun and he stumbled to the other side of the passage, gulping in the cooler air.

"Have you no greeting for your lord, Cristophe?" the dark knight asked.

The bald head lifted, and dull gray eyes regarded each man's face before settling on that of the dark knight. "No more do I trifle with scum such as you and yours, Tremayne. Begone with you."

One of the other knights surged forward, but the clout he intended to give never landed. The dagger in Brother Noir's hand pierced the knight's wrist, driving him backward until the blade buried itself in—and pinned his hand to—the stone wall.

Horrified, Frémis shuffled backward and covered the scream that wanted to burst from his mouth. Despite the vicious injury his dagger had inflicted, Brother Noir himself had not moved a muscle.

"As I recall," Tremayne said, "when you left England you vowed never to ply your gift again. I had hopes for your son, but his talents have proven to be quite the opposite of yours."

"Did that bitch send you?" Brother Noir slowly rose to his feet. Surely the tallest man Frémis had ever seen, the reclusive brother stood a head above the knights. "Is that what you do here?" Before Tremayne could answer, he spit on the floor. "That is all I have for her and her little bastard."

"Pity. The boy is the image of you, Cris." The dark knight seemed unmoved. "A crime for which Blanche has punished him all his life. But no, that is not why I have disturbed your prayers."

At that Brother Noir seemed to shrivel, his shoulders drooping, his chin dropping until it touched his chest. When he spoke, his words rasped with defeat. "Say what you would have of me and be done with it."

"Tomorrow Philip the Fair intends to move against the order," Tremayne said. "Every one of our brothers across Christendom will be arrested and imprisoned. The temples are to be seized and sacked. The pope has given his blessing."

Brother Noir eyed the dark knight. "So at long last Rome makes a choice."

Tremayne inclined his head. "I fear the king, however, has more earthly motives. He has finally emptied all of France's coffers, and now owes far more than he could repay in a dozen reigns."

"You should have turned him when you had the chance." Brother Noir lifted a hand, and the dagger pinning the knight's hand to the wall grew invisible wings and flew back to his fingers. "Now he will empty the temples of life and treasure."

"Life, perhaps."

The monk's eyes turned the shade of a newly minted silver coin as they shifted toward the odd shape of the cloth sack one of the knights carried. He then regarded Richard Tremayne. "You *dare* bring this to me."

"I dared bring this to no one else." When Brother Noir did not speak, the dark knight spread out his hands.

"Tell me, then, which mortal shall I entrust with our greatest treasure?" He swung a hand toward Frémis. "Perhaps the little monk cowering in the corridor there. He seems an honest if simple fellow."

Brother Noir shouldered his way out to loom over Frémis. The weight of his silver gaze made the smaller monk sink to his knees.

"Forgive me, I beg you," Frémis pleaded as he stared up. "I cannot tell you why I brought them here. It was as if demons possessed me. I could not help myself."

A hand as wide as his skull settled over his bristled tonsure. "Peace, brother." Brother Noir closed his eyes for a moment before he turned his head. "You and your men cannot remain here, Richard. Aragon is riddled with Philip's spies, and doubtless they have been told to watch all of the monasteries."

"Then you must come with us."

"To take up the sword and shield again? Or to armor you for eternity?" The monk's mouth bent at the corners. "I would sooner go to Marseilles and fling myself before Philip the Fair's throne." He went back into the room and took the sack from the knight. "If I am to give form to this damnation, then you will meet my price." He looked at the other knights. "Leave us."

When Tremayne nodded, the other knights filed out of the room and disappeared down the corridor. No one paid any attention to Frémis, who dared not twitch an eyelid.

The dark knight frowned. "What will you have? Gold or blood?"

"Protection." Brother Noir hefted the sack. "Once it is done, I shall conceal it from the eyes and the greed of the world. Only I will know where it is hidden."

Tremayne shook his head. "It is too dangerous a thing for only one to know."

"Those who share my name will shoulder the burden," the monk said. "And when the day comes that I am no more, their finest will serve as its guardian."

"You ask too much." Tremayne's gaze dropped as Brother Noir offered him the sack. "You would have us rely on the honor of mortals."

"The honor of my name. Those who bear it have never betrayed my trust." He cocked his head. "But you would know nothing of that, would you, my fine lord? For Blanche told me the brat was yours."

"As she told a dozen others they were his sire." Tremayne let the words hang between them for a long moment. "Your kin will betray you, Cris. Just as she did."

"That is my concern, not yours," Brother Noir assured him. "Those who prove disloyal will die by my hand. Even as I am gone from this world."

The dark knight fell silent for a time, and then slowly nodded.

"From here we travel to England," Tremayne said. "The king will be persuaded to offer us sanctuary during the trials. By spring we will divide the territory and establish our strongholds."

"When the work is done I will return to France and begin the education and training of my kin." The monk glanced at Frémis. "You will not kill this one. He is an innocent."

"They always are." The dark knight stepped out into the corridor and helped Frémis to his feet. "Come, brother. Come with me now."

The heavy scent of cherries made the monk's head spin. "Where do I go, my lord?"

A strong, hard arm steadied him. "Back to your post."

Chapter 1

During the day the waitresses at La Théière Verte delivered filling but forgettable meals from the cramped kitchen of the restaurant to the table of any hungry tourist who had wandered in through the old green doors. The owner, Madame Eugenie, prepared all the dishes herself, using the cheapest ingredients and as much garlic as she dared. She considered this blatant desecration of God's bounty an economical measure as well as her patriotic duty.

The tourists, ignorant cretins that they were, never seemed to notice. As long as they were served a plate close to overflowing, they happily handed over their euros.

Only after dark did madame's chef arrive to cook for the villagers who came to dine, and whose standards were French. The local residents could not be appeased by a stew of shredded lapin smothered beneath a *montagne* of carrots, the blandest of radishes glued by oleo to day-old black bread, or gallons of cheap Spanish wine funneled into empty, French-labeled bottles. If in a moment of madness Eugenie ever dared to serve such swill to her neighbors, they would consider it *their* patriotic duty to lock her and her staff inside the old restaurant before setting fire to the place.

For these reasons madame was not at all pleased when her waitress Marie nudged her and nodded toward a tall, flaxen-haired stranger standing just inside the threshold.

"*Zut*, not a German at this hour. He must have run out of petrol. Unless he is an American." Eugenie almost spit on the last word. To her, the only thing worse than the Berliners were those loud, nosy imbeciles from across the Atlantic, forever thumbing through their phrase books and mangling her native tongue. Or the ones who waddled in, their rotund bodies shiny with sweat and sunscreen, to demand to know whether she served *low-fat* this and *sugar-free* that.

"Whatever he is, he's handsome," Marie said, and shifted to get a better look. "Such a big man, too. Look at those shoulders, and all that hair. It must fall to his waist."

"*Et alors?*" Eugenie gave the girl a hard pinch on the arm. "Forget his hair. Ask if he has a reservation. He will say no, and you will tell him to call for one tomorrow."

Marie rubbed her arm and said in an absent tone, "We do not take reservations, madame."

"Does he know this, you goose?" she hissed, and then saw it was too late. "There, now, because you are lazy and stupid, he is already sitting down. Go and see what he wants. If he asks for the cheeseburger do not tell me. I will choke him with his own hair."

Korvel stopped listening to the conversation between the women behind the bar and checked the interior of the restaurant. Only a third of the tables were occupied, most by couples and some middle-aged men. One delicate fairy of a schoolgirl sat picking at her food while her parents bickered in half whispers. Apart from sending a few uninterested glances in his direction when he had walked in, no one paid any further attention to him.

As transparent as a bloody specter, but not half as interesting.

When the young, smiling waitress approached his table his empty belly clenched, but years of self-denial quickly dispelled the involuntary response. He listened as the girl stammered through a brief recital of the evening specials before he ordered a bottle of a local Bandol and the vegetable soup. The wine would not satisfy his ever-present hunger, and if he attempted to eat the soup he would puke, but they would buy him a half hour of quiet and rest before he continued his journey.

Or I could have the waitress and be gone in five minutes.

He had no time or particular inclination to give his body what it needed: a woman. There had been a time when any woman would do, for no matter how different they were from one another, they all shared the same soft warmth, the same intense fragility. He had thought mortal women as lovely as an endless meadow of flowers.

So it had been until he had fallen in love with Alexandra Keller. The only woman he had ever truly wanted for himself, now gone from his life and forever beyond his reach.

For a time, being caught between his physical needs and his broken heart had produced ungodly urges that had nearly driven Korvel out of his head. Fortunately those, too, were now gone. His will, or what remained of it, permitted him to don a brittle mask each day and carry on with this imitation of life.

God in heaven, he had wearied of this charade, of everyone and everything in it. More than that, he was sick unto death of himself.

"Monsieur?"

Korvel glanced up at madame, who had brought a dark bottle to his table, but seemed more interested in examining him than in pouring the wine. She measured every inch of the hair he kept forgetting to cut, and the garments he had tailored to fit his overlarge frame, which cost more than the average tourist spent on ten vacations. Doubtless she could also name his weight to within five kilos' accuracy.

Her gaze flicked down to dwell with disapproval on the mark that encircled his throat. It resembled a garrote of dark green thorns, and as most mortals did she would assume he had been tattooed. He could not explain that being hanged for weeks in a copper-barbed noose had caused the marks. Copper proved lethal to his kind only when it entered their veins or heart, but its poisonous effects were such that even touching it caused burns. Any extended surface contact with the dark metal left permanent, green scars on immortal flesh; grim reminders, in a sense, of humanity's loathing of their dark Kyn.

He also doubted she would care. *"S'il vous plaît?"* He gestured at his glass, earning a mild frown from her before she filled it to the rim.

"You are American?" she asked in English as she wiped a dribble from the bottle's neck.

Another reminder of what could never be. "No, madame. I am from England."

"Ah, *les anglais*." She nodded to herself with some

satisfaction, and the lines bracketing her mouth softened. "You come with the caravan, *oui*?"

"I am here on business." The business of playing courier for his master, for reasons that had never been adequately explained to him. "Thank you for the wine."

"*Il n'y a pas de quoi.*" She bobbed her head and smoothed her hands over the sides of her apron before reluctantly turning away and resuming her post behind the bar. He saw the flicker of confusion that passed over her narrow features before she returned to her task of sorting flatware.

Korvel reached over to open the window a little wider before sampling the glass. Mortals considered Provence a fine-wine void, something the residents likely encouraged to protect their supply of some of the best red and rosé wines in the world. Madame had brought him a Mourvèdre-based red wine with a pleasing amount of spine to it, and Korvel breathed in its tannic perfume while he removed a flask from his jacket. He had to sip some of the wine before discreetly adding a measure of the darker, thicker liquid from the flask to the glass, but his next swallow instantly eliminated the leaden sensation the first swallow had left in his gut.

The mixture of blood and wine went to work, spreading slowly through him to warm his cold flesh and loosen his stiff muscles. It would tide him over until he reached his destination, where he planned to see to his needs once he retrieved his master's property. He took out the small GPS device that had been attached to the car's dashboard to check his current position.

"That no work here, monsieur."

"Indeed." Korvel eyed the plump face of the waitress as she set down a steaming bowl of soup. "Why not?"

"The wind very bad Sunday. The tower, send signal?"

When he nodded his understanding, she straightened her hand and then let it fall to mimic something toppling over.

So it seemed the GPS was useless, and the French he spoke hadn't been used in this region for half a millennium or better. He reached out to rest his hand over hers. "Do you know the road to Garbia?"

"Mais oui." Her expression brightened. "Go this way" — she pointed north — "until you reach the second turn. Then go this way." She pointed east, but this time her fingers quivered under his, and her breathing grew fast and uneven. "I come with you. I show you. Madame, she not care."

Korvel eyed the scowl being directed at them from the bar. "Actually I do believe madame will mind."

"You take me. With you?" She released one more button of her blouse, which exposed the sweat beading between her full breasts. "I want go with you."

He knew exactly what she wanted, and carefully removed his hand from hers. "You have been quite helpful," he said as he deliberately shed more of his scent to bring her under his command. "Thank you. You should return to your work now."

The light vanilla fragrance of larkspur enveloped the two of them as *l'attrait* caused the waitress's pupils to dilate.

"Oui." She backed away, bumping her ample hip into the edge of another table. The pain released her from Korvel's control, and she clapped a hand over her giggles as she fled toward the kitchen.

Once he pocketed the GPS, Korvel drank the last of the bloodwine and sat back to let it finish its work on him. While he waited, he checked his mobile for messages. Stefan, the senior lieutenant Korvel had assigned to serve in his place during his absence, had texted him a brief status report before Korvel had left Paris. The men had been drilled, the night patrols assigned, and the high lord had retreated to his study for the night.

All was as it should be, as it would have been if Korvel had never departed. It should have reassured him, but it only made the hollow sensation inside him grow.

Since becoming one of the immortal Darkyn, Korvel had served Richard Tremayne as the high lord's seneschal as well as the captain of his guard. Seven lifetimes he had devoted himself to his duties and honoring the oath he had made to his master. Eight, if one counted his mortal life.

Now it seemed his absence was not even noticed.

"You look sad, monsieur."

The ethereal little girl who had been sitting with the bickering couple slipped into the empty chair beside his. Confusion filled her eyes, as if she weren't quite sure why she was speaking to him.

Korvel knew exactly why the child had come to him. She must have been just on the verge of puberty; his ability to influence female mortals never affected the very young. "I am well, thank you."

"You are a Viking, no?" The girl darted a look over her shoulder. "My *maman* said you look like one, which made my papa very mad. But I think you are more like the beautiful angels."

Korvel glanced around the room and saw he had gained the avid attention of the child's mother and every other female in the place. He'd made a serious error shedding so much scent to influence the waitress, for he had not considered that the cold air outside might have acted as a natural barrier at the ventilation points. His scent saturated the inside air now. If he did not leave at once, all of the women would come over to his table, drawn to him like moths to a burning lantern.

"I must go now and continue my journey." He managed a smile for the little girl. "*Au revoir,* my sweet."

"Take me with you." Tears welled up in her eyes. "Please."

He could not explain to her that what she felt would disappear as soon as he departed, but he would not see her suffer even a few seconds. "What is your name?"

"Tasha."

"Tasha." He touched his hand to the side of her little neck, where the connection of his will to her mind was the strongest. "Go back to your parents. Forget me. Be happy."

"Go. Forget. Happy." She turned like a sleepwalker and shuffled away.

Quickly Korvel took out enough euros to pay for a case of wine and dropped them on the table before he rose to his feet. The habits of many lifetimes compelled him to attend to one final detail: the memories of madame and the waitress, who intercepted him at the door.

As they were both already bespelled, he had only to command them. "You will attend to your work and your patrons. Once I am gone, you will forget me. It will be as if I never came here."

The women spoke in monotone unison. "Attend. Work. Gone."

Korvel left the restaurant, checking the street to ensure it was empty. As the chill of a dark wind streamed against his coat, he turned his head to look back through the front window and saw the waitress taking an order from an older couple. Madame stood once more behind the counter, her expression no longer as sour as it had been when he had walked into the place. For them he no longer existed; he had never existed.

He envied them.

In all the centuries Korvel had lived since rising from his grave to walk the night, he had never considered his own memory to be anything but useful. Indeed, every bit of knowledge he acquired he carefully added to, stockpiling all he knew like weapons. Now he would gladly empty his head of all of it, if it meant he could forget forever what had been. What would never be.

You're supposed to love me.

He had put so much practice into banishing Alexandra Keller's voice from his thoughts that he could silence her in an instant. Her scent, however, still haunted him. But no, what filled his head came on the wind, scoured from acres of blooming lavender. Provençal farmers grew so much of the fragrant herb for the wine and perfume industries that one couldn't drive a mile without passing one of the vivid amethyst fields.

He walked down the deserted street to the spot where he had parked the gleaming black Audi he had rented in Paris. Most of his kind preferred to travel on horseback rather than by automobile, and many refused to learn how to drive, but the demands of serving his master had forced him to make regular use of modern technology. A horse had to be frequently rested, fed, and watered on a long journey; the car required only brief stops for petrol.

As he took out the keys to the vehicle, Korvel stared at them. As the first Kyn ever to be made seneschal, Korvel had set the standard for all the others, one that had yet to be fully matched. He had personally trained every warrior who had ever served in the high lord's garrison, and had taught his methods to the captains of other *jardins* around the world. His unwavering loyalty to the high lord had earned him a spotless reputation as the most trusted and valuable second among all the territories. None would be shocked to learn that he had been sent to France to attend to his master's wishes and retrieve a priceless artifact before it fell into the wrong hands.

To serve Richard again, this time as his errand boy.

Korvel did not succumb to sudden and bizarre urges; nor did he intend to start. He would never turn his back on his duty to walk into the shadows and disappear into the night. Such a thing would violate his oath and break faith with his master, and his honor forbade him to behave in such a cowardly manner.

But oh, how he wished he could.

As he unlocked the car, he could imagine the keys dropping from his hand to the ground. As he got in and started the engine, the sound of grass brushing against his trousers whispered in his ears. As he tightened his grip on the steering wheel, he could feel on his skin the fearful silence that would fall over the forest creatures as they witnessed his departure from the world of Kyn and man to enter their peaceful realm.

It would be so simple. So uncomplicated. And there, where no one could command him, the loneliness and despair would do their final work.

"Turn around," a muffled voice ordered from his pocket.

Korvel removed the GPS, which he had switched off in the restaurant, and tried it again. The screen displayed his current position as being in the middle of nothing. As he reached to reprogram it, the screen blanked.

He swore softly as he shifted the Audi into drive and executed a three-point turn. The faster he reached Garbia and retrieved the scroll, the sooner he could return to the island, and his duties, and the sanity they preserved.

"Do you know what time it is?"

In complete darkness Simone Derien lifted a mass of worn, cream-colored cloth from her washbasin and gently twisted it to wring out the water. "Time to buy new bedsheets. These have so many holes they are turning into lace."

With the slow but sure steps of a person who could not see in a very familiar space, Flavia Roux came in and sniffed the air, then bent and groped until she touched the clean, damp wash Simone had placed in a basket. "You should be sleeping, child."

"The wind, and the broken shutter outside Terese's room, would not allow it." Simone dropped the sodden sheet onto the top of a basket before drying her hands on the threadbare towel pinned to her skirt. "Just as well. I wanted to get an early start so I can weed the winter vegetables."

"That is Nichella's responsibility," Flavia scolded. "You have taken on enough chores."

"Nichella hates bugs, and the last time I asked her to pick some potatoes, she brought me morels." She reached for the clothespin bag hanging over the rust-edged sink and clipped it to her belt. "Besides, I have to pick out a baking pumpkin for you. Father Robere will be here for dinner tomorrow, and you know how much he loves your autumn bread."

Flavia picked up a basket and followed Simone out to the moonlit yard. "I suspect the wind was not all that drove you from your bed tonight."

Simone shook out the wrinkles from a pillowcase before she clipped the left corner to the clothesline. "I did try, as you suggested, to count sheep jumping over a fence. They ignored my wishes, stampeded over the pumpkins, and disappeared down the hill. I expect now they are grazing their way through Madame Lambert's beet patch."

"Child."

She smiled down at the petite tyrant whom she had loved all her life. "You worry too much about me, Mother. You know I will sleep when I need it." She bent and kissed her furrowed brow. "Now go back to bed, and I will see you at breakfast."

"Which no doubt you will cook," Flavia grumbled as she picked up an empty basket and went back to the laundry.

Simone continued hanging up the wash, but kept her eye on the old woman until she made her way safely back into the convent. Aside from the common ailment they all shared, most of the women who resided at La Roseraie suffered from the various frailties of advanced age.

Flavia, a former teacher from Milan, had still been quite young when her illness had ended her career. La Roseraie, an inheritance from her last living relative, had first provided her with a sanctuary as she learned how to cope with the abrupt change in her circumstances. Her faith had done the rest, and over the next thirty years she had opened the doors of the convent to other sisters who, by illness or injury, had found themselves in the same condition.

As soon as Simone's father had brought her to live with him, he had taken her to the sisters to receive instruction. As young as she had been, Simone still remembered that brief, tense meeting.

"The girl is to be versed in all mathematics, sciences, literature, and world affairs," her father said. "Teach her every language you and the others speak. She will come every morning except Sunday, until she is of age."

"Monsieur, what you ask is simply impossible," Flavia had protested. "No child could master so many subjects in so short a time."

"I am not asking, madame." He handed her a folded slip of paper. When she had passed her fingers over the strange bumps that covered it, he said, "I will send her to you at dawn tomorrow. My driver will return at noon to collect her."

Whatever the bumpy paper had meant, it had convinced Flavia to accept the impossible demands of Simone's father. For the next twelve years the little girl spent nearly all of her mornings among the sisters, and had soaked up their teachings like a withered sponge.

Simone had always been a quiet, obedient child who devoted herself to her lessons. Only gradually did the sisters discover the bruises and cuts, the sprains and bumps. This distressed them, most particularly when Simone had trouble walking. Finally Flavia had taken Simone into the garden for tea and butter cookies. As the little girl nibbled on the unexpected treat, the old woman touched her arm.

"Did your papa do this to you, child?" the old woman had asked as she gently skimmed her fingers over a gash just above Simone's elbow.

"No, madame," she answered truthfully. "It was my fault. Sometimes I am too slow."

"I know you are trying not to limp in front of us, but I heard your shoe dragging on the path from the house." When Simone didn't reply, Flavia took hold of her hands. "Does your father beat you, child?"

"No, madame." Simone couldn't imagine her father doing anything to hurt her. "Papa never touches me."

"I hear the truth in your voice, but these wounds . . ." Gentle fingertips caressed Simone's cheek. "You must learn to be more careful with yourself, child."

"*Oui*, madame." Simone wanted to press a kiss against her palm, but such things were not permitted. It was enough to imagine that she did. "Will you be teaching me today?"

Over time Simone did learn to be faster, and her frequent injuries dwindled and then vanished altogether. By the time she was eleven, her father dispensed with sending her to the convent by car and instead had her run up the hill each morning. Like so many of his requirements, it had been difficult at first, but then her body grew accustomed to it.

In between her lessons Simone fell into the habit of helping Flavia and the other women by performing small chores for them. At first they had objected, but she begged to be allowed what were for her true pleasures.

"Papa does not keep chickens or cows, and all of our food comes from the market," Simone had explained to Flavia. "I am good at finding eggs, and very fast. The hens never have a chance to peck my hands."

Her lessons had been interesting, but it was those little chores she did that brightened each day. The women in turn taught her how to do many things that her father knew nothing of, from cooking to gardening to sewing.

When she was sixteen, Simone worked up the courage to ask her father whether she could join the sisters permanently. "There is plenty of room, and they like me. I can work for my keep. They have some land they are not using, and I can plant lavender and herbs to sell at market."

For the first time since coming to live with her father,

Simone did not run up the hill the next morning. Nor did she return for her lessons until a week later.

"We were so worried about you," Flavia said as she met her at the gate. "What happened? Were you sick?"

Simone blinked back hot tears. "I am well, madame," she lied. "Father needed me to stay at the manor with him."

"Why?"

She could tell Flavia only what her father had instructed her to say. "It is family business."

Flavia, ever sensitive to her moods, never asked her again about her absence, and in time Simone made peace with what had happened. Yet from that day she never called her father Papa, or the manor where they lived home.

Simone finished hanging the last load of laundry as the black sky slowly lightened. When she returned to the convent, the stars had winked out and a dusty orange glow hemmed the horizon. In the kitchen she found two sisters, Manon and Paulette, preparing the morning tea and toast and as usual bickering over which preserves to put on the table.

"Your hibiscus jelly is too sour this year," Manon complained. "It puckers everyone's mouth."

"And your fig jam is not too sweet?" Paulette admonished. "Who complained that it made their teeth ache? Oh, yes. I remember now. Everyone except you."

Simone smiled as she went to the sink to wash her hands. "You should mix them together, sisters. They might taste sweet and sour, like Sister Terese's strawberry-rhubarb tarts."

Manon chuckled. "As quickly as you eat, child, I'm surprised your mouth has the time to taste anything."

The water spilled over her hands as she remembered

how quickly they had been made to eat their meals at the château. Cinq had always made a game of it, racing with her other brothers to finish before her, teasing her in a whisper whenever their handlers were distracted. *This time I will win, sister. . . .*

"Simone, there you are." Another sister appeared in the kitchen. "Flavia wishes you to come to the library."

Simone stopped drying her hands. As the only person in the convent who used the library, she occasionally visited at night to rummage through the old collection. The sisters kept their books in their rooms or on the shelves in the salon where they all gathered after dark. Flavia used the library for only two reasons: to receive official visitors from Rome, or to deliver news she didn't want anyone else to hear, for it was also the only sound-proofed room in the convent.

It had to be someone from Rome.

"*Merci, ma sœur.*" Quickly Simone unpinned the towel from her skirt and smoothed back the tendrils that had come loose from her braids before she hurried up to the second floor.

When Simone reached the door, she stopped and took several calming breaths. The first year she had lived at the convent full-time had been the worst; she'd been convinced that every stranger who came to their door had been sent with a message for her. Only after another year passed did Simone begin to hope that the bargain she had made with her father would last a lifetime.

Her hand stopped shaking as she knocked twice and opened the door.

The stranger inside with Flavia was a young man who wore the casual clothes and backpack of a tourist. At first glance Simone thought he might be a wandering Spaniard who had gotten lost, until she noted the Rolex on his left wrist and the excellence of his grooming. The slight bulge under the right seam of his denim jacket made her close the door and flip the bolt.

Flavia spoke to Simone in English. "Thank you for attending us, sister. This is Brother Rudolpho, who brings from Rome a message of great importance."

The Italian rose to his feet and dipped his head. "My superiors directed me to deliver a message from our brother Helada. Madame advised me that it should be relayed to you."

Simone forgot to breathe.

The courier produced a folded sheet of parchment sealed with a black-and-white oval, which he broke as he opened and read it aloud. "Helada writes, 'The frost has ended, and so the harvest must begin.'"

Helada is the frost that descends everywhere. That kills everything it touches, her father had said so many times. *The snow that falls from the heavens to cover everything in death.*

I cannot do this. She had refused her father once, twice, a dozen times. *I will not.*

The last words he had spoken to her had been his terms of the bargain. *Swear to me you will do this, and I will let you go.*

The courier frowned as he looked up at Simone. "I do not understand the message."

"I do." In her misery Simone felt a small pang of sympathy for the courier. "Forgive us, brother."

"Why should I—" A heavy thud proceeded Rudolpho's groan, and he fell forward into Simone's arms.

Behind him, Flavia lowered her cane. "Is he unconscious?"

"Yes." Simone hauled the man's limp body over to the window seat and placed him in a comfortable position on his side. "My father said the message would be sent only if our ruse had been discovered. The scroll is no longer safe here. I must leave at once."

Flavia went to the desk, unlocking it to remove another key, which she placed in Simone's hands before she embraced her. "I will pray for you, child."

Not even God could intervene now, Simone thought as she removed the cross she wore around her neck and placed it in Flavia's hands. "Would you put this in my room for me?" When the old lady nodded, she kissed her brow. "Good-bye, Mother."

Simone ran from the room and down the hall to the linen closet. In the very back she moved three stacks of heavy quilts aside to expose a padlocked niche; she opened it with the key Flavia had given her.

The niche held a custom-fitted harness, a neatly folded habit, and a steel case. After donning the harness and habit, Simone opened the case and began removing the weapons inside. The short, razor-sharp blades she slid into each of the harness's sheaths; the box of ammunition she opened and used to load the magazines of three semiautomatic pistols.

Twice a year she took out the guns to clean them before she took them into the hills to practice and check their accuracy. Whenever she'd considered discontinuing the unpleasant task, her father's voice would begin ringing in her ears.

You must be prepared at all times.

She was not ready for this; she would never be ready. Yet as her father had predicted, her feelings didn't matter in the slightest degree. He had once told her about Pavlov's famous experiment in conditioned behavior, something that as a child of eleven she had not quite understood.

When the bell rings, the dog feeds.

Running downstairs, she had to dodge around several startled sisters, and kept silent as they called out their concern to her. From the convent she went to the stables, where the three horses they owned were placidly enjoying their morning feed. She took out the quickest, Georges, whom she used to pull the vegetable cart when they took their herbs to market. The gelding didn't object to being saddled, although he seemed puzzled when Simone yanked up her skirts to mount him.

"Come, Geo." She walked him out of the barn to the back of the yard, where a footpath led back into the hills. Three miles away, protected by fences and private-property signs, and nearly hidden among acres of ancient hundred-foot-tall plane trees, lay her destination: Château Niege. Her father's house, her childhood home.

The prison she would never escape.

Chapter 2

As he deftly avoided yet another crater, Korvel decided the waitress at La Théière Verte had sent him down the worst road in southern France. Already half-caked in mud, the Audi had lost a hubcap and gained a crack in its windshield, thanks to gravel shed from an overloaded construction lorry. Twice the gendarmes had stopped him for speeding. Now the road's condition had deteriorated to the point where he was obliged to slalom back and forth between the grassy shoulders to spare his tires.

When his mobile rang, Korvel pulled off onto the side of the road before he answered it. "Yes."

"Captain." Static crackled across the line but failed to drown out the unsettling power of Richard Tremayne's voice. "Have you arrived at your destination?"

He glanced at the GPS. "Not as yet, my lord. I should reach it before dawn." He hesitated before he asked, "Has something changed?"

"I have just received a report from our Italian associates," Richard said, referring to the *tresoran* council, which was based in Italy. The council, which governed all the *tresori* who served the Darkyn as their human servants, would contact the high lord only in the event of a real emergency. "Our competitors have organized the means with which they intend to acquire the property in question."

Korvel's jaw set. Whoever had taken interest in the scroll would be making a direct attempt to steal it. "When do they make their bid?"

"Our friends believe they will try within the next several hours." The high lord's voice grew sharper. "Upon your arrival, you must secure the property at once."

What had been an annoying errand might now result in an unwanted confrontation—one Korvel was hardly prepared for. "Are there any of our associates in the immediate area?"

"Our friends have family there," Richard said. "They will instruct them to meet you and provide whatever assistance you need."

"I would rather they not, my lord." Although the *tresori* had been serving the Kyn for many generations, and were trained from birth to become operatives with a variety of skills, Korvel disliked depending on them. For all their loyalty they were still mortal. In a fight he preferred to have his own kind watching his back. He thought for a moment. "Could you call on Gabriel and his lady to meet me, perhaps?"

Richard's tone grew disgusted. "I would, if I knew where the devil they are."

Two of the finest trackers among the Darkyn, Gabriel Seran and Nicola Jefferson had been devoting all their time to rescuing and relocating Kyn who had been targeted by their enemies. Nicola, who had been attacked and accidentally made Darkyn by Richard's former wife, Elizabeth, had later found and saved Gabriel from a horrible and slow death. The two had bonded, and

while Nicola remained fiercely devoted to her lover, she
had little love for the Darkyn, and showed no respect for
Richard whatsoever.

The high lord's voice faded in and out. "You will
report . . . me as . . . you have . . . the property."

"Yes, my lord." The connection lost, he switched off
the mobile and frowned.

Something is wrong, Korvel thought as he drove back
onto the road.

The scroll Richard had sent him to retrieve had once
been the subject of much speculation among the Kyn,
primarily because it was said that only the high lord
knew what it contained and where it was located. Korvel
had believed the same, until Richard himself had informed him to the contrary.

"I entrusted it to an old friend," the high lord said.
"He kept it in the family."

Of course, the usual wild rumors about the artifact
abounded, but only among the Darkyn. The passage of
the centuries had slowly scoured away the scroll's existence from the memory of the mortal world, at least until the human scholars and scientists had discovered a
mention of it, written in an ancient text unearthed from
the rubbish left behind in the bowels of an abandoned
English monastery.

One of Korvel's responsibilities was to monitor all
news reports regarding the Knights Templar, which often contained information Richard found useful. The
high lord also exercised his authority to bury any story
that could lead to exposure of the Kyn and their inter-
ests, in particular anything that could be used by their
enemies to identify any immortal or locate their strongholds.

The mention of the scroll had been confined to a few

speculative lines by a medieval scholar who had proposed that it contained descriptions and possibly maps to treasures hidden by the Templars just before their arrest and the disbanding of the order in the early fourteenth century. Kyn memory did not deteriorate with age, so Korvel considered the scholar's presumptions nothing more than the greedy hopes of yet another treasure hunter.

After listening to his report, Richard had dismissed the story. "Had I a shilling for every treasure we are said to have buried," the high lord said, "I could buy controlling interest in Microsoft and IKEA."

Korvel printed and filed away the AP report, and forgot it until three nights past, when Richard had summoned him and insisted he go to France to personally retrieve the scroll.

"Helada is the guardian of the scroll, but apparently he has disappeared," the high lord said. "The treasure cannot be left unattended, so you will bring it to me."

"My lord, we have a number of trusted couriers in Paris who in the past have served us as reliable transporters," Korvel said, perplexed that the high lord would have him leave Í Árd island to perform such a menial task. "Permit me to contact one of them, and I will—"

"You will do as I tell you, Captain," Richard told him flatly. "When you reach France, you are to travel alone and only by land. Once you are in possession of the scroll, you are to return directly to the island in the same fashion. That is all."

With all his heart Korvel wanted to know his master's reasons for such odd and specific instructions, but the high lord did not take kindly to being questioned, even by those he most trusted. "As you command, my lord." He bowed low and turned to leave.

"Korvel." Richard waited until he faced him again before he said, "The Scroll of Falkonera is a priceless treasure, forged from solid gold. That is not why our enemies are trying to steal it."

He waited, but his master offered nothing more, so he had to choose his next words carefully. "Then perhaps I should know what value it has to them, my lord, that I may properly safeguard it."

Richard inclined his head. "The scroll contains the writings of an alchemist of the first century, one who discovered the formula that bestowed immortality on a mortal. To protect the secret, the smith who forged it also placed a curse upon the scroll. Any unworthy human who touches it will die an agonizing death."

Most of the alchemists who had lived during Korvel's human lifetime had been practiced charlatans; most had wrapped themselves in secrecy and mystique to make their doubtful art seem more legitimate. "You do not believe in curses, my lord."

"All that concerns me is how the scroll may be used against us," Richard said. "Under no circumstances are you to permit it to fall into the hands of any mortal, friend or enemy. Is that understood?"

Korvel nodded and bowed again before leaving to make the arrangements for his journey, which now was coming to an abrupt end, thanks to a tractor-trailer that effectively blocked the entire road.

After he pulled over for the second time, Korvel parked the Audi and climbed out to inspect the disabled vehicle. Although crates of loudly squawking chickens and geese crowded the open-sided back of the trailer, the cab proved to be empty.

Once he had searched in vain for the keys, Korvel glanced over at the horizon. The hot orange crescent of sun blazed in the east; he slid on a pair of sunglasses designed to block most of its rays that would otherwise irritate his light-sensitive eyes. He could do nothing about the dawn or the weariness it inflicted on him except bear it. Fortunately a check of the GPS, which had decided to function again, showed him to be less than a mile from the château.

He had brought only one case with him for his garments, which he would not need until he returned to Paris. His two-handed broadsword and the other weapons he always traveled with lay inside the boot. He had not anticipated arriving at the château on foot; nor did he know whether he would encounter anyone along the way. Arming himself was second nature, but the sight of his sword would definitely alarm the resident mortals, and might result in alerting the enemy to his presence. He settled on taking just two daggers with forearm sheaths, which the sleeves of his coat completely concealed, before he started off toward the château.

Once Korvel squeezed past the back end of the trailer, he saw the road branch off in two directions, one toward the distant blur of Garbia and the other curving around into the heavily wooded hills. Small but plainly lettered signs that read PROPRIÉTÉ PRIVÉE had been nailed to the trunks of the outermost trees. By the time he had walked half a kilometer the road virtually disappeared from sight, obscured by massive silver-trunked trees with twisting, riotous branches that formed an effective natural barrier.

Korvel smelled wood smoke tinged with the sweet-tea scent of sycamore, but the leafy canopy barred his view of the sky, so he couldn't see from which direction it came. He stopped and listened for several minutes, intent on discovering the source of the smoke, but heard

and smelled nothing out of the ordinary. The local farmers would have lit their fireplaces, he decided, to dis-
pense some of the morning chill from their homes. With
the high price of heating oil and coal, and France's per-
petually dismal economy, it made sense that they would
burn wood.

He knew why every little thing was setting him on
edge. He had entered territory unfamiliar to him—a
strategic disadvantage he always attempted to avoid.
While the Darkyn no longer actively occupied southern
France, centuries of respecting the boundaries between
immortal strongholds had become a matter of form for
his kind. Thus traveling into strange lands made every
Kyn warrior uneasy. That, and without his sword Korvel
felt almost naked. But he knew he could bespell any
mortal who saw him before they could expose his
presence—

The smell of hot, sweet, smoky tea grew stronger, dis-
tracting him from his thoughts, and he realized a faint
opaque haze was now visible in the air. A lightning strike
might have set some of the woods ablaze, but then the
birds and the other creatures inhabiting it would be
making a racket. All he heard was birdsong and the flutter of leaves in a breeze.

A breeze that felt a few degrees warmer than it had
by the main road.

Korvel eyed the nearest sturdy tree, measuring the
width of its branches before he went to it and jumped up
to catch the lowest bough. He boosted himself up easily
and began to climb in search of a better vantage point.
Forty feet from the ground the branches began to thin,
and another ten feet higher a gap from a broken limb
afforded him a view of the surrounding hills.

Frost had begun to kill the grazing grasses, leaving

behind wide, irregular brown patches on the gentle slopes like some giant's muddy, erratic footprints. From his position he could see a stretch of road leading up to a high stone wall and iron gates; beyond them shrubbery and shorter trees masked the grounds around a large structure with a tiered roof of gray slate shingles. Steady streams of white smoke poured from the slate roof's three chimneys.

It had to be Château Niege. It seemed Helada's mortal servants also disliked the cold October mornings.

Feeling once more like a fool, Korvel stepped off the branch and dropped to the ground. Once he had the scroll, he would go to the nearest city and take his rest there until nightfall. Then, when he rose, he would find a willing female and feed. Perhaps he would fuck her, too, and relieve his other, long-denied needs. Sex had never been a particular pleasure for him, not when he could have any woman just by willing it, but he had let too much time pass. He could no longer remember the last time he'd taken a female to his bed.

He knew he had not touched any female in an intimate fashion since his master had abducted Alexandra Keller and put the American doctor in Korvel's care. Another painful indicator that it was high time he dispensed with the last dregs of his idiotic adolescent obsession.

Korvel picked up his pace and in a few minutes arrived at the gates of the château. The guardhouse stood empty, and the gates had been opened. Fresh tire marks left twin tracks in the dirt before disappearing on the concrete slab of the drive.

The unmistakable reek of mortal blood made Korvel halt and draw in the smoke-fogged air. A trace of the wet-scarlet bloom came from inside the gates, but a stronger source was much closer. He shrugged out of his coat, letting it drop to the ground as he spun around to face whatever had crept up behind him.

Two mortals dressed in military fatigues and black cloth masks stood silently watching him. Both held combat blades in their hands and carried handheld radios. The automatic weapons slung over their shoulders had not been fired, but the dark red spatter on their uniforms was still wet.

Korvel felt a crowding sensation as more men emerged from the tree cover and spread out, encircling him. Their efficient movements and effortless formation testified to their training and experience; this ambush was not their first. A whirring, mechanical sound brushed against his ears as the only avenue of escape they had left him, the open gates behind his back, began to close.

"This one has hair like a little girl," one of the mortals said.

"He smells like one, too," another muttered. "We should slice off his cock and put him in a dress."

"I like his mouth." Another man openly massaged the bulge in the front of his trousers. "You save the head for me, eh?"

The men spoke in gutter Italian with Napoli accents, something Korvel would have to ponder later. The easy certainty with which they spoke of desecrating his remains gave him pause; they already assumed they would prevail. He studied them again, and saw that their combat blades had been greased black, a tactic foreign to him. As one turned his dagger, Korvel saw beneath the coating the rosy glow of copper, the only metal on earth that could inflict injury and death on him.

They not only knew what he was; they had learned how best to deal with and dispatch him.

All Korvel had left to him was his Darkyn ability to compel any female to desire him. Unlike *l'attrait,* his power was not based on scent, but on touch or proximity, obliging Korvel to lay hands on or move close to the mortal he wished to bespell. Although it usually had no effect on men, some who were attracted to their own gender occasionally fell under his power. He focused on the man with the obvious erection and imagined Alexandra Keller standing in his place, her arms extended, her petite, naked body gleaming in the pale sunlight. Forcing himself to visualize her filled Korvel with self-disgust, but channeling his own desire into his ability made it strong enough to cross the physical gap between him and the aroused man.

The blade fell from the man's hand, and he took an uncertain step toward Korvel. His movement drew the attention of the other men, one of whom spoke sharply.

"Watch hi—"

The warning ended in a gurgle of blood as Korvel's blade buried itself in the man's neck. The others rushed in, hoping to close the circle, but Korvel crouched and jumped, soaring over their heads before he flipped and landed on his feet behind them.

He cut the throat of the man closest to him, pushing him into another and relieving both of their blades, throwing them into the bellies of two more. The terror of the remaining men radiated as they collided with one another and retreated in a desperate attempt to elude Korvel's counterattack. He opened the femoral artery of one with a single sweeping strike; another shrieked and toppled as the long dagger sliced across the back of his knees.

Korvel put his back to the gate as the three remaining men regrouped, one fumbling as he pulled around his

assault rifle to aim and fire. A spray of bullets pinged
against the iron gates and the wall stones while Korvel
dropped and rolled behind one of the injured, rising to
hold the gasping mortal in front of him. Now a living
shield, the body writhed as more bullets pierced his
clothing, and Korvel threw his second dagger into the
chest of the shooter, who staggered backward. He then
pulled free the automatic weapon from the shoulder of
the bullet-ridden body, dropping the dead man to fire on
the last two left standing.

One managed to fling his knife before he fell, a move
Korvel did not anticipate. He turned, but not quickly
enough, and felt the weapon strike the back of his thigh.
The burn of the copper did not end when Korvel reached
back to yank out the dagger; from the jagged condition
of the blade it was evident that part had broken off and
remained lodged in the wound. He fired one final time,
turning in an uneven circle to finish off the wounded before he threw away the weapon and staggered toward
the gates.

The scent of smoke made Georges rear his head, his ears
flicking back and forth as he tasted the air.

"Doucement, mon ami." Simone tugged back on the
reins to slow him to a walk as she looked ahead. The
path wound through the back of her father's property,
and lack of use and maintenance had caused weeds and
shrubbery to overgrow and narrow it. "They're just
keeping the old place warm for the mice now."

Simone dismounted as soon as she was within sight of
the château's walls, and slapped Georges on the right
flank, sending him back down the trail to the convent.
During her father's absence Piers, the butler, had taken
to secretly lighting the fireplaces. Although Simone had

never enjoyed such comforts when she had lived here, she didn't blame him. Her father had always believed physical comfort dulled the senses and encouraged complacency, which he regarded as intolerable. He never considered the comfort of his staff, all of whom were in their sixties and seventies now. Enduring the long winter months in a house with no central heating had simply become too much of an ordeal for them.

Purpose, Quatorze. The only fire you will ever need.

She went to the section of the wall ten paces from the end of the path, where she pressed three bricks in sequence. Unseen hinges groaned as internal locks released and a three-foot-wide section shifted slightly. She had to push hard to create enough space to step through—she would have to speak to Piers about oiling the rusting mechanism—and once inside the wall, she pushed it back in place. As she reached to reverse the sequence of bricks to lock it once more, she heard a series of rapid pops and froze.

Gunfire?

She spun around and ran along an unmarked path through thorny hedges, not stopping to free herself when untrimmed branches tore at her fluttering habit. The burning scent of wood grew intense, and smoke whitened the air, until she emerged from the ground cover at the front of the château.

Several new, black all-terrain vehicles and an enormous unmarked truck blocked the drive, while smoke poured from the eaves and window seams on the château's top floor. One of the maids lay by the front door, her sightless eyes staring at Simone, her features painted with congealing blood that gravity had drawn from the small black crater in the center of her brow.

She heard glass smashing and wood ripping from inside the house, sounds so shocking to her ears they made her cringe. She slipped behind a tree trunk, pressing her back against it as she tried to catch her breath. They had killed, and now they were inside. They had set fire to the attics.

Somehow her father's message had come too late. That, or the courier had given it to someone before coming to the convent. But she had seen the seal, intact—

A cry of pain broke through her horrified confusion, and Simone flew across the drive, pulling her veil across her nose and mouth as she stepped over the dead maid and went inside. A few feet down the hall an old man crawled toward her, his body leaving a wide smear of blood on the marble floor.

"Piers." Simone went to him, crouching down to scoop his thin, frail body into her arms. Blood immediately soaked through the front of her habit from innumerable gunshot wounds in his torso. She carried him out of the smoke to the drive, where she dropped down with him and pulled up his shirt.

The old butler groped for her hand, squeezing it weakly when he caught it. "God have mercy on me, but there was no time." His mouth became a straining O as he gulped in air. "I saw them outside the gate. The next moment they were at the door." His grip tightened. "The master will be so angry, Simone. The master—"

"I know, Piers."

"You must stop them. For Hel—" A sharp crack cut off his words, and his body jerked as the bullet struck his chest. He slumped against her, his last breath leaving his lungs in a thin rush.

Simone looked up at the wisp of smoke rising from the barrel of a rifle. The priest holding the weapon shifted it to aim at her head, but as his dark eyes met hers he lowered the barrel. He spoke in Italian, but not to her.

Two other men converged on her. One dragged away the old butler's body while the other kicked her from behind, knocking her flat with such force she barely had time to protect her face. The same man grabbed her shoulder and wrenched her over onto her back.

The priest drifted closer, the skirt of his black cassock swirling with each step. The sun painted an oily gleam over his thin black brows and trim mustache, and his smile displayed his small, pearly teeth where two diamond-studded gold crowns winked at her. He handed off the rifle to the man who had kicked her, and then removed a red silk handkerchief from his pocket, using it to wipe his hands before folding and replacing it.

"Hello, Quatorze."

Simone tried to sit up, but he planted his boot between her breasts and bore down on it to keep her in place. She did not recognize the priest's young, handsome face, which seemed flawless. Only when he spoke had she noticed a degree of unnatural immobility that suggested he had not been born with such perfect features.

The voice, however, she knew as well as her own. *"Pájaro."*

"You remember me." He seemed delighted by this, his mouth curling up in a Cupid's bow as he produced a dark blade and bent down to cut open the front of her robe. "I had not thought he would permit it. He made you put all the others out of your mind, didn't he? After he cut their throats."

"I've never forgotten you." She saw the murderous glee in his eyes, and in it recognized her last chance to escape. "I am glad to know you are still alive."

"Still the little liar." He made a chiding sound as he bent down and used the blade to slice through her harness, stripping it from her and throwing it into the bushes. He did the same with the two pistols he removed from her pockets. "I considered taking you with me when I left, but my chances of successfully faking *two* deaths seemed rather improbable." He tugged on a torn piece of her robe. "He finally gave you to the convent, I see. Has locking you up in the nunnery kept you from becoming a five-euro whore, like your mother? Where is he?"

"Helada."

Simone looked at the man who came out of the château.

"Did you find it?" Pájaro asked.

The mercenary nodded. "In the back."

"Recall the men." Pájaro looked down as Simone seized his combat boot, clutching it. "You have something else to offer me, Quatorze?"

"I will go with you and your men, and do whatever they want. Whatever *you* want, *mon frère*." The beseeching words tasted like acid in her mouth. "If you and your men will leave with me now, my body and my life are yours."

He looked down at her with visible pleasure. "What happened to the girl who never lost a battle?"

"That is not my life anymore."

"You sound like your mother." Pájaro reached down and hauled her to her feet, jerking her close. His hot breath touched her face as he whispered, "I found her in Paris, you know. Yes, there she was, still peddling her diseased cunt under bridges and behind rubbish bins. I bought her with a swig of cheap wine and the promise of a needle. She pleaded for her life in the first five minutes. It took another hour before she begged me to end it."

He put his mouth next to her ear. "I was generous. I gave her another two weeks to live."

She swallowed hard to keep from vomiting on him. "I will last longer than she did."

"Anything is possible." He clamped his hand around her throat, applying just enough pressure to make her vision dim. "Now, *where is he*?"

She had to gasp out her reply. "Everywhere."

"*Maudite garce.* I don't need you to tell me. When he discovers I have the scroll, he will run to me." He shoved her at the waiting man. "You and the others can amuse yourselves with this one for a few minutes. She won't fight you. She won't fight anyone."

The man grinned. "Can we take her with us? It is a long drive to Marseilles."

Pájaro shook his head. "I have another slut to deal with there. When you've finished, gag her and tie her up inside. She can burn with the rest of the bodies."

Chapter 3

After tearing off and using his sleeve to temporarily bind his still-bleeding leg wound, Korvel limped through the gates and started up the drive toward the burning château. The broken copper blade lodged inside his flesh wouldn't kill him immediately, but until it was removed its poisons would continue to weaken him. The cursed metal also affected his ability to move; already he felt numb from knee to hip. Soon he wouldn't be able to remain upright, much less walk.

He came up behind a large unmarked truck, using it as cover when he heard men shouting and laughing. He gripped in each hand the greased blades he had recovered from the corpses by the gates and shifted his position from one side of the truck to the other. Silently he inched forward until he had a better view of the front of the château.

On the ground lay two elderly mortals; both had been shot and appeared dead. Four other mortals stood on the drive in a quad formation, shoving back and forth between them a young female in a long gray dress and white-banded gray kerchief. She cringed and stumbled but did not resist them, her features as tight as the hands she used to clutch together the remains of her bodice. They'd already ripped open her dress.

Not a dress, he realized, but a habit. The girl was a nun.

The game the men were playing became immediately obvious as well; they pushed and snatched at her, pawing and groping her body as she tried to evade them. Their laughter and the girl's struggles breached Korvel's self-control, igniting and feeding a killing fury, until the rage wiped clean every calculated thought from his head. Now he wanted only to feel bones snapping beneath his fists, and flesh parting against his blades.

One of the men, apparently impatient to be the first to inflict real harm on the girl, finally caught her and threw her to the ground, straddling her as he tore at his belt buckle. He had just begun to drop on top of her when Korvel reached them.

"Animal." With one motion he hauled the mortal off the girl and snapped his neck. As the other men reached for their weapons, he used the dead mortal's pistol to shoot two in the head.

The last man he shot in the knee as he was running away. Grim pleasure spread through him as he hobbled over and aimed at the back of his skull.

"Please don't shoot him," a low, soft voice said in French-accented English.

The next breath Korvel took came with the scents of green rosemary, thyme, and something sweeter and darker, warming his chest and stirring his hunger. It came from the nun, who was no longer cowering but moved with purpose as she came to kneel beside the groaning man and turn him over onto his back.

He wondered whether she was in shock. "You would show mercy to this one, sister? He had none for you."

"I don't care about that." The nun leaned forward and murmured something in Italian to the man, who said, "*La serre,*" and jabbed his finger toward the side of the château.

Korvel reached down to help the girl to her feet, but with one fluid movement she stood and brushed past him, running in the direction the man had indicated. "Sister, wait."

The nun didn't look back.

"Damn me." He drove his boot into the wounded man's temple, knocking him out, and then started after the girl.

The tangle of shrubbery and hedges crowding the grounds formed an impromptu yet effective labyrinth, forcing Korvel to track the nun by her scent. That led him to the open door of an enormous glass greenhouse behind the château.

Broken glass crunched under his boots as he stepped inside. The men had left the place in ruins; what they hadn't smashed they'd knocked over or thrown through the glass panels of the walls. He worked his way back to the gardener's benches, where the nun crouched beside a large pot that had been cracked in two. Spilled black soil and the pale green, broken wands of paper, whites littered the ground around her.

"Sister, what are you doing?"

She did not respond as she used her hands to claw through the contents of the shattered pot, stopping only when her fingernails scraped the bottom. She rose quickly and looked all around her.

"Sister." He didn't want to touch her, but she seemed unaware of his presence, so he reached for her dirty wrist. "Please, stop—"

The moment his fingers began to curl around her

wrist she pivoted, sliding her hand out through his so quickly he ended up with only a little soil in his palm. She moved around him as if he were nothing more than an object in her way, her eyes still searching the floor, until she made a strange sound and bent to pick up something.

Korvel looked over her shoulder. The long green sack had been fashioned out of velvet and embroidered with golden thread. A symbol worked in the fabric, a tiny triad formed of three circles, had been stitched over and over to form two long cylinders side by side.

"What is it?" he asked her.

She removed the long gray metal case inside before dropping the sack. The hasp on one side of the case had been carelessly pried apart, and when she opened it he saw that the inside had been lined with the same embroidered green velvet.

Whatever the case had once held, however, had been removed.

With some difficulty Korvel bent and picked up the sack to examine the design again. Touching the fabric sent an unpleasant tingle through his fingers, but it faded almost as soon as he felt it. The arrangement of the two embroidered cylinders, however, finally made sense to him. "This was used to hold the scroll."

"It was." The nun's eyes shifted up, and in them he saw a strange weariness. "Who are you?"

Since she knew where the scroll had been, she had to be an ally, but he would be sure of it. "I mean you no harm." He reached for her, resting his fingertips against her throat. "Give me your name."

"Simone Derien." She turned her head and took a deep breath. "You smell of larkspur."

She had a Frenchwoman's discerning nose; the few

mortal females he encountered remarked most often that he smelled like a pastry shop. Korvel frowned as his body swayed, and only then realized that his leg was buckling. The nun was too slight to bear the brunt of his weight, so he removed his hand and reached for the edge of a plant stand to brace himself. "Were you sent here?"

"I was summoned." She stared down at his leg. "You are bleeding all over the ground, Englishman."

He glanced at the small, wet red pool in which he stood. "So I am."

The plant stand insisted on tipping over at that moment, and took Korvel with it. He marveled that such a flimsy object could fell him, a feat not even the shrewdest, most skilled warrior among the guard had ever achieved.

He landed on his side, his vision alternately blurring and sharpening, which allowed him to snatch glimpses of Sister Simone as she dropped down beside him. Why had he not noticed until this moment how unusual and lovely the green of her eyes was, or the intense perfection of her fair, delicate skin? Every feature on her face shouted purity, from the smooth arch of her pale brows to the sweet bow of her full, rosy lips.

"It is good that you chose the Church," he told her. "You have the face of an angel."

"You are delirious," she replied, removing her head veil to reveal what seemed to be a crown of braided copper and gold. "Were you shot in the leg?"

"Stabbed." And with him on his back as he was, she could not remove the broken blade from the wound. That no longer seemed to trouble him as he fixed his gaze on the wondrous treasure she had been hiding. "God in heaven. Is that your hair?" He tried to touch it, but his arm refused to obey him.

"Be still." Her strong, capable-looking hands tore a long strip from her veil. "I will see to your wound, but then I must go. The others will notice the smoke and come for you."

"Everyone leaves me." The thought of her doing the same seemed to penetrate the muddle of his thoughts and bring back a measure of sanity. "You cannot go. The mortal's blade broke off in my leg. Unless you remove it, I will sicken and die."

She sat up, trailing her fingers through the blood that had soaked through his trousers and then lifting them to her nose. "You are one of the Kyn."

"Aye. Korvel, seneschal to Tremayne." He heard his voice slurring the words, and seized her wrist, using the last of his strength to drag her down atop him. His blood loss had filled the air with his scent, but he focused, releasing even more until he saw her eyes go dark. "You will not leave me like this. You will take the copper out of my body. You will remain with me until nightfall." He kept his eyes on hers until he heard her slowly agree with him, and then brought her hand to his lips. "Thank you, my angel."

"I don't get what the big deal is," Nicola Jefferson said as she peered through the bulletproof glass between her and the portrait on the museum wall. "She's yellow. She's crackly. And she's not smiling; she's smirking. Seriously smirking. Like she's been stepping out on the sly with her brother-in-law or her best friend's husband or something."

"Perhaps she did." Gabriel Seran tugged on one of Nick's white curls. "The lady's contemporaries considered her a great beauty of her time."

"A beauty?" Nick made a rude sound. "She doesn't

even have eyelashes or eyebrows." She glanced at him. "Oh, I get it. You knew her?"

"Her name was Lisa del Giocondo, and no, I never met her," he admitted. "The artist, however, accepted an invitation from the king and came to stay at Clos Lucé, near my home in Amboise."

"You met Leonardo da Vinci." Nick chuckled. "Get out of town."

"I did meet him several times, thanks to his insomnia, which often compelled him to go walking at night." Gabriel eyed some approaching Japanese tourists before taking her arm. "You would have liked him, I think. The two of you share many qualities."

She followed him to the next exhibit. "Is that a diplomatic way of saying I'm as cranky and bad tempered as he was?"

As the tourists began snapping photos of the *Mona Lisa*, Gabriel bent his head and brushed a gentle kiss against her lips. "As old as he was when we met, he still had the incandescence of a much younger man. You could look into his eyes and see all the passions and fires inside him, waiting to be unleashed." He touched his mouth to hers again. "Exactly like yours."

"Keep kissing me," she warned, "and I'll get very hot on you. Right here in public." With a sigh she scanned the room. "I don't like this. Our informant should have been here an hour ago. Assuming she is an informant and not some double agent for the holy freaks."

Gabriel ran his fingertip along the curve of her jaw. "Our friends investigated her thoroughly, and confirmed her as a reliable source."

"Baby, she's a Paris street hooker. That tends to put a big 'un-' before reliable." Nick caught a trace of something salty and unpleasant in the air: the smell of old blood and fresh fear. She turned around, zeroing in on a woman who stepped inside the entrance to the Salle des États. "Trouble at six o'clock."

Gabriel breathed in and his mouth tightened. "She's injured."

The two immortals casually approached the veiled woman, who wore a heavy coat, hat, and sunglasses with enormous lenses. As she noticed them she shuffled back a step and looked from side to side before closing the gap between them. "You are *les détectives*?"

"That's us," Nick said, studying the puffy lips and swollen nose under the other woman's heavy makeup. "I'm Detective Nick. This is Detective Gabe. What've you got for us?"

"Not here," the woman snapped. She turned to walk out of the gallery.

Nick caught her arm. "Hold it, sweetie," she said when the woman flinched and whimpered. "We're not going to hurt you." She focused on the sunglasses, and the scent of juniper enveloped the three of them. "Why do you want to take off?"

"I'm afraid he has someone following me," the woman said, her voice soft and drowsy. "If he catches me with you, this time he'll kill me."

Gabriel eyed the Japanese tourists, who had lost interest in da Vinci's masterpiece and were now watching them. "Nicola."

"Yeah, I see them." She held the woman's hand. "Why don't we go find a quiet place where we can have a drink and talk?"

The woman flashed a smile and a broken front tooth. "I'd like that."

A half hour later they sat down outside a mostly deserted café to share a bottle of wine. As Gabriel kept watch on the pedestrians and the waiters, Nick poured a full glass for the woman.

"What's your name, honey?" she asked as she handed over the wine.

"Oksana." The woman gulped down three swallows before she took off her sunglasses. Someone had blackened both of her eyes and left a nasty graze across the top of her left cheekbone. "Oksana Gravois."

Nick nodded toward her wounds. "Who worked you over?"

"One of my clients." She took another gulp. "Antoine. The shithead. I want him to pay."

"We'll see what we can do." Nick wondered whether this valuable information was going to turn out to be nothing more than working-girl spite. "You told the police that you had information about an arson job."

The prostitute nodded. "Antoine bragged about it. He said he'd been hired onto a crew that was going to rob an old place in the country, and then burn it to the ground."

For the last several years the Brethren, a group of fanatics who posed as Catholic priests while they hunted, captured, and tortured the Darkyn, had been using arson to cover up their attacks on immortal strongholds. Nick knew they also hired muscle outside the order to help them, muscle that sometimes took the blame for the crime when things went down the wrong way. "What old place, and where in the country?"

"A château in some country pisshole called Garbia." Oksana gingerly toughed the swollen lid of her right eye. "Antoine said they were going to kill everyone in the house before they took the treasure."

"Treasure?"

"Something like a book, but rolled up." She paused to

think. "A scroll. He said it was made of solid gold, and worth billions of euros." She flicked her fingers. "Nothing in the country is worth that kind of money. Then he said it was written by some magician who knew how to make someone live forever. He was going to steal the secret of eternal life. That's when I laughed at him."

"Really." Nick saw her lover turn his head to stare at the prostitute. "Then what happened?"

"What do you think? He started hitting me with his fists until I blacked out." Oksana sniffed. "When I woke he was gone. He took all my money and ruined my face." She pressed her fingers against her lips. "I can't work like this. Do you know how much crowns cost?"

"We'll get you fixed up. Drink your wine." Nick shifted around to face Gabriel. "The Brethren never share this kind of information with their hired muscle, and they're interested only in vamps. Sounds like we've got some new rules and players."

"Can you attend to this female?" When she nodded, Gabriel rose. "I'll meet you at the hotel."

"Sure." Nick watched him go before she spoke again to Oksana. "Honey, I think you just scared the pants off my boyfriend."

The prostitute's eyes filled with tears. "I'm sorry."

"It's not on you." Nick shook off the feeling of dread and took hold of the other woman's hand. "Now, let's talk about what you're not going to remember in about two minutes."

Once she had compelled the prostitute to forget everything she had told them, Nick gave her all the cash she had on her and sent her to the safe house they used in Paris. She then used her mobile to call the *tresora* who managed the safe house, and instructed him to relocate the prostitute in the morning.

"Have your people give her some TLC, and see if you can get her in to see a dentist, too," she said as she walked up to the hotel where she and Gabriel were staying.

"It will be as you say, my lady," the *tresora* promised.

"Thanks, and don't call me 'my lady.'" Nick switched off the phone and spoke to the elderly doorman. "Have you seen my guy?"

"He arrived a few moments ago, madame." The doorman gave her a cheeky smile. "He went directly upstairs."

As Nick did the same, she went through everything Oksana had said about Antoine and the arson job. Gabriel hadn't reacted until the prostitute had mentioned the treasure, and then he had looked . . . stunned? Scared? Both?

Nick didn't care for surprises, and she *really* didn't like her lover feeling frightened. After being captured by the Brethren, Gabriel had spent two years at their mercy, being tortured and questioned daily. In the end they'd bricked him up in the cellar of an abandoned house and left him to starve to death—something that for a Darkyn took years. If not for Nick finding him, he still would be there, slowly withering away.

If this were some kind of Brethren setup, Gabriel would have told her immediately. Nick's instincts told her it was something else—something that he might try to keep from her.

Inside their suite, Gabriel stood by the windows. He was speaking quietly in the old language over the satellite phone they used to communicate with other Darkyn. Nick went to the bar and poured herself a measure of bloodwine, knocking it back like bad-tasting medicine while she watched his reflection on the mirrored wall and waited for him to finish his conversation.

"Forgive me."

"Nothing to forgive. So far." She deliberately finished the drink and rinsed out the glass before she turned to him. When he began to speak she held up a hand. "Is this something that is really going to piss me off, or something that you don't want me to know because I'm not one of the boys? Tell me that first."

He hesitated before he said, "It is both."

"Okay, that explains why you were talking to the vampire king." She went to him, propping her shoulder against the window frame. "Let's hear it."

"Nicola, this is a very delicate, potentially volatile situation—"

"And when is it not?" she asked. "Just spill it."

"This dilemma has nothing to do with the Brethren. At least, we do not believe they are involved." He sounded tired, the way he did when anything reminded him of his long captivity. "The woman spoke the truth. The man who beat her was part of a group hired to kill a Kyn lord and steal the treasure he guards for us."

"This treasure would be the solid-gold scroll thing?" When he nodded, she sighed. "Wonderful. Who's the Kyn lord?"

"You don't know him," Gabriel said. "His name is Helada. Cristophe, the maker of the scroll, entrusted it to him. We must go to Provence tonight and retrieve it."

"Oh, must we?" This was just getting better and better. "Is this because we'd like to donate it to a museum?"

"The Scroll of Falkonera contains directions to create an elixir that is supposed to bestow eternal life on a worthy mortal," Gabriel said. "Over the centuries many have attempted to make and drink the elixir. Most of them died a very unpleasant death."

"But not all of them," she guessed.

"No."

"Marvelous. So we're off to Garbia." She went to the closet and began removing their clothes, carrying them over to the bed. "Do we have any friends there, or are we flying solo?"

"Richard sent Korvel to France two days past to secure the scroll."

"He sent Big, Blond, and Badass to get it?" She stopped on her way back to the closet. "Then why do we have to go?"

"Korvel apparently arrived at Château Niege early this morning, but has not been in contact with Richard since," he said slowly. "The authorities in Garbia also responded to a fire at the château this morning. They found all the servants murdered."

Nick had met the captain of Richard's guard only a few times, but she had liked him. She'd even hoped the vampire king would lend him out to work with her and Gabriel. "Did they find Korvel's body?"

"Richard does not know the fate of his seneschal; nor does it concern us," Gabriel told her. "We are being sent to track the mortals who did this, and to recover the scroll."

"Oh, give me that phone." When he wouldn't, her temper rose. "Gabriel."

"Richard is our lord, Nicola."

"He's *your* lord. Not mine." She began to pace. "I think what Richard really needs is a little refresher course on what you and I do for the Kyn. Last time I checked, baby, we don't risk our lives in territory overrun by the enemy to save stupid fucking golden scrolls." She stalked over to him. "Now give me the goddamn phone."

He held it out of reach. "You do not understand, *ma belle amie*. It is not simply a treasure."

"I don't give a shit what it is." She was shouting, and she never did that. She turned down the volume before she said, "Look, all I care about is Korvel. You remember, the really loyal guy who's been keeping Richard's ass safe for the last seven hundred years? So fuck the scroll; we need to find him. If you don't agree, tell me now and I'll go track him by myself."

Gabriel looked at the phone, and then threw it across the room before he took her into his arms. "Nothing comes between us, Nicola. We will find Korvel together."

"Good." She felt a little better. "Start packing."

Chapter 4

Although the château's stables were far enough away from the main house to prevent the fire from spreading to them, the smell of smoke had made most of the horses nervous. Simone entered the stall of the sturdiest, a dappled gray used as a plow horse, who like all her father's animals had been trained to do much more than till the soil. She bridled him before leading him out of the stall, soothing him with her hands and her voice when he fought the reins. She eyed the tack room, tempted to retrieve one of her father's expensive saddles, but they were all too small. A coil of rope and a blanket slung over the gray's broad back would have to do.

The plow horse allowed her to lead him up to the greenhouse, where she tethered him securely before returning inside. The Englishman still lay where she had left him, his big body unmoving and his chest still. When she placed her hand over his heart she felt nothing.

He weighed too much for her to carry or drag to the horse, so she would have to revive him, and only one thing would do that.

She took down a pair of pruning shears, opening them and using one sharp tip to pierce a small vein in her forearm. Once the blood began to flow, she knelt down and pressed the wound against his lips. The first few drops trickled down the side of his jaw, and then his lips moved, pressing and then clamping against her arm. She let him drink until his hand moved sluggishly to grip her, and then lifted her arm out of reach. By the time she had bound her own wound, he had begun to breathe again.

"Wake up." She shook his shoulder gently until his eyelids opened. "We have to leave here, Englishman. You must stand up and walk."

Confusion clouded his gaze. "Alexandra?"

"They will find us when they come to put out the fire. They will want to take you to the hospital." When he didn't respond, she used his name. "*Korvel.* We have to go *now.*"

He rolled onto his side, pushing himself up from the ground. Once she got her arm under him, he braced his hand on her shoulder and bent his legs, pushing himself to a crouch. She kept him from falling on top of her when he swayed, and worked her shoulder under his arm, biting her lip as she struggled to get him to his feet. He had to be twice her weight, and while she was strong she couldn't carry him to the horse.

Once he stood Simone didn't wait but pulled at him, supporting and guiding him as he shuffled along. When he tried to stop, she tugged harder. "It is only a few more meters; then you can rest again."

Korvel nodded, not wasting his breath on words, and hobbled forward.

His wounded leg barely functioned, she saw as they made their way out of the greenhouse, something she would have to deal with as soon as they reached safety. He would also require more blood by nightfall—if he lived that long—which presented another problem: Garbia had only a small clinic; anyone with serious injuries had to be transported to the hospital in the city. She couldn't call down to the village to order blood; nor could she ask the sisters to provide for him.

He will have to take what he needs from me.

The horse shied nervously as they approached, but went still as the Englishman's scent reached his broad nostrils.

"Agenouillé-toi," Simone said, shifting to keep the man braced against her. After the gray slowly lowered himself to the ground, she brought the Englishman beside him. *"Reste."* To the man, she said, "Lay yourself across his back."

When she tried to ease Korvel down, he resisted.

"I am a warrior," he muttered. "I will mount and ride."

His stubbornness reminded her of her brother Vingt, who had received twice as many beatings for defiance as any of them. In the end Vingt had not gone quietly, either. The handlers had been forced to drag him away.

"You are hurt, and you will fall on your face." She wriggled out from under him, steadying him as he sagged to his knees. She swung around him, latching onto his shoulders and digging her heels into the soil as she eased him front-first onto the gray's back. Once he was in place she bound his wrists with the rope, threading it under the gray's belly and looping the other end around his knees. She tightened the rope as much as she dared before she told the horse, *"Lève-toi."*

The gray's muscles bunched as he lifted up and stood, snorting as she adjusted the man to better center his weight.

Simone rested her forehead against the gray's strong neck, closing her eyes in relief. The distant sound of a clanging bell forced her to straighten and take hold of the bridle.

"Doucement," she told the gray as she led him around the château toward the front gates, the only exit large enough to accommodate them. As she passed the corpses littering the drive she paused here and there to retrieve more weapons. Although she doubted anyone would be waiting on the trail back to the convent, she could assume nothing.

As soon as they spotted her, some of the men Flavia had hired to ready the fields for winter came hurrying from their plows. She untied the rope and directed four of them to carry the Englishman inside.

"Should we call down to the village for the doctor, sister?" one of them asked.

"No, it looks worse than it is," she lied. "Carry him upstairs to my room, and put him in my bed." She looked over as she heard Flavia's cane sweeping from side to side along the path from the house. "I will be there in a minute."

The old abbess said nothing as she joined Simone, until the men had gone into the convent. Then she reached out and touched her face as unerringly as if she could see it. "We must talk, my child."

Simone guided her to the little rose garden where Flavia had conducted many of her lessons, and there told her what had happened. "He came for my father. He's taken the scroll in order to draw him out." She looked down at the ground. "I offered him my life. He left me to his men."

Flavia took hold of her hand. "I spoke with our superiors while you were gone. They will be sending someone to relocate us. They also gave me new instructions for you."

Simone glanced at the top floor of the convent. "What do they wish me to do?"

Flavia's lips formed a tight, bitter smile. "You are to use the Englishman sent by Tremayne to secure the treasure."

"His name is Korvel, and I rescued him," Simone told her. "He is wounded, and too weak to be of any use to us."

"Then you must revive him, child. You are to use his gifts so that you may track the thieves and retrieve the scroll."

"So he can take it to his master in England?" Simone shook her head. "They have gone mad."

"He will not be taking it anywhere." The old woman's voice went flat. "Once you have recovered the scroll, you are to destroy it . . . and kill the Englishman."

"They command me to *kill* him?" Simone stared at her. "But he has done nothing wrong. He has no more knowledge of this than that courier you clouted."

"You know that does not matter," Flavia said.

"To them, no. To me?" She got to her feet. "Mother, Korvel killed for me. He saved my life." When Flavia said nothing, Simone crossed her arms over her churning stomach. "I can't murder an innocent man. I won't do it."

"You made your oath to the council, child, as we all did," the old woman reminded her. "You are *tresori*. Your first obligation is complete obedience to your masters."

"Who are sworn to protect the dark Kyn," Simone

countered. "How does killing one of them serve that oath?"

"Such things are not explained to me," the old woman admitted, "but I can guess. If the high lord possesses the scroll, he will find out the rest. And he will have the means with which to create a new army to move against the Brethren. If Tremayne learns the council has destroyed the scroll—which his warrior would tell him as soon as he returned to England—then our other purpose will be revealed."

For seven hundred years the *tresoran* council had walked the impossibly narrow line of faithfully serving the Darkyn while ensuring that the immortals did not inflict irreversible harm on the mortal world. Their Darkyn lords depended heavily on the former but had no knowledge of the latter. Every generation of *tresori* took not only an oath of loyalty to the Kyn, but swore to protect the future of mankind by any means necessary.

All the fight went out of Simone, who sat down beside the abbess. "So the Englishman must never leave France."

"Not alive," Flavia agreed, and turned her head toward the convent. "His wound and the daylight will have him at his most vulnerable now. The council need never know that he survived the confrontation at the château." She groped for Simone's hand. "If you will guide me, I will do it."

"No." The thought of them going upstairs to kill the man while he was helpless made Simone sick. "I do need him. Pájaro is telling his men that he is Helada."

Flavia made a disgusted sound. "Why didn't your father kill him like all the others?"

"The night before he was to be tested, Pájaro stole Piers's wallet and car and ran away." Simone remembered how angry her father had been when he had opened the door to the empty cell. "A month after that the police in Marseilles called. They had found Pájaro drowned. He had been in the water for weeks, but they found Piers's identification as well as his keys. Everyone knew that Pájaro could not swim; water was the only thing he ever feared. Father told them to burn the body and never spoke of him again."

"He must have killed a boy who resembled him, and planted the evidence on his body." Flavia made the sign of the cross over herself.

"He knew if Father thought he was still alive, he would never stop searching for him." Simone looked at one gnarled, dead-looking rosebush. It seldom had more than a dozen leaves on its spindly canes, but still steadily produced the largest and most exquisite flowers at the convent. The reason for that made her get to her feet. "I must tend to the Englishman and then rest while I can."

"He will want blood when he wakes tonight," Flavia warned. "I will provide it."

"You can't risk—"

"Nor can you." She reached out and touched the strip of cloth Simone had bound around her forearm. "I may be blind, child, but I am not stupid. Nor have I forgotten how much I may safely take from my own veins to mix in some wine. Now go to him."

Simone retrieved some tools from the garden shed before she went upstairs and sent the field hands back to their work. Once inside, she bolted her door and laid out the tools on the end of her pallet.

Her bed was too small for a man Korvel's size, and provided no room in which to turn him. She tore her sheets by using them to drag him half over the edge before she rolled him onto his front.

Time was running out for him, so she discarded the idea of cutting off his bloodstained garments, and instead tore the rent in the back of his trousers wider to give her easier access to his wound. Pájaro's man had buried his blade deep, and only a tiny piece protruded from the still-bleeding gash.

Simone picked up the slimmest pair of pliers and clamped them around the protrusion. She tugged carefully on the thin metal, wriggling and easing it at a slight angle rather than pulling it straight out. Fresh blood streaked with black grease welled up the broken blade.

She knew the risk she took. If the metal snapped and even the tiniest sliver of copper entered his veins, it would lodge in his heart and spread poison from there into every other vessel in his body. He would die in minutes.

The metal remained intact, although she could feel the serrations tearing anew through Korvel's flesh. As soon as she saw the tip of the broken blade, she pulled it free and tossed it to the floor. She inserted her fingertips into the wound, holding it open as she used her teeth to pull the cloth wound around her forearm away from the cut.

It hurt to bite around the cut, but she applied only enough pressure to make herself bleed again before holding her forearm over the open wound. As soon as her blood dripped into the gash, Korvel's bleeding stopped, and the tear slowly began to shrink inside.

Korvel's hair began to rapidly darken, turning from flaxen gold to a dark red. Like all *tresori*, Simone knew that Kyn with copper poisoning often shed the metal through their scalp, which caused the color of their hair to change. Because the copper now staining Korvel's hair would also cause irritation to his skin, she used her sewing shears to cut off most of the length.

Exhaustion, not all of it from her own blood loss, turned Simone's limbs to lead. Her hands shook as she ripped clean strips from the remains of her sheets to bind his leg and her forearm. After that she intended to climb off the bed and get a blanket from her chest so she could sleep on the floor, but Korvel's arm encircled her waist to pull her down beside him. He did not wake, but when she tried to move away from his big body, his arm tightened and he shifted, tucking her head in the space between his shoulder and neck. The coolness of his skin felt good against her hot face.

Of course, he needed her warmth, she decided, too tired to fight his hold another moment.

The universe had become gray sludge.

Korvel no longer permitted himself to pass into the nightlands, where the Darkyn went to rest and recover from the brutalities of the world. Too much of that strange territory reminded him of Alexandra, whom he had lured there more than once.

Nor could he sleep as once he had during his mortal life, as one of the prices of immortality was perpetual awareness. Even when blood loss and injury shut down his physical form, his mind remained active.

Being nowhere, he sensed only what there was: nothing.

Korvel knew the brief battles in which he had engaged had not harmed him greatly, but the poisonous effect of the copper lodged in his flesh had rendered him weak and listless. In another time he would have fought his way back to life and his place in it, but his current apathy made it a difficult thing to desire. Why leave the dull gray void in which he lay suspended, only to return to a world that no longer held any interest for him?

His dismal thoughts conjured images of the young nun with the angelic face. She had been tormented and nearly raped; she remained alone on the other side. He suspected he hadn't killed all of the men who had attacked the château, and if they came upon her while he was helpless . . .

Korvel reached for consciousness, and at once the void dragged at him, becoming a sea of muck through which he waded, one infuriatingly slow step at a time. He was much weaker than he had guessed, dangerously so; if he were to awake it would have to be by will alone.

Once more he thought of the green-eyed angel who had tended to his wound. Whatever faith had compelled her to abandon life and serve an uncaring God, she was still an innocent. As such she needed—no, deserved— his assistance. *I will go to her and keep her safe.*

He could feel her, close to him now, her presence like a muted caress. Even through the gnashing teeth of fresh pain, she calmed him. His weakness grew as his sense of her faded, and he reached out blindly, capturing her warmth and enfolding it against him. There she remained, unresisting and silent, until his thoughts dwindled and he entered a darker corner of the void to rest and heal.

Sometime later, the setting of the sun roused Korvel to consciousness. He sensed this time that he had more strength to draw on, and crossed the emptiness with only a brief effort. He felt her warmth slipping away, and opened his eyes.

Cracked hand-carved moldings framed a rough plaster ceiling spotted with small water stains and draped in one corner with the dusty remains of some long-dead spider's trap. The soft amber light illuminating it came from fat beeswax candles set in crystal goblets half filled with pretty pebbles and shells, which had been spaced like treasures across a stone shelf. A muslin pinafore hung from the knob of bolted door, over which a plain wooden cross had been nailed. A basket with balled wool and knitting needles sat beside a shabby tapestry chair; a chipped blue stoneware jug sat inside a matching basin in an iron stand.

He turned his head to see a small shrine built atop an old secretary: flowers and votive candles in punched-tin holders surrounding a diminutive statue of the Virgin Mary in her blue robes and white headdress. A rosary of gray stone beads and blackened silver lay draped around the base of the statue.

If this were the cloistered cell it appeared to be, then the nun had brought him to her convent. If this were a jail cell, the French police had greatly improved the living conditions within their prisons.

A flutter of fabric drew his attention to the foot of the pallet, where the nun stood with her back toward him. She was in the process of undressing, and while Korvel knew he should look away, he couldn't stop watching her. She pulled the bloodstained gray habit over her head to reveal the long line of her spine. She tugged at the drawstring of her only undergarment, a pair of loose cotton drawers, before sliding them down her legs.

Now naked, she went to the basin stand, where she poured water from the jug into the bowl and began to wash the blood from her body.

The tightening of his muscles didn't distract Korvel from watching her, but the knotting in his groin did. His shaft hardened and swelled, inching back his foreskin from the tight dome of his glans.

Carnal desire racked him, demanding relief, and it stunned him. It had been so long since he had wanted any mortal female that his arousal seemed utterly alien, as if some unseen predator had burrowed under his skin and decided to amuse itself by infesting his cock.

The nun's body beckoned to him, an oasis of pleasures yet to be had, but he could resist her by thinking of her innocence. She belonged to God, not him. It was when she took down her braids and unraveled them, combing through the long, bright strands with her fingers, that he crumpled the bed linens in his fists. Once free, her hair fell in luminous waves all the way to her hips, glinting like fiery gold in the candlelight.

Korvel had not seen a woman with such hair in centuries, not since mortal females had lived out their entire lives without once cutting a single hair from their head.

He frowned as he saw that the light had also chased the shadows from her skin, and revealed a collection of odd, pale marks all over her. The random positions of the marks and the fact that she was a nun made it highly unlikely they were tan lines. The marks themselves formed a variety of shapes; on her left hip one narrow stripe curled like a lock of hair, but a few inches above it a broader, straight slash bisected her shoulder blade.

Only when she dried herself and went to kneel before the shrine did she come close enough for him to see the faint ridges of the marks, which made Korvel realize at last what they were.

Scar tissue. Someone had grievously abused the nun, so harshly and often that they had left her scarred from her nape to her knees.

Lust ebbed, scoured away by shock, shame, and an empathy he had never felt for a mortal of the modern world. As she took down the rosary and began murmuring her prayers, Korvel recalled the years of punishment he had once endured, the dismal human life he had never been able to forget. Small wonder she had turned her back on the world to cloister herself. Perhaps, like him, she had never received a single kindness from her birth family.

As Korvel pushed himself into a sitting position, the nun glanced over her shoulder and then kissed the rosary before replacing it. Instead of scurrying for clothing to cover her nakedness, she fastened a silver chain around her neck and came to the pallet, climbing up onto it and pushing him back against the pillows.

Shocked anew, Korvel stared at her. "What are you doing?"

"Attending you." She pushed her hair back over her shoulders and produced a small folding knife, opening it and plying it against her forearm.

Her body heat combined with the blood scent and slammed into him, as merciless as it was enticing. Korvel managed to turn his head away as she brought her arm to his mouth. "No."

"Take it." She pressed against his cheek with her free hand, guiding his mouth along her thin skin until his lips parted.

As hot as it was luscious, her blood coursed inside him as if it were molten sunlight, eating away at his coldness and flaring in every shadowy corner of his soul. He wanted nothing more than to roll her beneath him and take her completely, his teeth piercing her throat, his body pushing into hers, drinking from her and moving inside her until she knew and wanted nothing but him.

He was descending into the thrall of bloodlust, which seemed as bizarre as his sudden desire for this mortal. Never had he been tempted to drain a human upon whom he fed, for he knew the act that would send them both into the nightlands. There she would die, and he would be trapped, senseless and unmoving, for days. Now at last he understood the terrible temptation of that thrall and rapture, and how it destroyed all reasoning, all will.

Korvel wrenched his mouth from her, and for an instant it was if he tore the heart from his own chest. "Stop."

A line formed between her brows. "Am I not to your liking?"

Her taste had nearly reduced him to a beast, not that he would frighten her by saying so. "You have given enough to restore me. That is all I can ask of you." Because his voice sounded so harsh, he caught her hand and brought it to his lips. "I am grateful for your kindness."

"Kindness." She seemed bemused, and ran her fingertip across the tight line of his mouth, wiping away a trace of her blood. "You have a very strange way of speaking, Englishman."

"Korvel." He wanted to hear his name on her lips.

She tilted her head, spilling a cascade of rose-streaked gold over her bare shoulder. "I am obliged to call you 'my lord,' or at the very least 'Captain.'"

He couldn't keep his hand from brushing back the fine flax of her tresses, or from curling around her nape. "Call me any damn thing you wish," he murmured as he brought her head down to his.

Kissing her was his worst mistake, for while she had the face of an angel he discovered her lips were all fiery

softness and womanly delight. She made a faint, aston-
ished sound in her throat as he used his tongue, stiffen-
ing one moment and then opening for him the next.

Korvel's eyes closed as he savored her, his hand
clamping over the back of her skull as he slanted her
face for better access. The wet heat of her mouth was
made for sex, for making a man ache with all the things
he might teach her to do with it.

He would take her back to Ireland with him, he decided, and install her in the castle as his bedmate, so that
he could have her whenever he wanted her—

Simone pressed her hands against his chest, lifting up
and gazing down at him, the cross around her neck
swinging gently. "Do you want me?"

Her, yes, endless nights with her under his hands, eager and straining, always ready to provide him with all
the pleasures she had sacrificed to become a bride of
Christ. His eyes went to the cross she wore. Instead of a
depiction of Christ, the exquisitely worked silver held a
tiny jewel in its center. If he did not get her off him in the
next three seconds, he would begin to destroy her reasons to wear the symbol of her faith, along with everything of importance to her.

"No." He took his hands from her hair. "I do not require that of you."

Now, thanks to his ability, she would beg and plead
for it, unaware that she had fallen under the worst of his
power. Korvel clenched his teeth, ready to endure her
pleading, only to go still as she bobbed her head like a
polite peasant and climbed down from the pallet. She
knelt to open the trunk and retrieve some clean garments.

He had not enraptured her, Korvel realized. He
doubted she was even bespelled—and then it occurred

to him why she hadn't fallen under his command. "You are *tresori.*"

She slipped into a fitted undershirt and panties before turning to him. She lifted her left arm out, turning it to display the tattoo of a black cameo. Instead of the profile of a Kyn lord, a mariner's compass had been inked in the center of it.

Korvel recognized the rare design, a designation given to sentinels, mortals sworn in service to the elders of the *tresoran* council. Only the most trusted of the Kyn's human servants were permitted to take the oath, which elevated them above all other *tresori.*

It also made her a mortal equal to Korvel in rank, something that completely astounded him. "Why did they send you to France?"

"They did not send me. I live here." She tugged on a pair of dark trousers. "The men who burned the château have taken the scroll to Marseilles. I must go prepare some supplies for the trip." She pulled on a knitted long-sleeved sweater before she took a stack of clothing and placed it on the bed. "These should fit you."

His long hair should have fallen in a curtain around his face as he reached for the garments, but only a few dark red strands spilled over his forehead. He rubbed a hand over his shorn head. "You knew to cut my hair."

She nodded. "Until your body sheds all the copper in your blood, it is best to keep it short. If you wish to bathe before we leave, I saved you some clean water in the pitcher."

He started to tell her he didn't need her to accompany him, but she walked out of the cell, quietly closing the door behind her. Rising from the pallet to follow her, he felt a twinge from his leg wound, and reached around to probe it. Thanks to her ministrations and the blood she had given him, it would be completely healed by morning.

Korvel went to the basin, first splashing his face with the cold water and then drying it on the towel she had used. It smelled of sunshine and her, and he breathed in deeply.

"How are you feeling, my lord?"

He dropped the towel to see an old woman standing a few feet away. "I am well. Who are you?"

"Flavia Roux, the abbess of this convent." She dropped into a polite curtsy before holding out a dark bottle toward him. "For your needs, should any still linger."

"Sister Simone attended to me." He noticed her expression as he took the bottle. "She did so freely."

She sniffed. "From the smell of you I expect they all do. You should know that Simone has never been called on to serve, and has no practical experience with the sort of demands your lot make."

"But you do," he guessed.

The old woman inclined her head. "Thirty years I served in the household of Seigneur Tristan. Had I not lost my sight, I would still be there, explaining the bizarre nature of social behaviors among mortals, and the inexplicable delights of modern sexual freedoms. But I came here and created a haven for other *tresori* women blinded by illness or injury. I brought them back to God. And I have taught Simone everything I know."

No wonder the nun had thought nothing of her nudity. No one here could see her. "The girl is of your bloodline?"

"No." Flavia listened for a moment. "Our sisters are awakening, so I must be brief. Pájaro, the coward who orchestrated this butchery, was once in training to serve as a sentinel. He failed, but before he could be dealt with properly he fled. Make no mistake: He is not simply another ignorant mortal."

That explained the copper-clad weapons his men had used. "Has this traitor allied himself with the Brethren?"

"No. The only allegiance he has is to himself and the vengeance he seeks. Do not underestimate him, for he has had ten years to prepare for this day." She took a step closer, and reached out to touch his arm. "Whatever happens, you must not allow him to take Simone alive."

He stiffened. "Madame, I have no intention of —"

"I speak for the council now," she said, cutting him off. "If you cannot keep her safe in this life, then you must send her on to the next. It will not be an easy thing, but it must be done."

"Do you know what you are asking of me?" he demanded. "That girl saved my life."

"These are the wishes of the council. No sentinel may be taken alive. As for me . . ." She stopped, and with some difficulty went down on her knees. "I love Simone like a daughter, and I would gladly take her place. But I cannot. So I beg you, my lord, spare her the suffering Pájaro will inflict on her. For the sake of your kind as well."

Over the centuries Korvel had heard stories about the sentinels and their vast knowledge of the Darkyn. While all *tresori* were trained from birth to serve, only the council and their sentinels were permitted complete knowledge of their masters, from the location of their strongholds to the number of sworn immortals in the Kyn lord's household and garrison, collectively known as the *jardin.* Under the duress of torture, Simone could be forced to reveal all she knew about the Darkyn.

He lifted her back to her feet. "I will look after her,

and when this is done, I will bring her home to you. But if that is not possible, then I will see her safely to the next place."

She blinked back bright tears. "You have my eternal gratitude, my lord." She extracted a thick envelope from her skirt and pressed it into his hands. "Money for the trip, as well as a map to our safe house in Marseilles. I will pray for you both."

Chapter 5

Simone checked the fuel gauge on the courier's Land Rover before she opened the hood to inspect the motor and its oil and fluids. Although it was almost new, she had learned never to assume that any vehicle was kept in good operating condition. This one, at least, had been maintained, and when she started the engine it ran smoothly.

She searched the interior, removing two loaded handguns that had been taped under the front seats and a bundle of cash in various currencies and several expertly forged passports wedged behind the false back of the glove box. She pressed her lips together as she found one final stash, a lozenge box with a variety of capsules, vials, and even a small syringe, all neatly concealed beneath the top layer of cough drops.

So the courier served another master, one who wanted to deliver more than a message no one could understand. Whoever had sent him must have thought her an idiot.

She shut off the car and sat looking at the convent. The Englishman's kiss had left her lips tender and her thoughts in a tangle. He had wanted her; she'd felt the evidence of that pressing like an iron bar against her bottom. So why had he refused her? Had she not offered herself properly? She knew the Darkyn had strange ideas about correctness and protocol; Flavia had never tired of recounting her years with the Italian lord she had served. Simone also knew that when in dire need the immortals always wanted sex as much as blood.

Perhaps he prefers men to women. But if that were so, then she should not have aroused him. He had kissed her and touched her with such passion, in fact, that she had expected to be taken without any discussion at all.

Simone understood physical desire, and how to control and channel it, but his mouth on hers had caused all her training to vanish. In the space of a heartbeat she had been rendered mindless, all flesh and feeling. Her father had always said mastering the art of physical pleasure was to gain an enormous weapon against which there was almost no defense. In this as in all things, he had been right, and she had nearly become a victim of her own senses.

Would it have been so terrible?

Living in a house of women for so long had made her forget what strong and beautiful brutes some men could be. Even in that Korvel had surprised her, for while his strength far surpassed her own, he had handled her with restraint, as if she were something precious.

What would he think of her if he knew what she had burned to do to him? As he kissed her she had clenched her hands and her teeth, not to resist, but to keep from using them to tear at his clothes. She had wanted to make him as naked as she was, to see the column of his shaft so that she might stroke it and hear him groan before she guided it to the clenching ache between her thighs.

She had never known a desire for sex. Even as she wanted to blame him for her bewildering emotions, she knew the fault was her own. He had no power over her other than his physical superiority; he could make her do nothing against her will.

He can't make me do anything.

She got out of the car and walked to the old chapel, where she slipped in through the side door. Because the sisters had no need of light she had learned to move through the small, dark sanctuary just as blindly, and made her way instinctively to the simple altar where the village priest sometimes stood to deliver one of his out-dated sermons.

She knelt down behind it, tracing the outer seam of the pedestal until she found the hidden latches to release it. The bag stuffed inside had not been removed from its hiding place since she had placed it there. At times she had amused herself by imagining it being found someday, far off in the future, to puzzle whoever had wrested it from the convent's ruins.

Now it would vanish from those distant sands of time, just as she would.

"I do not hear you praying, child," a querulous voice admonished from the pews. "You must be taking out that bag from the altar."

Simone slung the bag's strap over her shoulder and walked down to where Sister Marie sat in the front pew. "There is no bag, sister."

"Of course not. Just as there is no hidden panel in the upstairs linen closet, nor a very large man who drinks blood in your room." Marie closed the Braille Bible in her hands. "The truly pitiful thing is how often you treat us like ignorant children. We were all once *tresori,* child."

"You are too good at making me forget that." Simone

sat down beside her. "Is something wrong back at the house?"

"Other than that horrible marmalade Paulette insists is not too tart? No. Flavia sent me to give you this." She handed a sheathed blade to Simone. "Into the heart or through the spinal cord will see it done. Strike quickly, and it will be virtually painless."

She removed the slim, long knife from the leather, and saw that it had been forged from copper. "Did she tell you?"

"What the council demands of you? I can guess." She turned her head toward the altar. "Once, when I was young, I thought them nothing but silly old men who saw monsters in every dark corner. They are not that, child, but they are mortal. As such, they sometimes make mistakes."

"What are you trying to tell me?"

"Anyone may give you a blade, Simone." The old woman knelt down and folded her hands, positioning the first bead of her rosary between her fingers. "Whether or not to use it is always your decision."

After washing himself and donning the garments Sister Simone had set out for him, Korvel tested the strength of his leg on the stairs. While the wound still throbbed, he felt none of the numbing coldness that would indicate any copper remained in his flesh. The young nun's blood as well as the bloodwine the abbess had brought to him had done much to restore his strength, although he would need to feed several more times before he fought again.

Not from her, Korvel decided. He would not risk causing either of them to fall under the spell of thrall and rapture.

Outside the convent he saw Simone loading a bag and several boxes into the back of a Land Rover. She moved with speed and efficiency, and while she still appeared pale she demonstrated no signs of weakness. During her *tresoran* training she had probably been conditioned to withstand the effects of regular blood loss. Over the centuries mortals who were born to serve the Kyn had gradually developed tolerances and immunities that ordinary humans lacked, such as a resistance to *l'attrait*.

She cannot resist my ability. No mortal female ever had. *I could have had her a dozen times, and she would only have begged for more.*

Her unremarkable clothing and the black cap she had used to cover her braids should have rendered her unnoticeable, but Korvel found his gaze drawn to the trousers, which emphasized the elegant length of her legs. When she bent over to arrange something, the sweet curves of her buttocks made him clench his fists, but he didn't look away.

Lust roiled inside him, but he could withstand the longing of his body. He knew why he wanted Simone: because he could not have her. *Tresora* or not, she was a nun. His honor would not permit him to violate the innocence of her body or the vows of chastity she had already taken.

She glanced up as he joined her. "It is only a few hours' drive to Marseilles. We have friends there who will assist us in tracking the thieves."

"Before we go I must return to my car and retrieve my belongings," he advised her. "I left it on the road by the turnoff into the hills. Give me the keys."

"I know all the roads, as well as the quickest routes, Captain," she pointed out. "You do not."

Centuries of commanding instant obedience from the most vicious warriors among the Kyn had not prepared Korvel to be questioned by a mortal female. That she was right only further annoyed him. As he ducked into the passenger side of the Land Rover, he asked, "Can you drive faster than a cabbage farmer?"

"I don't know." Now she sounded irritated. "I've never raced one."

As soon as Korvel shut the door she started the engine and made a three-point turn, driving around the convent to a gravel-and-dirt road that divided two fields. He saw several men with large canvas bags slung across their torsos; each stood crouched over the short, leafy rows of vegetables. All the dead mortals he had seen at the château had been elderly, and all the women at the convent were blind. "Sister, why did the council not send men to protect the scroll and its guardian?"

"Until yesterday, no one knew it was here." The Land Rover bounced as she turned onto a narrow dirt road. "Helada has no need of protection."

"You know the guardian personally?"

Her lips twisted. "All my life."

He saw a wispy column of smoke rising in the distance. "Among the Kyn, Helada's reputation is legend. In more than six centuries no one has ever laid eyes upon him. It has been said that he kills anyone who docs. Now you tell me that you have known him for years." When she didn't reply, he added, "Why did he spare your life?"

"That is a very long story, Captain," she said as she braked to a stop. "One that will have to wait for another time."

"Why?"

She nodded at the windshield. "Your car is on fire."

Korvel turned his head and swore as he saw the flames and smoke pouring out of the Audi. One of the rear windows had been smashed in, and the smoke carried with it the stink of grain alcohol.

Simone walked to the back of the Land Rover, where she retrieved a small fire extinguisher and walked down to the Audi. By the time he reached her she had begun spraying foam through the broken window.

"Sister." He caught her arm. "The petrol tank."

"It hasn't spread that far yet." She continued using the extinguisher until the flames disappeared and all that was left was a smoldering ruin. She lowered the nozzle, peered inside at the sooty foam coating the interior, and then glanced down each side of the road. "Were you followed here?"

"No." Korvel wrenched open the driver's-side door to see what could be salvaged. The heat had melted his mobile phone into a blob of plastic, and the nylon bag containing the rest of his belongings had been reduced to a pile of ash. As the foam dissipated he saw the glitter of glass spread across the backseat. The soot-blackened shards were too curved to have come from the smashing of the window. "They used a bottle of alcohol for the firebomb."

He went to open the trunk and found it filled with smoke. The flames, however, had not reached his sword.

Korvel removed his coat to strap on his blade harness. As soon as the sheathed sword pressed against his shoulder blades the damnable sense of feeling naked disappeared. "What sort of field training did the council give you, sister?"

"Field training?" She frowned. "None."

He eyed her. "But you are *tresora*. You must have had some instruction."

"I know what my duties are, Captain, and I am capable of attending to them." Her expression turned bleak. "We should go."

"I need a satellite phone." When she didn't produce one, he made an impatient sound. "Take me to a secure phone line, then. I must contact the high lord and relate what has happened to the scroll."

"This is a farming village, Captain, not Paris. Your call will have to wait until we reach the city." She started walking back to the Land Rover.

Korvel followed her to the vehicle. "What was the council thinking? You are completely unprepared for this."

She stopped in her tracks and slowly turned around. "How is it that you were prepared?" Her eyes shifted past him. "You came here alone, with no one to have your back. You tried to fight mortals armed with copper blades, and you're still limping from a wound that should have killed you. You don't know where they are or how to find them. Oh, and now you have no phone."

He clenched his jaw. "I did not try to fight those mortals," he told her. "I killed them. All of them."

"Did you? Then tell me, Captain, where is the scroll? And who burned your car?" She tossed the fire extinguisher into the back of the Land Rover and got in, waiting only until Korvel was inside before taking off.

He reined in his temper and breathed deeply until he felt calm enough to speak without shouting. "Forgive me, sister. I spoke without thinking. I never intended to insult you or your service to me."

"I do not serve you." Now she spoke through gritted teeth. "I belong to the council. They command me."

"As you say." He had no experience with sentinels; she was as much as mystery to him as the Scroll of Falkonera. "But with no combat training, you cannot hope to retrieve the scroll on your own. It took only four of those men to render you helpless, and if I had not come upon you, they would have violated and killed you." He saw her hands tighten on the wheel until the knuckles whitened. "I am sorry to remind you of your ordeal. What matters now is the scroll. I need your help to find it, just as you will need me to take it back. I suggest we focus on working together to . . ." He trailed off as he realized how much his scent had intensified, and stared at her. "Why am I arguing with you?"

She gave him an odd look. "Because you are English, and a man?"

"You should be agreeing with every word I say to you." Indeed, even an experienced *tresora* with years of service could not hope to evade its effects in such a small, confined space. He caught her chin and made her look at him. Both of her pupils were normal size, and all he saw in her lovely green eyes was annoyance. "You are not merely resistant to *l'attrait.* You are entirely immune to it."

"All sentinels are. The council considers it a prerequisite, so they test us to see whether we were born with the immunity before we enter training. *Tresori* of our rank could not carry out some of our duties if the Kyn were able to influence or control us."

"You mean you could not spy on us for the council."

"I am not a spy." She jerked her chin away and turned her face back toward the road.

"At the château, and later, in your room, you were not bespelled." When she said nothing, he demanded, "If I cannot compel you, they why did you behave as if I had?"

She moved her shoulders. "I serve the council."

"Is that your answer to every question?"

"There is nothing more I can tell you." She pressed her lips together before she asked in a softer voice, "When your master gives you an order, does he explain it to you? When you command your guard, do you offer them reasons as to why they should obey?"

"No," he admitted. "Never."

"It is the same for us." She touched the place on her sleeve that covered the *tresoran* tattoo on her inner arm. "We take an oath. We are commanded; we obey."

She wasn't lying—her scent would have changed— but he sensed that a much more complicated version of the truth lay concealed by her simple statements. Since he could not bring her under his influence, he couldn't compel her to elaborate, either.

"You have never engaged the enemy," he guessed out loud, and was surprised again to see her nod. "That is why the council ordered you to bring me along. To serve as your guard and your blade."

One corner of her mouth curled. "You sound as if you are insulted."

He should have been, and would be, had he not come to the same conclusion. "The Kyn are more accustomed to having mortals serve *us.*"

"We must both do things unfamiliar to us," she agreed. "But we can take comfort in that we serve the same purpose."

They both lapsed into silence. She had clipped short the nails on her long fingers, Korvel noted, and more of the faint, odd scars covered both hands from knuckles to wrists. Despite the evidence of the wounds she had suffered in the past, her hands looked strong and capable, as they had felt when she had touched him. He dragged his thoughts away from those moments and instead wondered why her fingers were bare. She should have been wearing the traditional plain gold band presented to a novice when she took her vows and became a bride of Christ.

Perhaps she left it behind at the convent, with her habit and her rosary. Why had the council permitted her to become a nun in the first place? *Because no one would suspect her.*

She did not look at all like a nun now, however. Korvel eyed the boy's cap on her head, wishing she would take it off. No mortal female he had ever known, not even Alexandra Keller, had possessed such long, beautiful hair.

"Why do you never cut your hair?" he heard himself ask.

"It is a personal vanity," she said. "My father always kept it short when I was a child. Why was yours so long?"

"I kept forgetting to attend to it." Korvel decided her father was an idiot. He wanted to unpin her braids and unravel them, one by one, so that he might comb his fingers through the fiery golden strands and feel their silkiness against his skin once more.

Stop thinking about her damn hair.

She turned off the road from Garbia to take a ramp onto a wider, busier roadway. "Do you know Marseilles?"

"I have not been here since the monarchy fell," he said, glad for the distraction, "and then came only to smuggle my kind across the channel."

She frowned. "That was a terrible time to visit."

"It was." He didn't want to think about the mortal madness and mass murder he had witnessed during the French Revolution. "How did you come to be so familiar with the city?"

"My father frequently traveled there on business." She pulled into the next lane to pass a slower-moving van and just as deftly changed the subject. "I have never been to England. Is it as miserable as my countrymen say?"

Korvel felt amused. The poor opinion the French held of his homeland was one that had been perpetuated since the time of William the Conqueror, and still showed no signs of ever changing. "Most of our cities are as old and crowded as yours, and the people equally self-absorbed. Our weather is not as fair as yours, but the countryside is not so different. Garbia reminds me of the village where I was born."

"Never tell anyone in Garbia that," she advised. "Do you ever go back to visit your people?"

"No." Korvel's eyelids drooped as he thought of the night he had been dragged from his bed by the old baron, who had informed him of his mother's death simply by tossing him out into the snow before bolting the doors against him. "The last of my mortal kin died many centuries ago."

"I forget how long you have lived." She glanced at him. "I don't mean to offend you, Captain. I know that I should speak only when spoken to in your presence; I have simply never met one of you in person."

"I do not mind your talking to me." Something about what she said vexed him, but he didn't know why. Nor did he want to talk about the Kyn. "What is it like living in a convent filled with blind women?"

"I'm never scolded for getting a sunburned nose when I forget to wear my hat in the garden," she said, her voice wry. "Nor does anyone complain about the stains I can't get out of their aprons, or the poor quality of my mending. Well, except for the time when Sister

Paulette forgot to close a gate, and Saint Paul decided to pay a visit to the laundry."

"You had a visitation from a saint?"

"A goat," she advised him gravely. "The sisters named them all after the apostles. Saint Paul is the largest and noisiest, and he hates everyone but Father Robere. I think that's why he's always the first one to stray. He's forever trying to escape all these women around him."

Korvel watched her face as she described some of the wayward goat's antics. Every nun he had ever encountered had been stern faced and thin lipped, but not Sister Simone. As she spoke her pretty features came alive, while her mouth curved and pouted and framed every word as if it were something delicious to be tasted. In her chamber she had not fought nor returned his kiss, but her lips had parted for him and surrendered her mouth to his. He imagined her atop him, her mouth caressing a path down his chest, her breath warming his flesh, her hair entwined in his hands as he guided her, gently but deliberately, until she opened those lovely, soft lips to taste the aching swell of his cock head—

God in heaven, would he never stop thinking about having her?

Simone seemed oblivious to his silent plight as she continued her story. ". . . and, of course, I had to lure them out of the vegetable garden. Luckily for me they like blackberries more than turnip tops. It wasn't until I had the last of them penned that I noticed Saint Paul was still missing. I am boring you."

"No." That came out too harshly, so he tried again. "Not at all. What happened next?"

"I searched the fields, the barn, the drying sheds, and even the house, but there was no sign of him." She sighed. "By noon I decided he had made good his escape, and went to start the laundry. There I discovered every basket chewed and trampled, and shreds of what had been the laundry scattered to the four corners. All of the aprons had vanished. Finally I found Saint Paul sleeping peacefully under the washbasin, his belly swollen, and an apron string still caught in his teeth."

"They will eat anything," Korvel said. "What did you do with him?"

"First we waited to see whether he would explode," she admitted. "When he didn't, Mother said the crime would also be the punishment. And it was, for Saint Paul soon learned that what goes in must also come out."

"How many aprons did he eat?"

"After three days of bloating and belching, he finally slung out three in his cud, strings and all." Her lips twisted. "Now all I have to do is flap my apron at him and he runs for the pen."

Chapter 6

Simone liked the sound of the Englishman's laugh. It curled around her, silky and warm, like a cashmere shawl. Like his voice, it also had a rasping quality to it, as if it hadn't been used in a long time. As soon as it trailed away she wanted to hear it again, to feel its deep resonance before the coldness of her duty froze the last feeling from her heart.

My duty. Her eyes stung, and her throat grew tight.

For all the years she had lived at the convent, Simone had always known this would someday happen. She had carried the threat of it every day, like an invisible yoke. The weight of her duty, like the irrational guilt she felt over failing to be a true Derien, dragged at her. Not once in all the generations that preceded Simone had anyone refused to carry on the family's obligations; her rebellion had put an abrupt end to seven hundred years of tradition held sacred by the Deriens. She carried so many unforgivable sins, but the bargain was the worst. She had tried to convince herself that it was the price of her freedom, but she had been its prisoner ever since making the promise to her father.

Simone didn't have to look at Korvel to know he was

watching her again. He would also know how miserable she felt; Flavia had said the Kyn could smell emotions and lies. But he would assume that she was merely missing her home, and she could divert his attention as simply as he had hers. "What is it like being captain of the high lord's guard?"

"I never sunburn or garden," he admitted gravely. "But once a hungry mare forced me and the entire garrison to improve the quality of our mending."

He told her a story about a practical joke played by one of his men on another that backfired badly. The warrior had borrowed a mare from a neighboring farmer and left her in the quarters of another Kyn with whom he had quarreled. Scattering grain around the room in hopes that she would wreak havoc on the man's possessions, the joker had left to join the rest of the garrison for training. His only mistake was not securing the door, or knowing of the mare's fondness for eating anything shiny.

"She got out and went from chamber to chamber. By the time we returned from the lists we found she had been at every coat, shirt, shoe, and pair of trousers left out within her reach. Not a single button remained on any of them." He shook his head, remembering. "Only when I sent for the wardrobe master to repair the garments was I informed that he was away in London on a buying trip, and would not return for another week."

"What about the other servants?"

"It was near Christmas, and all had been sent to visit their mortal families for the month. We sorted out what garments the mare had left unscathed and found we had but a mere dozen changes of clothing left—not nearly enough to garb a hundred men—and the high lord due in less than an hour to inspect the garrison."

"Laundering what you were already wearing would have taken at least another day," she guessed.

"It would, had any of us known how to use the bloody machines," he agreed. "Which, of course, none of us did."

Simone couldn't imagine a solution to the embarrassing dilemma. "Did you go to your master and explain what had happened?"

He made a cutting gesture. "Sooner I would have fallen on a copper-clad sword. No, what I did was order the men to bathe their faces and then don full armor. When our lord came to the courtyard to inspect the guard, he asked me why they appeared prepared to march into battle. I told him that I had decided to conduct surprise readiness drills." He waited a beat. "For the entire week."

Shocked, she caught her breath. "You *lied.*"

"I saw to it that the men made it the truth. Every night for the next week, half the garrison ran drills in full armor," he told her, "while the other half became acquainted with the joys of sewing on buttons and mending seams. Never have needle and thread been so repeatedly, continually cursed."

His laugh invited Simone to do the same, but the sound that caught in her throat felt like a sob. All at once there was too much of him, too close to her, as if he had somehow slipped through her defenses and was only a heartbeat away from possessing her soul. No one, not her father, not even the sisters, had made her feel so open, so vulnerable.

And then her father's voice, as soft as a caress, snaked out of her memory. *Are you unworthy, daughter?*

She would not do this, not in his presence. A sign for a rest area appeared and she quickly moved into the exit lane, hoping she could make it before he suspected what was wrong.

"I must stop for a moment," she managed to say, and had the Land Rover parked and the engine switched off a moment later.

"I will accompany you."

"No, thank you, Captain." Without looking at him she pushed open the door and climbed out. "I will return shortly."

She did not run until she was out of his sight, and she made it as far as a sink in the women's restroom, where she doubled over and vomited. To cover the sound of her retching she turned on the tap, and then braced herself with her hands as she brought up the rest.

Finally the nausea receded and she could breathe again. She splashed her face and rinsed out her mouth, running the water until the sink cleared before she looked into the mirror, and then wearily rubbed at her pale cheeks until some color returned.

When the bell rings, the dog feeds.

"I am not a dog." The words came out on a whisper and ended with a single tear that welled on the edge of her lashes. She used the heel of her hand to dash it away.

Someone, probably the captain, was walking toward the restroom; the heavy footfalls made her straighten. She dried her face and mouth on her sleeve, set her cap to rights, and composed herself. If he had heard her puking, she would blame it on Sister Paulette's too-sour preserves, and tell him the story and make him laugh again. This time she would endure the warmth of it and let it pass through her without stirring her feelings or making herself sick.

Stepping out, Simone didn't see Korvel or anyone, and she glanced across at the men's restroom. *Why would he go—*

Something whistled through the air at her ear, and

she ducked as the hard, short object connected with her head. Although a glancing blow, it threw her off balance, her shoulder slamming into the concrete wall as a hand clamped onto her shoulder and an arm raised a lead-filled sap above her face.

With no time to assess the attacker, Simone dropped out of range, hunching over and rolling into his knees. Before he could adjust his stance, she hooked her arm around his ankles and jerked his legs out from under him.

He went down with a low grunt, breaking his fall with a rigid arm. She heard his wrist bones snap as she flipped forward, her head tucked low, and landed two feet away, pivoting as she straightened.

Halfway to his feet, the man pressed his damaged arm against his chest and kept his damp eyes on her face. He shuffled to the side, sweat popping out on the space between his reddened nose and whitened lips as he measured the gap between them and slowly reached down to slip a knife from his boot.

Simone mirrored his movements as she assessed him. His dark blue knit pullover and loose black trousers had been chosen to allow freedom of motion and conceal stains. He bobbed slightly as he made jabbing motions with the blade in an attempt to distract her. His flat eyes, however, never wavered from hers.

Simone had no doubt he had been sent to kill her. If he had chosen to strictly obey his orders, he would have first come at her with the knife. But he'd chosen to use the sap first in order to knock her unconscious, the hallmark of a rapist and torturer.

Such animals are easy to provoke, her father's voice reminded her. *You have but to question their manhood.*

The side of Simone's head throbbed in time with the

slowing beat of her heart. The belittling words lay on her tongue, impatient acid waiting to be spilled. She could have his life in her hands in five seconds, and end it in three moves: Shatter the knee, splinter the ribs, and stop the heart.

He came at her, head lowered, eyes up, pistoning his legs and then lunging across the last half meter, the hand holding the knife sweeping out wide. At the last moment Simone shifted and kicked, knocking the blade from his grip. As she turned back toward him she clamped her hand around her wrist and drove her elbow into his throat, knocking him backward. He clutched at his neck as his eyes bulged and his body dropped to his knees.

Simone kicked the knife away. She had no use for his weapon. By crushing his trachea, she had ensured that he would suffocate within three minutes.

Finish it.

She moved around him, encircling his neck with her arm and applying pressure to the arteries, cutting off the blood supply to his brain. He brought his fist down against her leg, hard enough for her to feel the thick ring he wore on his smallest finger, and then the shocking sting of a needle in her flesh. She tore his hand away, but not before a burning sensation spread across the top of her thigh.

She felt his pulse stutter, but held on until it stopped. He slumped over and did not move again.

She grabbed the body under the arms and dragged it into the men's restroom and into one of the stalls. Her arms and legs began to shake as she hefted up the body and positioned it on the toilet. She searched through his pockets, finding them empty. An unnatural heaviness began to weigh on her as her vision blurred.

She locked the door from the inside, and then crawled

out through the space underneath. Soon Korvel would come looking for her, or the drug would take effect; she wondered which it would be. If the captain discovered the body of the assassin, he would know she was not the harmless mortal he assumed her to be. He would definitely ask questions that her oath to the council would not permit her to answer. She risked the time it took for her to clean up again at the sink and check the knot on the side of her head for blood before she staggered out of the restroom.

She breathed through the numbness the drug caused and quickened her steps, lifting her aching head and moving as naturally as she could. When she reached the Land Rover, her head was spinning and shadows crowded in on the edges of her vision. She went around to the passenger side and opened the door.

"Would you mind driving, Captain?" she asked in what she hoped sounded like a tired voice as she held out the keys. "I'd like to rest."

"Of course." He took the keys and climbed out.

As he went around the car and got in behind the wheel, he glanced over at her. "Are you feeling unwell?"

"No," she lied as she reached for the handle to adjust the seat back. The little white stars spiraling down to light upon the windshield came from the effects of the drug, not the sky. She was forgetting to do something, but it was too late. The shadows had stretched out and now were dimming the stars. "Wake me . . . in an hour."

She closed her eyes as he said yes.

"Wake up."

The guard nodding over his clipboard jerked to attention and swiveled on his stool to face the truck. "No one in after dark; come back . . ." He hesitated as he looked at Pájaro's face. "Oh, it is you, Monsieur Helada."

Pájaro considered shooting him in the face, but the sound of the gunshot would attract unwanted attention. "Let me in."

"*Oui,* monsieur." The security guard hurried out of his little shack and nearly dropped his keys as he removed the padlock and chain and pushed open the rusty gate.

The facility appeared deserted, except for two vehicles: a large truck and a small red Fiat, which had been left outside the only warehouse with its windows lit. Pájaro drove past them to the end of the dock, where he parked his BMW between two pylons.

Pájaro removed the pistol he carried, emptying the bullets from it before returning it to his pocket. Such precautions annoyed him—he should no longer have to trouble himself with mortal banalities—but he was not yet invulnerable. Nor would he be until he had taken the elixir of eternal life.

You are unworthy, Pájaro.

The old man had done his best to terrify him with his warnings and his judgments. For a time Pájaro had even believed him, and worked all the harder to master the skills necessary to survive the final trial.

The other boys at the château had tried to befriend him at first, but he knew their game and remained aloof from them. In time he had become the old man's finest student, faster and deadlier than any of the others. He knew he would emerge from the severance with victory and honor. There had never been question of it.

No one talked about the girl at the château, or how she managed to win every battle she fought. Once two handlers joked about the real reason the old man had taken the girl from her prostitute mother in Paris. As pretty as she was, she was less than nothing, a whore's castoff. It had disgusted Pájaro to see her behave as if she had a right to be there. The château was to be his, and the night before he faced the last challenge of his training, the final bout known as the severance, he decided he would show her exactly what her place would be in his household.

He could still see her sitting up on her bed, naked under one of the butler's old shirts, her deceiving eyes wide, her voice trembling as she dared speak to him.

What are you doing in my room?

Pájaro still did not know how she had done it. One moment he was dragging her to the floor; the next his back struck a wall. There must have been someone else there, he remembered thinking, before she appeared over him, her small face pale and troubled.

Why do you want to hurt me?

Snapping her neck and silencing her forever should have been a simple thing, but in his haste he did not use the correct hold. That allowed her to rake her nails across his eyes and drive her tiny foot into his balls. By the time he finished puking she had fled.

He had not run, but walked back to his room and changed his clothing. The throbbing ache of his balls and the gritty pain of his scratched corneas tormented him, but he returned to his bed and waited for the old man to come for him. For hours he had waited for the door to his room to open.

Get up.

The light made Pájaro squint as he rose from his bed, but he stood straight and tall as the old man inspected him.

What happened here?

Pájaro calmly explained how the whore's brat had come to his room to viciously attack him while he slept.

His training had prevented her from blinding him, but he had been compassionate, too, and allowed her to escape with her life.

Is this all you have to say?

Pájaro had felt a moment of uncertainty before he admitted that naturally he would need time for his eyes to heal before he could begin the final trial. Only then did his voice falter, for he had not considered what might happen if the old man refused to give him time to recover.

You are unworthy, Pájaro.

Hearing his birth name had shocked him; here at the château he had always been called Huit. The old man had left, and Pájaro had followed him, hurrying to catch up, insisting that what he had said was the truth, begging for the chance he had earned to prove himself. When he had grabbed at his arm, the old man had knocked him to the floor.

The next minute was one he had lived over and over for the last ten years.

"Master, please," Pájaro shrieked. "She attacked me. I swear to you that is what happened."

"I don't care how it was." The old man sounded impassive, as if they were discussing a simple training technique. "You were defeated by my daughter. This *was* your final trial."

The girl was his daughter?

In that moment Pájaro knew he had lost everything that mattered to him, and desperation drove him to seize the old man's ankle. "Then kill me. Kill me now, before the others awake."

"I would not wipe my ass on you." The old man had kicked him off before walking away.

Pájaro got out and walked to the warehouse's back

entrance, where he paused and listened before going inside. Only a handful of the men he had hired in Paris stood in various positions with their backs against plastic-wrapped pallets of boxes labeled in Italian as restaurant supplies. Pájaro noted that half eyed him while the others kept watch on the front entrance.

"He is here," one of the men called out.

Antoine came out of the office carrying a reinforced case, and placed it on the top of a crate before regarding Pájaro. "We were worried about you, Helada. We thought you might have run into trouble leaving the château." He opened the case. "As you see, the raid did not go so well for us."

"You knew the risks." He eyed the empty case. "Where is the scroll?"

"I have it." Antoine swiped the back of his hand over his sweaty brow before he tugged open his vest and removed a bundle of cloth tucked inside. Instead of transferring it to the case, he weighed it in his hand. "It is heavier than it looks, but gold always is."

"Put it in the case," Pájaro told him.

"First, we talk." Antoine cleared his throat. "You said there would be only a few old servants at the château. So who was the Englishman?"

Pájaro saw how it would be, but kept his expression bland. "I don't know. I never saw an Englishman."

"The big son of a bitch was hard to miss. He took out half the crew by himself." Antoine nearly dropped the cloth bundle, and tossed it in the case before wiping his hands on the sides of his pants. "I never saw anyone move like that. Except you."

The old man had no hair and was neither big nor English. That left only a few possibilities. "Did he move too quickly for you to shoot him?"

"Nothing stopped him, which is why we left, and why we still live." Antoine coughed into his fist before pointing a finger at Pájaro. "You hired him to kill us so you wouldn't have to share the gold. Didn't you?"

"There is blood on your hand," Pájaro said mildly. "And your mouth."

Antoine's damp face went white as he wiped his fingers over his lips and looked at the smear of blood. "What is this? What's wrong with me?" Before Pájaro could reply, he took out a gun, which rattled in his shaking hand. "You poisoned me."

"No, *mon ami*," a feminine voice said, and an elegant brunette in a low-cut red dress appeared. "The scroll has killed you."

The presence of the Italian woman drew all of the men's eyes, and Pájaro darted forward, slipping behind Antoine and seizing his trembling hand, directing the shot he squeezed off at the closest man. He neatly removed the gun and rapidly fired, killing each man in succession.

Burned gunpowder turned the air acrid as Pájaro shoved Antoine away from him, at the same time sweeping his legs out from under him so that he fell to the floor. Antoine tried to scramble back, but another fit of uncontrollable coughing overcame him, and he curled over, covering his mouth and throwing an arm over his face.

Pájaro drew his blade as he looked down at the dying man. "You took your time, madame."

"I chose my moment." Leora sauntered over, frowning as she inspected the now-babbling Antoine's ashen features. "This one looks like death."

Pájaro liked the Italian, who was as cold and practical as a Frenchwoman. He didn't know how she had discovered that the old man had left the scroll unguarded at the château, but he knew exactly why she had come to him with the information, and given him the resources he needed to retrieve it. She thought he was entirely disposable. "If you wish to observe his decline, I can let him live a little longer."

"That isn't necessary." She walked around Antoine, stooping to study his bloodstained hands. "How long was he in possession of it?"

"A few hours." Pájaro bent down and sliced open Antoine's carotid, enjoying the neat way Leora stepped to one side to avoid the arterial spray. "At least we have proof that the curse is intact."

"I don't believe in curses." She removed a small pistol from her purse and walked to each body, firing a single shot into each head. "You did very well. Now I will take the artifact to Paris. We have a lab there where it can be analyzed."

So she was making her move now. It was sooner than he had expected—he assumed she would first use him to transport the scroll to Paris—but he could accommodate her here just as well.

"Why are you wasting bullets on them?" he asked idly. "They'll bleed out in a few minutes."

"Anyone can talk, even if they're spending the rest of their life on a respirator." She went to the next man.

Pájaro guessed the last round in her weapon was meant for him. He entertained the thought of allowing her to attack so he could play with her at his leisure, but the new threat to his plans made any extended dalliance unwise. The unstoppable warrior Antoine had described had to be a Darkyn lord sent to protect the scroll in the old man's absence. Now that Pájaro had possession of it, the Kyn warrior would stop at nothing to find him.

And the council would send the little whore along to help him.

As soon as Leora turned her back on him, he threw the blade in his hand. It struck her between the shoulder blades, lodging between two vertebrae and partially severing her spinal cord. Once she collapsed he went to her, tugging the blade out of her flesh and rolling her over onto her back.

As he knelt between Leora's thighs, he pushed her skirt out of the way and ripped off her silk panties.

"Why?" she gasped out.

"I do like you, so this is best," he told her as he unzipped the front of his pants. "I don't have to tie you down, and you won't have to feel even a moment of discomfort. Not even after I'm done, when I cut your throat." As he shoved inside her, he wallowed in the horror in her eyes. "As you said, *chérie,* survivors can talk, even when they are on a respirator."

Chapter 7

His infrequent contact with mortals had made Korvel forget that they normally slept through the night. He suspected Simone was much more tired than she had claimed, for she hadn't twitched a muscle in over an hour. Likely the blood she had fed him also contributed to her exhaustion.

He had promised to wake her, however, and he would keep his word. "Sister, it is nearly midnight." When she did not stir, he reached over and gently shook her shoulder. Her head bobbed with the motion, but her eyes remained closed. "Simone?" As he released her she slowly slid to one side until she slumped against the door.

She was not sleeping. She was unconscious.

He seized her hand. Her flesh felt as cool as his, and when he pressed his fingertips against her pulse point, he could barely detect a heartbeat.

"Fuck me." Korvel cut off another car as he swerved onto the shoulder, and ignored the shouted obscenities of the driver as he put the Land Rover in park and turned to the nun, pulling her upright and tipping her head back so that the dome light illuminated her face.

"Angel. Look at me. Simone."

He saw no wound and smelled no blood on her, but when he cradled her face between his palms he felt a swelling just above her ear. He tore off her cap and turned her face to one side, probing the area and tracing the contours of a large contusion. When he parted her hair over the swelling, he saw the purplish red color of her bruised scalp.

The injury could not have come from her struggles with the men at the château. Someone had hurt her when they'd stopped at the rest area. He had thought she had taken too long. Now he recalled how slowly, how carefully she had been moving when she returned to the car. He had even asked her whether she had felt sick.

Why didn't she tell me?

He drew back and began using his hands to check her from the neck down. Korvel stilled as he reached her midriff, and felt a strange arrangement of straps and objects beneath the knit fabric. He didn't believe what his hands were telling him until he reached beneath the hem of her shirt and felt the sheaths attached to a fitted weapon harness buckled around her waist.

He unfastened the harness, lifting her slightly in order to safely remove it. She wore seven daggers of various sizes, three spaced on either side of her waist and one that had nestled against the small of her back. He also found a coiled wire garrote, a pouch containing drug-filled pressure darts, and several small metal spheres that he guessed to be some type of grenade. He found no marks to indicate that any of the weapons had been used for the purpose they had been crafted, but from the scent traces left on them he could tell that at least three mortals—including Simone—had handled them.

Of course the council would have ordered her to arm

herself, Korvel reasoned, but why hadn't she used the weapons against her attacker?

He bent down and placed the weapon harness under the seat before he completed his inspection of her. When he found no other injury, he bent his head to smell her clothing, and discovered the scent of another mortal's sweat on the inside of one sleeve. He slid up the sleeve and found another, fresh bruise on her elbow.

Why hadn't she called for him? How had she eluded her attacker? Why hadn't she told him when she came back to the car?

Korvel climbed into the driver's seat and started the engine, pulling out onto the roadway. He pressed the accelerator to the floor as he sped past the few remaining cars and saw a sign, AVIGNON SUD. He moved over into the exit lane and left the highway.

As he approached the city, Korvel considered turning around and going back to the highway. He didn't know how badly Simone was hurt, and while he could probably reach Marseilles within an hour, the girl needed medical attention now. At the same time he was reluctant to take her to a hospital, where one or both of them might attract unwanted attention—the scrutiny of the authorities and perhaps even the notice of the Brethren.

The road leading into Avignon branched off around the old walled portion of the city where popes had once come to take refuge. Korvel followed the yellow signs that directed visitors to the appropriate gate and drove slowly until he spotted the front facade of the Hotel Vue.

He parked on the street outside the service entrance and got out, going around to the passenger side. He took out the weapon harness from under Simone's seat, slinging it over his shoulder before he shrugged into his coat.

Carefully he lifted Simone's limp body out of the car and carried her to the tradesmen's entrance. He clasped her against him as he tried the knob, found it locked, and then forced it open, stepping inside into a storage area and loading platform. The sound of a clanging alarm cut off a second after it started, followed by the shrill sound of a woman scolding someone.

"I did lock it," a man's petulant voice complained. "You must have unlocked it again."

A middle-aged woman in a stained apron came through the swinging doors. "Who is there? We are not . . ." As she saw Korvel she stopped and put a hand to her throat. "Monsieur."

"Madame, my wife has had an accident." He walked slowly toward her, holding her gaze with his as his scent flooded the air around her. "You will show us to an empty suite and summon a doctor at once."

Her pupils expanded under her fluttering eyelashes as she slowly smiled. "A suite, yes. The doctor, at once."

He followed her into the hotel's kitchen, where she took down a set of keys from a pegboard next to the door and beckoned for him to follow her. Korvel carried Simone through the hall to the service elevator, where the woman took them up to the top floor.

"This is the Napoleon suite," the cook said, giggling a little as she went in to turn on the lamps. "Your wife will love the bed. The mattress is all feathers. Would you like to know how it feels to—"

"No." Korvel carried Simone over to the bed, pausing to pull back the quilted blue coverlet before lowering her onto the rose-colored sheets. "Find a doctor and send him to me," he ordered as he began to undress her. "Now."

"*Oui,* monsieur." The cook wandered back out.

Korvel knelt beside the bed, holding the nun's cool hand in his. "Simone, can you hear me? I've brought you to a hotel. Help will be here soon."

She did not respond to his touch or the sound of his voice. He put his hand to her throat, where the beat of her heart pulsed too slow beneath his touch.

She couldn't die, not here, not like this. Korvel moved his hand to her brow and leaned close. "Angel, why didn't you cry out for me? You know I would have heard you. I would not have allowed you to be harmed. I would have . . ." He stopped and drew back.

She had not called out for help at the rest stop, Korvel realized, nor when he had first seen her being attacked by the men at the château. As a nun she would have taken a vow of chastity, yet she had freely offered him sex as well as blood. She carried on her body the scars of grievous abuse, and under her garments enough concealed weapons to kill a dozen men. When she had hobbled to the car, hurt and drugged, she had pretended to be only tired.

What had made her like this? Her faith? Her duty to the council? Was she somehow torn between the two?

Korvel sat on the floor beside the bed and leaned his head back against the wall. Vengeance and death had been an integral part of his immortal life—he was bound to his duty to protect the high lord and his household. Like most of his kind, he had risen from his grave believing his soul had been cursed by God to walk the night forever. What little faith Korvel had possessed as a mortal gradually faded over time, and his belief in the superstitions of the Kyn vanished along with it. No rational explanation had ever filled that void, not until the high lord had kidnapped Alexandra Keller, who believed the Kyn were infected, not cursed.

The door to the suite opened, and a short, thin man carrying a bulky case stepped in. "I am Dr. Pavel, monsieur. Your wife is ill?"

He got to his feet. "She slipped and fell at a rest stop and struck her head." He bent over the bed to turn Simone's face to the side and touched the swelling on her scalp. "Here. She walked back to the car, but then she fell unconscious. I have not been able to wake her."

The doctor nodded, setting the case on the end of the bed and opening it. "Has she vomited? Have you seen any blood coming from her ears?"

As Korvel answered those and his next questions, the doctor examined Simone, listening to her heartbeat and then using a penlight to check her eyes, her ears, and her mouth. Once he had felt all along her scalp and neck, he performed a quick inspection of the rest of her body, and paused as he reached her right thigh, using his light to inspect a tiny mark there. He then turned and took a small bottle from his case, removing the stopper and holding the sharp-smelling contents under her nose.

Simone's eyes fluttered, and she made a low sound as she turned her face away.

The doctor replaced the bottle's stopper. "Your wife does not appear to have a concussion, monsieur. There are some indications she was attacked." He pointed to her thigh. "She was also drugged."

Korvel inspected the needle mark. "What was used?"

"Since she was at a rest area, I would think flunitrazepam, or perhaps ketamine. Such drugs are often employed in assaults to make women less resistant." Pavel glanced at Simone, who was pressing her hand against her temple. "You must keep her here until the effects wear off. By this time tomorrow she should be herself again."

"What effects?"

"Nothing dangerous." The doctor looked a little embarrassed. "The drug removes certain inhibitions, especially among women. That is why you should keep her here, alone with you, and see to her needs."

As soon as the doctor left, Korvel went to Simone and stopped her from trying to sit up. "Stay where you are."

Her eyes shifted from one side to the other. "Where am I?"

"A hotel in Avignon. When I could not wake you, I brought you here. The doctor has just examined you." He touched the back of his hand to her cheek. "How do you feel?"

She shifted her arms and legs. "Only my head hurts."

"Someone struck you," he told her. "You were also drugged." When she didn't respond, he asked, "Do you remember what happened when we stopped?"

"Yes. I was careless." She closed her eyes. "It won't happen again."

Her scent said she was telling the truth. So did the note of self-disgust in her voice. But once again Korvel sensed that she held back more than she said, as if she were using the truth as a means of protection rather than revelation, and not merely to prevent him from knowing who had done this to her.

What did she fear? Surely not him.

"It is only an hour to Marseilles. We should continue on." She rolled to her side and levered herself up with her hands, but Korvel kept her from trying to stand on her own by scooping her up and holding her against him.

"The doctor said you should rest." He lowered her to her feet and steadied her with his hands. "Marseilles will wait, sister."

She squinted up at him. "Why do you call me that? You're not one of my brothers."

"I am trying to be respectful." He followed her away from the bed as she took a short, wavering turn around the room. "How many brothers do you have?"

"I don't know."

"Are they stepbrothers?"

"No." She halted and reached out as if she saw something in the empty air in front of her, and then her hand trembled and dropped to her side. "I would not do it; I would never do it. He had me corrected and taken away and locked in my room. I could not leave until I recovered enough to train again. When I did, they were gone."

She spoke clearly, but her words made no sense to him. Korvel wondered whether she was talking to him or some hallucination. "What is my name, Simone?"

"You call yourself Captain. Korvel sounds like a surname." She gave him a curious look. "Do you have a Christian name?"

"I was never given one," he admitted as he steered her around the desk.

"You should choose one. Oops." She chuckled as she stumbled over an ottoman. "When I came to the sisters, I did. I picked Simone out of a wonderful book."

"Your family never named you?"

She shook her head, taking in a sharp breath. "I have no family. I was just the girl. Or my number." She held her head with her hands. "*Quatorze.* Fourteen. I was number fourteen."

He bent down to check her eyes. "I think you should go back to bed, angel."

"What for? I will recover. I always do. And you will need me. You need me now, don't you?" She staggered away from him, groping for the chair. "You should have said. That is why I'm with you."

Korvel didn't realize she had taken a dagger from the harness until he heard the blade cutting through the fabric of her sleeve. "Sister, stop."

He reached to take the dagger from her before she cut herself, and in the struggle that followed felt a slash of pain across his palm as the blade turned and cut his flesh. He finally gained control of it, and held it up to see his blood staining the dark metal.

He threw it away and seized her, turning her to face him. "Why are you carrying a copper blade?"

"It's the only way. Therese told me." She swayed, smiling blindly. "But I know the real reason she gave it to me. To put an end to it forever." She leaned forward to tell him in a theatrical whisper, "As soon as the scroll is safe, I'm going to use it to kill Helada."

"Simone." He cradled her head between his hands. "You don't have to kill anyone. Do you understand me? You don't have to do anything."

"I don't want to kill," she whispered, her eyes fever-bright. "I swore that I never would. But if I don't, Helada will never die."

He caught her as she collapsed and swung her up into his arms, swearing as he felt her body heat. She was suddenly, inexplicably burning up. "I'm taking you to the hospital."

"Please, no." She clutched at him. "There is no one else. My brothers are gone. I think he killed them."

"You're not making any sense, and this is not your responsibility," he told her. "Helada is charged with guarding the scroll. Where is he?"

The question made her go rigid, and she pulled back from him, her tear-streaked face suddenly calm. "Everywhere. In the frost that withers, and the snow that buries. No one can escape the winter, or the shadow of the valley of death."

Now she was misquoting Bible passages. "Simone, is he the one who did this to you? Was it Helada?"

A strange smile touched her lips before her body drooped against him. One last crystalline tear escaped her lashes before she went still and silent.

The weary village police chief only glanced at the counterfeit identification before handing it back to Gabriel Seran. "The fire inspector has not yet given permission for anyone to enter the château, Detective."

"That's all right, Chief." Nicola leaned close, suffusing the smoky air with the sweet-sharp scent of juniper as she rested her hand on his shoulder. "You know we'll be careful, so you're going to give us clearance."

"Careful." Dazed, he nodded. "Clearance."

She patted his shoulder. "Now, go ask the fire inspector to take a walk around the grounds with you to see whether anything else was torched. Be sure to walk around the outside of the walls first."

As the remaining firefighters were busy packing up and securing their equipment, no one challenged Gabriel or his *sygkenis* as they slipped inside the burned-out château.

"Two killed outside." Nicola turned on her flashlight and surveyed the entrance foyer. "Three more in here. They were thorough."

Gabriel walked to each body, crouching down to examine the remains. "Mortals," he said. "Shot with standard rounds in the head."

"Looks like Antoine wasn't lying when he bragged about the arson job to Oksana." She sniffed the air as they made their way toward the stairs. "They splashed around a couple gallons of gasoline in here." She eyed the burn patterns on the walls, and then bent and picked up a broken piece of clear glass before handing it to him. "Then they set it off with Molotov cocktails."

Gabriel and Nicola had investigated dozens of suspicious arsons in France. When burning out a Darkyn stronghold, the Brethren had used very specific incendiary devices designed to leave little to no trace evidence behind. Most of the time the local authorities declared the fires accidental, or the result of vandalism. "Perhaps they did not have the chance to make their usual preparations."

Nicola shook her head. "This doesn't feel like Brethren. For one thing they've never chased down and shot the humans on-site; they sneak into their rooms, knock them out, and burn them in their beds." She stopped and looked in at two charred bodies that had fallen with their arms still clutching each other. "No, this feels much more personal. Like someone wanted to send a very nasty message. Someone who doesn't care about getting caught. Which is seriously crazy."

Gabriel put an arm around her waist. "What are you thinking? That this was a deed born in madness?"

She shrugged. "A changeling doesn't have enough brains or self-control to hire a crew and pull off something this sophisticated. A rogue operates alone, and he certainly wouldn't have to shoot the servants to stop them from escaping. Not when he could easily control them with *l'attrait*."

Gabriel tested the stairs, which, while scorched black, were made of stone and remained intact. "Is there anything upstairs?"

Nicola lifted her face, her eyes glittering as she reached

out with her ability. No matter how well they were concealed, she could detect the presence of other Kyn as well
as objects they had handled. "Something small . . . and not
old." She mounted the stairs slowly, moving from one side
to the other, until she reached the landing and turned
toward the east wing's upper level. "Over there."

Gabriel followed her as she picked her way across the
burned floorboards, skirting open gaps where the flames
had burned through. She stopped in front of an open
doorframe, switching off her flashlight before she stepped
inside.

Gabriel smelled it as soon as he crossed the threshold
behind her. "Blood."

The word echoed faintly around them as he became
aware of the size and emptiness of the space.

"I don't see any bodies." Using her flashlight, she
moved around, eyeing the smoke-streaked mirrored
walls before she stared at the irregular areas of dark
brown stains marring the center portion of the gray stone
floor. "It's all over the place." She stopped at one stain,
dropping down to press her hands against the granite.
"Here, mostly. Old blood. Human, not Kyn."

"Most of the servants were elderly." Gabriel reached
out with his ability to communicate with insects, but
whatever had formerly inhabited the château had either
fled the fire or perished in it. "Perhaps some were killed
here and their bodies moved."

"No, I meant old as in it's been here awhile." She
stood and absently rubbed her hand against her trousers. "Maybe years."

He didn't like the strange room any more than she
did. "There is nothing here. The object must be in an adjoining chamber."

"Trust me, baby; it's right here. The feel of it is just

about crawling all over my skin." She walked over to one of the mirrored walls and placed her hand against it. "Behind this."

He measured the wall and the single sheet of silver-backed glass covering it. "I do not see how we are to get behind it."

"That's because you're not the thief; I am." Using her flashlight like a small club, Nicola struck the mirror squarely in the center. Glass splintered, and an enormous web of cracks rayed out from the spot she had punched, but the wall remained intact.

Gabriel pulled her away from it. "It will fall on you."

"I doubt it. The glass is coated with a polymer, like safety glass." She studied the panel again. "I doubt an immortal guardian was worried about seven years' bad luck. So why go to all this trouble?"

"It must be where the scroll is hidden."

"Maybe." She put her hand to one side of the panel and felt along the seam. She found something and pressed it, and stepped back as the panel began to descend into the floor. "Hello."

The weapons hidden behind the panel had been carefully hung on custom racks, and ranged from small knives to two-handed swords. All had been fashioned from copper.

"Interesting choice of materials, considering he's Kyn." Nicola bent down to a storage unit and opened the doors. "Some clothes down here." She took out one folded black garment and shook it out. "Looks like pants, but they're too small for an adult." She took out a matching long-sleeved jacket and a long belt. "These remind me of kids' karate uniforms."

"They are sparring garments," Gabriel told her. "Sized for children."

"Helada has kids? How is that possible?"

"They likely belonged to his *tresora*'s children. They begin their training as soon as they can walk." Gabriel went to the next panel, found the side latch, and opened it to reveal another, identical cache of weapons and stored garments. He continued around the room until he had opened all twelve.

Nicola stood up and wrapped her arms around her waist as she surveyed the open caches. "I know Europeans like big families, but would his *tresora* really have this many kids running around this place?"

He felt as puzzled as his *sygkenis*. "It would seem so."

Nicola turned and eyed the first rack of weapons. "He didn't touch any of these." She took down one of the daggers, frowned, and peered into a hole where the blade had been hanging. She tugged on the rack, which swung out on a hinge, revealing video equipment and a television screen. "Here we go. He handled this."

Gabriel studied the equipment. "He was secretly filming something."

"This looks like the first VCR ever made." She touched the front panel of the boxy recorder, jumping back as the television screen illuminated. "Didn't they cut the power to this place?"

"There is the power source." He pointed to the rows of batteries and wires sitting on the lowest rack.

"Good, we can see what he was recording. Maybe he got the guys who did this." Nicola pressed the rewind button, and then played the tape.

The images that appeared on the screen were slightly blurred, and they both stepped back. Twelve children who were dressed in the black sparring uniforms sat in a large circle on the stone floor. Behind them, four men wearing gray versions of their uniforms stood against the wall. All of them watched in silence as a teenager and a man circled each other in the center. Without warning the teen lunged forward, swiping at the man, who easily avoided the blow.

What followed was like an intricate dance, like nothing Gabriel had ever witnessed. Both fighters moved faster than seemed possible, weaving in and out and around each other as their arms and legs landed dozens of blows.

"Wait a minute." Nicola peered at the screen. "Are they using—" She fell silent as a blade flashed and the man struck the teen in the face.

The boy darted backward, holding one hand to his bleeding brow. Almost at once he attacked the man, and a moment later was sent sprawling onto the floor. His blade skittered out of his hand and landed at the feet of one of the watching children, who didn't touch it or react at all.

The man stood over the teenager, but didn't try to help him up. In a colorless voice he said, "You did not protect your head. Scalp and facial wounds bleed heavily. Blood in your eyes will blind you, and then you are dead. Quatorze."

One of the smaller children rose and walked into the center of the circle. A foot shorter than the teenage boy, and very thin, the smaller boy had light hair cut so short he looked almost bald.

"Now," the man said, handing his blade to the wounded teenager, "kill her."

"That's a girl?" Nicola murmured.

Gabriel felt more shock over the man's order. No one, not even the most ruthless of Kyn lords, trained children to kill other children.

Nicola pressed a hand over her mouth as the teenager went after the smaller child. Just as he was about to stab her in the neck, she spun out of the way, clasping her hands together and striking the older boy in the small of his back. He went down hard and lay on the stone as if stunned.

The little girl walked up to the boy, kicking the blade from his hand before standing back. The boy rolled over and crawled toward the man in black.

"Please, master," the boy begged, trying to grab the man's leg. "I will practice more. I will—"

One of the men in the gray uniforms came forward, grabbed the boy by the hair, and dragged him out of the circle and then out of view of the camera. Gabriel heard his shrieks grow louder, and then stop suddenly.

The little girl went and picked up the blade she had kicked away, taking it to an open panel and replacing it on the rack before she rejoined the circle.

The screen turned to static.

Chapter 8

Nicola stood in silence for a moment before she reached down and shut off the recorder. "This is how you train *tresoran* kids? By forcing them to fight to the death?"

"Never." He went to her. "The children of human servants are taught many things, but not this. Never anything like this. It is . . ." He had no words for it.

"Fucking disgusting?" she suggested.

Nicola had been only sixteen years old when the high lord's former wife had attacked her and her family. A sadist who enjoyed inflicting mental torture on her victims, Elizabeth Tremayne had forced the terrified girl to dig graves for herself and her dead parents before she had drained Nicola and buried her body.

Thanks to a twist of fate, Nicola had not perished, but instead made the transition from mortal to Darkyn. Left alone, without any of the Kyn realizing she had been changed, Nicola had roamed Europe searching for Elizabeth. It took ten years before she had finally found her and obtained justice for what the evil woman had done. However, the mortal life that had been stolen from her, like her parents, could never be replaced.

He would not have her suffer this place and those memories, not even for Richard Tremayne's sake. "We will go."

She removed the tape from the VCR and tucked it inside her jacket. "There's nothing else in here. Did you pick up anything on Korvel?"

Their bond made Gabriel sensitive to Nicola's moods and emotions; now he felt nothing from her, as if she were completely indifferent to what they had watched. "His scent is outside, near the body of the old man."

She walked out of the room.

Gabriel retrieved two more of the tapes stacked on top of the recording unit before leaving the château. Outside he found Nicola examining the old man's corpse and the ground around it. When he joined her she moved out of his reach.

"Two sets of footprints here." She pointed to the ground. "They went around to the back of the house."

"I know you are very angry," he said to her. "So am I. Hurting mortal children is a violation of our laws as well as our beliefs. Helada will be made to answer for what he's done. I promise you."

"Yeah. Whatever you say." She followed the trail of the footprints into the brush.

The police chief and the fire inspector appeared, flanking Gabriel as they both began firing questions at him. He took a moment to reestablish his control over them, commanding them to ignore him and Nicola while they attended to their duties.

His *sygkenis* he found inside a greenhouse that had been extensively vandalized. She was sitting on the ground next to a large shattered pot; in her hands she clutched an empty green velvet sack. She didn't look at him or the sack, but stared blindly at the black soil strewn about the remains of the planter.

Before he could speak, she said, "The scroll's gone. Korvel's injured or dead; he left behind a lot of blood tainted with copper. A human woman was here with him, too. From the direction of the scent trails I'd say she took him out of here on horse, up into the hills." She moved away from the hand he held down to her and got to her feet. "You want to track them from here, or call the vampire king and see what he wants us to do?"

She sounded like a machine. "I want you to talk to me."

"We don't have time for chitchat." She tried to go around him, freezing as he caught her around the waist. "I'm fine."

"No," he said softly. "You are not."

"If you're waiting for me to have another tantrum, that's not going to happen," she said flatly. "When we find Helada, we'll take him to Richard, show him the tapes, and he'll chop off his head, or wall him up in a room and starve him to death, and everything will be just peachy again."

"You don't believe that."

"Laws have been broken, like you said. Richard will take care of it, Helada will pay, and we'll go on like always. Until we find the next vampire who likes torturing humans, or considers them nothing but . . . What do the really snotty Kyn call mortals?" She pretended to think. "Oh, right. *Fodder.*"

She wasn't shouting, but then, she didn't have to. Her words scalded him. "Nicola."

"It'll never end, and I'm part of it now. You'd think karma would kick in, and as a vamp I'd be tuned into humans being tortured the way I was by Elizabeth, but no. I can't save any of them. *I* get to rescue the fucking monsters who *eat* them." She saw his face, and regret instantly replaced her rage. "Oh, no, baby, I don't mean you. You could never be that." She dragged her hands through her white curls, yanking at them before she dropped her arms. "I'm sorry. I'm just . . . tired. I need to do something that doesn't make me feel like this."

Gabriel pulled her against him, holding her until she stopped struggling. "Never apologize to me for how you feel. When everyone had forgotten me, you found me. After all my kind took from you, you saved me. You brought me out of darkness, Nicola. How can you expect me to do nothing when you are lost in it?"

"I'm not lost." She looked up at him. "I know exactly where I am, and what I am. Every time I see something like this, I know that could be me. I mean, come on; I'm really not that different from Helada, am I? What if someday I decide little kids are nothing but toys for me to play with?"

"You would never do anything like this," he told her. "Not in a thousand lifetimes."

She moved her shoulders. "Maybe you won't be around to find out."

He kissed her forehead. "I will always be with you."

"Really? Do you honestly think we're going to be together forever? That this thing we have now will keep us going that long?" She drew back from him. "Unless we're stupid, we're never going to die. You've already been here for seven hundred years. I know you've had women who make me look like a dog by comparison. How can you *not* get bored with me?"

He glanced down at the scars on his arms. "I could ask you the same."

"That's easy." She ran her palms over his shoulders.

"You're beautiful and kind and intelligent, and just looking at you makes me hot. That and I love you."

"As I love you," he reminded her.

"You're also the only other vampire on earth who is as fucked-up as I am." She touched his chest, tracing the ridges of one of the scars he carried. "Humans did this to you. I know if they get the chance, they'll do it again. But they won't, because I will kill anyone who tries."

Now he understood. "The Brethren are human, Nicola, but they declared war on us. Defending ourselves against them is not the same as what Helada did to those children."

She rested her cheek against his shoulder. "I don't know how much longer I can do this, Gabriel. Whatever Elizabeth did to me, I'm still human inside, and I won't lose that. Not ever. If that means I have to leave the Kyn, you're going to have to let me go."

He stroked her back. "Then I will come with you."

"Forgive the intrusion, my lord."

Gabriel eyed the mortal male standing a few feet away. He spoke in French with an Italian accent, and on the lapel of his jacket he wore a black cameo etched with a rose, the symbol of the *tresoran* council. "Name yourself."

"Sergio Benetta, my lord. Field operative of Padrone Ramas of the *tresoran* council." He bowed low and then went down on one knee. "My master sent me and a dozen men to provide any assistance you and your lady might require."

"Secure the premises and search the house. Remove all video recordings from the mirrored room in the east wing." Gabriel looked down at Nicola. "Send them by private courier to Richard Tremayne. Keep your men here and wait for further instructions."

"As you command, my lord." Benetta stood, bowed again, and left.

Before Gabriel could speak, Nicola said, "We have to track Korvel, and it's going to be light soon. We'll talk later, okay?"

Gabriel heard the weariness in her voice, which troubled him as much as what she had said before Benetta had arrived. "The hill trails here are too narrow to drive. We'll need horses; can you ride?"

She nodded. "There's a barn full of them back that way."

Once they had saddled and mounted two of the stock horses, they followed the track of Korvel's scent out to the front gates and along the dirt path that circled around to the château's side wall. There he spotted the hoof prints left behind by the mount that had carried Korvel away into the hills.

"The horse was carrying a heavy burden," Gabriel said after inspecting the depth of the tracks. "I think it was the female mortal who walked alongside the mount."

"She was probably leading it." Nicola pointed to small, dark red stains forming an irregular line in the soil beside the mortal's footprints. "That's his blood."

They rode through the hills until the trail came to an old manor house surrounded by several small outbuildings and large gleaned fields.

Gabriel dismounted along with Nicola, and tethered the horses to a fence before they approached the house from the back. As soon as he saw the clothing hanging in the yard—among them several nuns' habits—he stopped. "This is a convent."

"Maybe." Nicola closed her eyes briefly. "Korvel was here, but he's gone now." She looked at Gabriel. "So is everyone else. The place is completely deserted."

* * *

Saint Paul stood over the basket of clean laundry as he chewed on a shred of gray fabric. Beneath his hooves lay the rest of Simone's best Sunday habit, along with all her white head veils.

She looked around the empty laundry before she spoke to the stubborn old goat. "That will only make you sick again."

Saint Paul swallowed the fabric. "You should have killed me the first time," he said in Pájaro's voice before he bent his head and tore another strip from her skirt.

Through the window she saw a shadowy figure walking back and forth in the yard. Too large to be Flavia or any of the sisters, the shadow moved in a jerky, agitated fashion.

She went out into the moonlight and saw it was the Englishman. He held a bunch of white roses against the side of his face and was talking to himself.

"... the lines will be restored?" He stopped and scowled. "That is unacceptable. I don't care about the storm."

"Girl."

Simone turned around and found herself out in the rose garden. Large, perfect blooms adorned every bush, but as she went to touch one it shrank in on itself, turning brown and then black as the entire bush withered.

A skeletal hand emerged from the soil and clamped around her ankle as her father's voice whispered, "You will keep the bargain."

Simone screamed, twisting and yanking as she tried to free herself, but the hand dragged her down, pulling her into the ground, into the earth, where everything was soft and silent and dark—

"Be still."

She gripped the arms around her, expecting to feel bones but finding cool, hard muscle. The dirt smothering her paled and flattened into soft linen, and the heavy weight holding her down eased back as she stilled. Aware now that she lay facedown in a large, comfortable bed, she opened her eyes and rolled over as an arm reached past her to switch on a lamp.

She stared up at Korvel. "What happened?" She glanced around the lovely but unfamiliar room. "What is this place? Are we in Marseilles?"

"I brought you to a hotel in Avignon." He studied her face. "Who attacked you at the rest stop?"

She touched the place where the assassin had clubbed her. The excruciating pain had vanished, along with the swelling. "I can't say." She sat up and assessed her surroundings. "How did you get a suite like this?"

"The way I usually obtain what I want from mortals." The side of his mouth curled. "I compelled them to provide it, along with a doctor. I told him that you fell and struck your head. The owner and the hotel staff believe we are married."

"We might as well be. Every time I wake up, I'm in bed with you." Mortified by her own words, she put a hand over her eyes. "I apologize, my lord."

A phone nearby rang, and the bed rose slightly as Korvel went to answer it. She listened, but he spoke only a few low words before hanging up.

The sound of something rolling across the floor made Simone lift her hand. Korvel brought a white cloth-draped cart to her side of the bed; the top of the cart lay covered with porcelain plates topped by ornate silver domes. Two crystal goblets sparkled on either side of a bottle of dark wine and a small pitcher of clear water.

"I have been attempting to contact the high lord, but

a storm has cut off communications to the island." He uncovered two of the plates, which were filled with fruit, cheese, and bread, and reached beneath the linen to take out a tray for the bed.

She sat up and watched as he set the tray over her lap and transferred one of the plates. "What are you doing?"

"The doctor said you should eat and drink something after you awoke," he said as he filled one of the goblets with water and set it beside the plate. "If this is not to your liking I will bring you the menu."

"I appreciate your consideration," she said, "but I'm not hungry, and we need to get back on the motorway."

"It will be dawn soon. You will have the day to rest and regain your strength. No," he said as she started to get out of bed. "Traveling in the daylight will also weaken me."

"You need blood."

"That can wait as well." He took a raspberry from the plate and held it in front of her lips. "If I must, I will pinch your nose."

She reached up to take it from him, but he caught her wrist. "I can feed myself," she told him.

Glints of violet shimmered in the blue of his eyes. "Open your mouth, angel."

Simone parted her lips, and he pressed the raspberry between them. As she bit down, the berry's fragrant juices filled her mouth, so sweet and luscious she felt almost decadent.

"I remember these." Korvel watched her mouth. "Do they still taste like wine and dark roses?"

"I can't say. I've never eaten a flower." Her throat felt tight, and she picked up the goblet of water and sipped from it. As she did, she smelled something faint and acrid, and realized the assassin's sweat was still on her skin. "I would like to bathe."

Korvel helped her up from the bed. "Do you require my assistance?"

The thought of his big hands on her naked body made her knees turn to jelly. "Thank you, Captain, but I can manage."

She walked calmly across the room, and only when she closed the bathroom door between them did she give in to the weakness of her limbs and slide to the floor.

Pain she could overcome. Her training had taught her how to withstand the debilitating effects of injury as well as hunger, thirst, and exhaustion. But this was something else, something she had never felt. She wanted to be naked in the captain's arms again, so that he could touch her the way he had back at the convent. She wanted it so much she was shaking with it.

If she did not regain control of her body it would betray her and render her useless.

Simone got up and went to the sink. The hotel had provided an enormous beribboned basket filled with pretty soaps, lotions, and other toiletries, and from it she took a soft cloth and soaked it under the tap.

The wet cloth cooled her hot face and cleared some of the frantic emotion from her mind. She would offer him sex again, and this time he would use her, and that would extinguish this unbearable longing.

But that had been Pájaro's sin: using the excuse of duty to indulge his own vices. She had seen the excitement in his eyes whenever he had stepped into the circle with her or one of her brothers. Hurting others gave him pleasure; he had taught her that the night he had come to her room.

Simone had no illusions about herself. She might live as a nun, but she was the daughter of a ruthless killer and a drug-addicted prostitute. She had so feared becoming like her father that she had forgotten her mother's blood also ran in her veins. Korvel had simply opened her eyes to the other half of her nature.

A close examination of her scalp in the mirror revealed no evidence of injury, although Simone found some flecks of dried blood in her hair. She had a blurred memory of Korvel wounding himself as he took away her copper dagger; the blood was likely his. That would explain her missing injury, if he had offered some of his blood to heal her. She brought a few strands to her nose and breathed in his scent.

She stepped into the shower to scrub the assassin's sweat from her body and the smell of Korvel from her hair. Once she dried off, she combed out and wove her hair into a long braid, tying off the end with a piece of ribbon from the basket.

Calmer now, Simone put on one of the clean, fluffy white robes hanging by the shower and readied herself to face Korvel again. Now that she had defined what was happening to her, she could pass through it and move beyond it. Desire was hardly different from a knife wound; both simply caused weakness and pain. Given time and care, both faded and were forgotten.

She stepped out into the bedroom to see that he had drawn all the drapes and switched off the lamps. It took her a moment to locate him where he lay on the bed. She moved silently until she could see his face, his brilliant eyes closed now, his chest barely moving.

He had fallen asleep.

Deciding she was relieved, not disappointed, Simone retreated to the broad, curved lounge by the windows.

She sat on one end, where she could see Korvel and the door. The padded armrest made a somewhat comfortable pillow for her head, and when she curled up the robe covered her bare legs and feet.

Simone closed her eyes, clearing her thoughts of everything but the need to wake in a few hours, and then drifted off.

Chapter 9

Korvel watched the nun fall asleep. His own need to rest remained, a sullen weight inside his head, but it could not overcome the stronger, more immediate demands of his body.

While she had bathed he had struck a bargain with his conscience: When she returned to the bed, he would determine whether she was aroused or frightened by him. If she feared his attentions, he would take his rest in the other room. If she wanted him, he would show her every pleasure that convent life had denied her.

Now she slept ten feet away, and his curiosity remained unsatisfied.

Because Simone was mortal, Korvel could not enter her dreams, or lure her into his. Nor could he bind her to him as his *sygkenis*. Although it would have been easier, he was glad Simone remained immune to his abilities and influence. If she ever chose to come to him, to give herself to him, it would be of her own accord.

He reached down to palm the bulge beneath the front of his trousers. His penis felt like an iron club, his pulse hammering beneath the head, and it showed no signs of subsiding. Korvel almost released it to deal with it himself, until he imagined the depths of the hell he would burn in if the nun woke to find him watching her as he stroked himself.

His cock thought it a fair trade and swelled another inch.

He got up to move into the next room, and Simone shifted, turning slightly. The white robe she wore fell open just enough to show the bend of her knee and the curve of one thigh. The fragrance of her body altered as well, growing deeper and sweeter, like herbs covered in dew at the first touch of dawn's light.

That is not the scent of fear.

Korvel moved to the lounge, easing down beside her, not certain of what he meant to do but unable to stop himself just the same. He reached for a fold of her robe so he could cover her legs, and watched his hand draw it back, exposing more of her thigh. She had strong legs, smoothly muscled, the pale flesh sheened by tiny, almost invisible blond hairs. Like the women in the time of his mortal life, she must have never put a razor to her legs.

Korvel wanted to feel that sweet velvet against his cheek, his lips, his belly. His *dents acérées* slid slowly into his mouth, full and aching, demanding another taste of her, and he had to look away until he could master the beast inside him.

Simone made a soft sound, drawing his attention back to her, and he saw that her eyes were open but unfocused. "Captain?" she murmured.

"Yes, sister." He bent over her, releasing his scent so he could see her eyes go dark. "It's me."

She reached for him, finding his wrist, bringing his hand to her cheek. "Thought you were sleeping."

If she only knew what had kept him awake, she would

run from the room shrieking. "I must go. I will return soon."

"Don't." She held on to him. "Don't leave me again."

He could release himself from her grip with barely a flick of a muscle; yet he felt as bound to her as if they were chained in copper. "The drugs are still affecting you."

"No." Her eyes, clear and bright now, held his. "Not anymore. It's you. *You* make me feel this longing."

Her scent did not change; she was speaking the truth. He wouldn't allow himself to take her, but he could attend to her needs. "I want to touch you and give you pleasure. This will please me as well. If you do not want this, I will leave and see to my own needs. You have but to tell me what you want, my angel."

Her hand left his wrist, and Korvel started to rise. He stopped as he watched her hands move down to the belt of her robe and untie it.

He felt a moment of shocked uncertainty, as if she had stripped the centuries away and made him mortal again. Perhaps it was fitting that a nun who had never known a man could reduce him to the state of an awkward adolescent with his first woman.

She pulled apart the robe, baring her breasts and belly and thighs to his gaze. He wanted to open the drapes and allow the dawn to illuminate every inch of her so he could see her skin in sunlight. He didn't care that it would further weaken him, but such a thing would doubtless embarrass her. He wanted her to remember this interlude with nothing but delight.

Afraid he would lose his head and pounce on her, Korvel moved from the lounge to kneel on the floor. She turned toward him, shifting down to pillow her head on one arm and stretch out full-length.

"You do not belong in this world." Using one fingertip, he traced the ridge of her collarbone, following it up to her shoulder and down the side of her arm. "In my time men would have taken up the sword and the lance to win your favor."

"No need," she murmured. "You have mine."

Korvel found the end of her braid and removed the ribbon, unwinding the long, thick cable until he could drape her with the vibrant strands. He felt her palm graze his cheek as she curled a strand of his short hair around her fingertip.

She had such an absorbed look on her face that he had to ask, "What are you thinking?"

"The red in your hair is fading," she murmured. "Soon it will be blond again. If you were human, our babies would all be fair."

The thought of his child swelling inside her made him feel a surge of regret. "As I am, I cannot give you children."

She glanced down and touched two of the slanted ridges on her belly. "Even if you could, I can never conceive."

He covered one scar with his hand. Given the circumstances of his own birth, he had never regretted being rendered infertile by the change, but he knew most mortal females desired children. "I am sorry to know that."

"Don't be." Her eyes shifted to his. "What do you want me to do?"

"Close your eyes." When she did, he brushed the ends of her hair across her lower lip. "Do you feel that?"

"Yes."

"That is what I want." He let her hair sift through his fingers before he put them to her face, following the sweep of her brows around to the arch of her cheekbones, the slant of her nose to the cusp above her upper lip. Her mouth parted for his fingers as he traced its contours before he feathered a caress along the line of her jaw and down the hollows of her throat.

Korvel saw her lashes flutter as she felt his breath on her body. "Tell me what you feel."

"I ache inside. It feels like fever, but I'm not sick." She dampened her lips. "I want to open my eyes."

"Not yet." He bent his head, stroking his tongue over the swollen peak of her breast before he blew a breath across it to watch the damp tip bead. "You ache here, don't you?" When she nodded, he curved his hand around the flushed mound. "This is what you need."

He put his lips to her hard nipple, working his tongue over it. As he suckled, he moved his hand down to her waist, and then to her thigh. He stroked the tight muscle in time with the tug of his mouth, until her legs relaxed and her hips shifted. The scent of her arousal rushed over him as he brought his hand to rest over the curls of her mound. When he parted her with his finger, she jolted, her breast escaping his lips and her hand curling into his hair.

Korvel kept his hand where it was and turned his face to kiss her palm. "You feel the ache there, beneath my hand, don't you?"

"If I say yes," she asked, her voice low and tight, "are you going to put your mouth there?"

"You have to say yes to find out." He stroked his fingers between her folds so that she heard the sound of her own slickness. "I want to feel you on my tongue." He bent his head, and she felt his words against the skin of her belly. "Say yes, Simone, and I'll make the aching go away."

She trembled and covered her face with her hand, but finally she whispered to him, "Yes."

Korvel slid his hands under her hips, bringing her to his mouth, stroking her open with his tongue and tasting the sweet wetness of her need. Her position on the lounge prevented him from spreading her thighs, so he took his mouth away and dragged her down to the carpet, pressing her knees up and back as he settled between her legs, his head dipping so he could get at her sex, his tongue licking at the tight ellipse at her heart before he laved his way to the hard knot of her clit, nudging back the tiny hood to expose it before he caressed and sucked.

Her nails scored the carpet, and she made a low, wailing sound, but even as her body writhed, her hands curled in his hair, tightening with every lash of his tongue. Korvel felt her foot brush the pulsing ridge of his penis and reached down, tearing open his trousers to free his cock. He caught her foot and brought it to his shaft, using the delicate arch of her instep against the tight sheath of his foreskin.

To keep from rising up and shoving his penis into her sweet dampness, he shifted down and pushed his tongue into her, sliding it back and forth as he fucked her with his mouth. The tips of his *dents acérées* grazed the tender flesh plumped out by his penetrating kiss, spilling a few drops of her blood, and Simone cried out, her body vibrating with the force of her pleasure.

Korvel drove her through that climax and brought her to another, and then rolled away as she went limp, licking the taste from his lips as he wrapped his fist around his shaft. He stroked hard and slow, and then felt her move, and the light, warm touch of her hand on his fist. He groaned as she threaded her fingers through his, and together they stroked, up and down, harder and faster, until he brought her hand up to his cock head and spilled himself against her fingers.

When Korvel found the strength to turn his head, he saw Simone on her side, her hand still resting with his at his crotch, her eyes almost closed. "You did not have to do that for me."

"I wanted to. I liked feeling you in my hand." She closed her eyes.

Korvel took her hand and wiped his seed away with the hem of her robe, and then lifted her and carried her to the bed. He wanted to take his rest beside her, but he had done too much to her already. If he woke with Simone naked in his arms he would be inside her before he knew what he was doing.

He made himself as comfortable as he could on the lounge, which still smelled of her, and fell asleep wondering what she would say to him tonight when he awoke.

Golden swans found Simone floating in a pool of warmth and swarmed around her, cooing in low voices as they extended their wings and wrapped her in their soft feathers. Charmed by the unlikely attention, she reached to pet them, caressing their long necks and curved backs. On the other side of the darkness they would have attacked her, hissing and pecking, but here they belonged to her, a living garment of gilded beauty, and shielded her against some great unknown presence lurking just out of her sight.

The swans stretched, their necks twining around her arms and legs, coiling and merging until they flattened into golden armor. A two-handed sword forged of copper appeared in the sky above her, shining in the dark like a beacon, and turned slowly as it fell, end over end, until she reached up with her gauntlet and caught the hilt.

Come to me, girl.

Simone rose from the waters, the heavy chain mail draping her skull shifting, the leather soles of her boots finding hard-packed barren soil. The dark figure that emerged from the shadows wore the robe of a monk but carried the hammer of a smith.

His green eyes glowed, emeralds set in rubies, and the smile he gave her displayed the long, sharp ivory of his dents acérées. The assassin and the whore are dead. You belong to me now, girl. You and your sisters.

I don't have any sisters. *Simone felt bewildered.* Who are you?

I was the maker of the scroll, and it was I who washed it in my blood.

Simone suddenly understood who he was. You were the smith.

Once my mortal kin numbered in the thousands. The monk circled around her. You and your mortal family were my army, my guardians, each sworn to protect the secrets of eternity. Now you number but three. You will not fail me as your father did.

Simone lowered the sword. I will not kill for you, Cristophe.

You have the courage to protect the mortal world from eternal damnation. *He grabbed the sword, wrenching it from her hand and throwing it into the water. He reached out to her face, and Simone saw blood dripping from the deep gashes across his fingers and palm.* But do you have the strength to do what needs be done?

I will keep my word.

The armor writhed against her body as her legs slowly sank into the earth. One by one the golden swans released themselves from their Celtic coils, spreading their great glowing wings to glide away, leaving Simone hip-deep in the muddy shore. She held out her hand to the monk, but he had become a statue of blackened copper, his sightless eyes weeping blood.

As the mud oozed over her shoulders, Simone struggled, fighting to free her arms, but the earth held her in a tight embrace, pulling her down until she was swallowed alive in its grave—

"No."

Fabric tore as she ripped her way out of the smothering cocoon, gulping air as she flung away the bed linens and pushed herself over the edge of the bed. She had not been buried alive; it had been only a nightmare. She was still in the hotel in Avignon.

"Captain?"

He had left her there alone, Simone soon discovered after a brief search of the suite. Outside the windows, only stars lit the sky; she must have slept through the entire day.

Too much sleep, she thought, stretching her stiff limbs, and then felt an unusual tenderness between her thighs. All at once the memory of what she had done with Korvel came over her, and she sat down on the lounge and stared at the carpet.

She remembered his coming to her as she lay half-asleep on the lounge, and the gentle way he had spoken to her. Only when he had told her he was leaving had she shaken off the drowsiness. The thought of him with another woman had caused a strange panic to come over her. She had not meant to confess her desire for him so bluntly, but she could not regret it now.

The sisters had shared their knowledge of everything, including the ways of men, but hearing a blind woman describe attending to her lord was not anything like being touched by Korvel. What he had done had been tender and shocking and nothing like what she had been taught to do. Her face grew hot as she recalled the moment when he had pulled her from the lounge. If he had not dragged her to the floor, she might have flung herself on top of him.

Simone still did not understand why he would do all of that to her and yet not expect her to give him sex in return. If she had not realized that he was relieving himself, he would have completed the act on his own.

He could not think her undesirable, not when he had ravished her with his mouth as he had. Did he never lie with human women? Darkyn females might possess some physical talent that Simone did not. Perhaps her scarred body repelled him.

Was that why he had left her to wake alone? Was he so disgusted by her or what had happened between them that he had to seek out another woman? She had done almost nothing for him, but she had thought that was what he wanted.

I don't know what he wants. But when he returns, I will find out and give it to him.

Her empty stomach made her look for the cart of food from last night, but when she found it in the front room she found a four-course meal under the silver domes. Beside the entrée plate lay a handwritten note and a room charge card beside the room service menu.

After you dine, go to the hotel boutique and purchase a dress for yourself. I will return in a few hours.

She put down the note, annoyed by his order. There was nothing wrong with her clothes; she had no need to go shopping. He'd been foolish to leave her behind. He knew nothing about Avignon, and his French was terrible; he should have woken her and taken her with him.

She ate quickly, just enough to quiet her belly, before she washed, dressed, and braided her hair. On her way out of the suite she hesitated and then pocketed the room charge card. She didn't need a new dress, but some hairpins would be helpful.

She took the elevator down to the lobby, where she stood out of sight behind a potted plant in order to inspect the faces of the guests, the pretty young women behind the reception counter, and the dignified middle-aged man speaking on the phone at the concierge's desk.

She went to the man, who ended his call abruptly and regarded her with his brows raised.

"Madame, how may I be of assistance?" His cool, lofty tone indicated that showing her the exit might be the only service he was interested in performing.

"My husband and I are staying in the Napoleon suite," she told him, allowing him a moment to compose himself. "He left a short time ago but did not tell me where he was going." She gave him a brief description of Korvel, and then asked, "Did he happen to ask you for directions anywhere?"

"*Non,* madame. I did not have the pleasure of speaking with your husband." The concierge's eyes shifted to the left. "If you wish, I can ask him to call your suite when he has, ah, completed his business."

He had told the man to lie for him? "That won't be necessary."

Simone walked to the left side of the lobby and heard the faint sounds of laughter and music coming from a corridor behind reception.

The concierge appeared in front of her. "I know madame would enjoy a complimentary visit to our spa." He produced a coupon with a flourish. "I will be happy to escort you there now."

She watched over his shoulder as a couple came walking out of the corridor. Both carried drinks and looked happily inebriated. "What is down there?"

"It is our nightclub, but at this hour it is very crowded." He took her elbow in an attempt to steer her back toward the lobby. "Did you know that our spa is the finest in all of Avignon, madame? Our masseuse, Claude, was trained in the Far East, and can help you relax—"

She shook him off and strode down the corridor, stopping at the open entrance to a large, dimly lit bar.

A mirrored ball surrounded by rolling lights flashed as it slowly spun above a dance floor filled with gyrating guests. Several men in suits stood clustered around two islands where bartenders in red satin vests and white shirts flipped bottles to fill glasses, while cocktail waitresses in red satin miniskirts and white vests carried trays of drinks out to the guests sitting at tables. Women wearing the scantiest of dresses orbited the dance floor and flirted with the men at the twin bars.

Simone surveyed the interior of the club until she spotted a group of five crowded around a corner table. One of the rolling lights briefly shone on the group, revealing four women's rapt faces and the short, copper-colored hair of the man sitting in the center of them. The man caught the wrist of one of the women and brought it to his lips.

Korvel.

Simone walked inside, moving out of sight behind one of the bars as she chose a path that would take her closer to Korvel and his new friends. Men turned in her wake, and a few tried to speak to her, but she ignored them as she crossed to a column and used its shadow as cover.

The four women surrounding Korvel seemed mesmerized by his face, as they stared only at him, their painted mouths smiling, their hands caressing his arms and shoulders. One insinuated herself under his arm, rubbing her breast into his side as she pushed her fingers into the open collar of his shirt. He turned to her, tipping her chin up before he put his mouth to the top of her breast.

Simone retreated, striding out of the club and back to the lobby. As soon as he saw her the concierge hurried over.

"Madame, if you will permit me, I will—"

"Where is the hotel boutique located?" she asked in as pleasant a voice as she could get through her teeth.

"Ah, it is on the basement level. We have a wonderful array of evening dresses, and I will be delighted to—"

Simone stalked toward the elevator, taking it down to the basement level, where she made her way past the gift and convenience shops to the glass storefront of the boutique. Two elegantly skeletal mannequins displayed evening dresses; one was a long steel blue gown with an angora wrap, the other a strapless tube of bloodred silk with a plunging neckline and side panels of scarlet lace that revealed the body from breast to thigh.

The shop attendant met her just inside, and only directed one arched brow at her clothing. "May I be of assistance, madame?"

"I need shoes, stockings, and undergarments." Simone pointed to one of the mannequins. "And that dress."

Chapter 10

"We should go to my room," Amelia the brunette said, her breath hot against Korvel's ear. "I have a very large bed and a bottle of champagne on ice."

"I'll join you two," Tina, the redheaded American, offered as she stroked his thigh. "A big guy like you needs all the girls he can get, right?"

"You can't leave me behind," Francesca said, shaking her short black curls as her red lips pouted.

"I want to go, too," Keisha, the dark-skinned girl, chimed in with her sultry islander accent.

Bored, Korvel looked out at the dance floor. The small amounts of blood he had discreetly taken from each of the four women had sated his hunger; he had no interest in sampling any of their other delights. He had lingered here too long, and needed to return to the suite to check on Simone. He also wished he could do anything else but that.

By now she is awake, he thought as he absently reached down to prevent Tina from slipping her hand into his trousers. *She will find the meal and the note I left for her. Once she has eaten and bathed she will probably go to the boutique. All women like pretty clothes. She will think nothing of my absence. Or she will think I am too craven to face her after using her.*

Unable to bear his own thoughts, Korvel borrowed a mobile phone from one of the women and tried to call Ireland. The answering static frustrated him on a completely different level, for by now the high lord would know something was amiss.

Death had been the only thing that could break the oath Korvel had made as a human to Richard. When his still-human master had returned suffering with plague from the Holy Land, he had summoned Korvel to his chamber, and asked that only he tend to him. And so Korvel had, for a day and night, before succumbing to the same sickness.

Days passed in a feverish blur, but Korvel had clung to life, determined not to fail his master, until the hour when from his pallet he had watched the gravediggers, their noses and mouths covered with rags, carry away the limp body of his lord. Only then did he surrender to the fever scalding his body, and go gratefully into the darkness. It had been a peaceful moment, filled with one final satisfaction: He had kept his oath to the end.

Only it had not been the end. Some days later, he had clawed his way out of the dark, out of his own grave, strangely alive but not alive, to find Richard waiting for him. His master had explained to him that they had both become the dark Kyn, immortals that would live forever.

Humans had discovered them in the graveyard, and Korvel had not even hesitated to sacrifice himself so that his master might escape. He had been dragged away and taken to a crossroads, where the mob had used a copper-spiked rope to hang him from the gallows tree. There he had dangled, too weak to release himself but unable to die, for three weeks. As soon as he lost the strength to struggle, the mortals grew bored and left him to rot—which was when Richard had emerged from the shadows of midnight to cut him down and carry him over his shoulder to a nearby abandoned cottage.

You I trust as no other, Korvel, his master had said as he sliced open his own wrist to feed him the blood he desperately needed. *You will be the eyes at my back, my third blade.*

The terror and joy of that second reprieve had preoccupied Korvel as he learned how to survive and protect himself and his master from humans who despised and hunted their kind. It would be another century before he discovered that somehow during Richard's last days as a mortal he had discovered he was not dying of plague, but making the change from mortal to Kyn. By commanding Korvel rather than one of the women to attend him, Richard had exposed him to the same sickness. His only reason for doing so had to be in hope that his captain would also rise to walk the night.

From that time on Korvel understood that his master had never had any true regard for him. In some ways it had acted upon him like diluted acid, slowly eating away at his heart until he had no feeling left for his master. Still he served the high lord, for even Richard's most grievous exploitations did not violate his oath. No matter what the high lord felt for him, Korvel would not sacrifice his honor. Only death would end it.

Perhaps that will be my punishment for what I did to Alexandra. He touched the green scar on his neck. *Because I would not free her from the bond between us, now I will never be free of Richard.*

A flash of red caught his eye, and Korvel turned his head to see a tall, willowy female step up to the bar. Red satin ribbons snaked through the long ponytail of her shining hair, the ends of which curled against the curve of her buttocks. He could see her bare skin beneath the panel of lace that raced down her long torso; she wore no undergarments beneath the clinging silk sheath. The dark-haired Spaniard standing beside her gaped at her breasts, which were all but falling out of the provocative bodice.

Korvel had seen a thousand women so lovely it hurt the eyes to look upon them, and yet somehow this lady outshone them all.

He briefly regarded the mortal females around him. "You will leave me and return to your rooms to sleep. When you wake you will have no memory of me."

Like sleepwalkers, the women agreed and rose to walk in single file toward the elevators. Korvel picked up his wine to finish it, but over the rim of his glass his eyes strayed back to the bar, and the elegant perfection of the blond siren's form.

The woman in red uttered a low, husky laugh as she put her hand on the Spaniard's shoulder. The man spoke rapidly, gulping down his drink between sentences before he anchored an arm around her waist and pecked at her cheek.

Korvel didn't know why he wanted to rip the arm from the mortal male's body. As lovely and tempting as the siren in scarlet was, he had no time to dally with her. Certainly not with Simone upstairs; by now she had to be fuming over his absence. Perhaps his unfulfilled desire for the nun had bloomed into an unreasonable, temper-riddled lust for any woman. But if that were the case, then why had it been so easy to send away the other four, who would have happily permitted him to do anything he wished with them? And why could he not stop looking at this vision in red?

The siren leaned close to her drunken companion, speaking to him as she gestured toward the exit. At that moment the flashing lights above passed over her face.

The woman with the Spaniard *was* Simone.

Disbelief held Korvel locked in stunned silence as he watched the nun behave as shamelessly as a courtesan with her lover, her lips smiling as she spoke to the mortal, her hands landing to pet and stroke and tease until he became overwhelmed and pulled her into his arms. She turned around, hugging his hands to her waist while she led him toward the exit.

Simone was leaving with him. In that dress.

Over my dead body.

Korvel rose to his feet, knocking aside the table as he went after her, growing more furious with every step as he picked up her scent mingled with that of an exotic French perfume. From behind he witnessed the artful sway of her hips and the coy manner in which she looped her arm through the Spaniard's; she was all but throwing herself at him. And where did she think she was going? Did she mean to leave the hotel? With a drunken stranger? It seemed she did.

The concierge stepped in front of him, temporarily halting his progress. "Monsieur, I must apologize, but—"

"Not now." Korvel brushed past him, his fists curling as he saw no sign of Simone or her easy conquest.

If she thought she could elude him, she was sadly mistaken. His Kyn senses could track her from a mile away.

Unless she gets into a taxi with that sodding buffoon.

Outside the hotel Korvel scanned the street, relaxing a little when he saw no cars passing. Simone's scent drew him down the walk and into a side alley, where several cars had been parked.

He strode up to a sedan at which her scent flared

strongest and grabbed the door handle. He jerked, metal ripped, and the sedan rocked as the entire door came off. He threw it aside and reached in to pull the Spaniard away from Simone and out of the car.

"Monsieur?" the man squeaked as Korvel lifted him off his feet and held him, legs dangling, in the air. "What are you doing?"

"Far less than I want," he grated, forcing himself to put the mortal on the ground. "Go back to the club."

"But . . . but . . . my *door!*"

Korvel bared his *dents acérées*. "Go back. Forget all of this. Now. Or I will tear out your throat."

The Spaniard's feet slipped and slid over the slush-wet stone as he ran from the alley. Only when he was gone did Korvel look back into the sedan. Simone had gotten out and stood on the other side, her hands braced against the vehicle.

"Are you going to rip out my throat now?" she asked, her tone insultingly polite.

"What were you thinking?" He flung a hand toward the clinging red silk. "And what is that?"

"You told me to buy a dress. I followed your instructions." She came around the car to stand before him. "Don't you like it?"

She must still be addled by the drugs, he decided. "Come inside." He closed the gap between them and took her by the wrist. "I will send for the doctor."

She didn't move. "I am not sick."

"Do the other nuns at the convent dress and behave like trollops?" He tried to pull her along.

She came around him, her skirt riding up as she delivered a side kick to his knee and another to his shin that sent him sprawling. As Korvel lay there, stunned, she walked up to him and planted one shoe on his chest.

"I am not a nun, and you are not my master," she said calmly. "So you may go back to your women and leave me alone."

Simone had reached the end of the alley when Korvel jerked her around. "Say that again."

"Leave me alone."

He shook his head. "The first of it."

She moved faster this time, but Korvel felt the coil of her muscles and countered the attack, using just enough strength to subdue her. When she stopped resisting he put his face close to hers. "Say it again."

"I am not a nun."

He released her and moved a short distance away, staring at the brick wall as he battled back his temper. He heard her come up behind him, her movements causing the red silk to whisper against her skin.

"I never told you that I was a nun, Captain." She stood close enough for her breath to warm his air.

"You live in a convent," he told the wall. "You wear nun's garments, and pray with a rosary, and do good works. There is — was — a cross hanging about your neck." He felt steady enough to look directly at her, which he realized at once was a mistake. "What the bloody hell was I supposed to think you were? An exotic dancer?"

"You're not supposed to think about me at all," she reminded him. "I'm nothing to you."

His fangs pulsed as they stretched out in his mouth, as aching and eager as if he had not fed in a week. "Why do you live at the convent, Simone?"

"When I was a girl the sisters were my teachers, and they became very fond of me. When I left my father's house they offered me a home and a purpose. I wear a habit when I leave the convent because that is what is expected." She touched the place at her throat where her cross usually hung. "I've never taken vows or joined the order. I can't. I don't believe in God."

"In your room, I watched you pray." His jaw tightened. "Another pretense?"

Simone shrugged. "Habit. I do it because it pleases Flavia to believe I have faith. It is easier than arguing with her."

"Why let me believe you were a nun?"

"You did not tell me what you believed." At last a flicker of shame passed over her features. "Besides, if you had asked, I would have told you."

"I have been calling you 'sister' for days," he said, snarling the words. "You knew precisely what I thought. You *wanted* me to believe you had taken vows. That you were an innocent."

The laugh she uttered had a tinge of self-mockery. "I offered you sex, Captain. *You* refused *me*."

"Another of your maneuverings," he countered. "You knew my honor demanded nothing less."

"I knew nothing of you, you oblivious ass." Her upper lip curled. "Your precious honor didn't stop you last night, did it?"

Simone regretted the taunt from the moment it left her lips. Last night Korvel had not forced or coerced her; she had wanted it as much as he had. If she had refused him he would not have touched her. Now in her anger she had wanted him to feel as wretched about it as she did, but she had succeeded only in shaming herself.

"I shouldn't have said that. I apologize, Captain." Unable to look at him another moment, she walked out of the alley.

The few pedestrians Simone passed stared at her, as if they knew what a fool she had made of herself. She changed direction, retreating to a narrow, shadowed lane that led between the gates and walls surrounding some private homes.

The sound of water tickled her ear, and she stopped outside the iron gates leading to a private courtyard. Inside a garden of ivy, lemon trees and evergreens surrounded a tall, tiered fountain. Simone gripped the bars of the gate, resting her forehead against them as she watched the silvery streams cascading into three basins cast to resemble blooming flowers.

The sound of approaching footsteps made her look down at the latch on the gate, which was not locked, and then up at the shuttered windows of the dark house. She opened the gate and slipped inside, ducking behind a lattice of leafy vines. As the scent of larkspur mixed with the greenery around her, she closed her eyes.

"My women."

Simone looked up at Korvel, and braced herself as he lifted his hand. When he caught a tendril of her hair and drew it away from her face, she shivered. "What about them?"

"You told me to go back to my women." He traced the contour of her cheek. "You meant the females from the club. You saw me with them, and it made you do this. Why?"

"I woke up and you were gone." She sounded like a sulky child, but she didn't care. "I came downstairs to find you, and there you were, with four of them crawling over you. How could you be with them after last night? What's wrong with me?"

"I used them for blood, Simone, not sex." He moved his hand to the back of her neck, where his thumb brushed over the fine hairs on her nape. "There is nothing wrong with you."

"I watched you put your mouth on one of them." She touched her breast. "Here."

"In public I must feed with discretion. I took blood from her there so that her dress would cover the marks from my *dents acérées.*" He glanced down. "Are you wearing anything under yours?"

Now he was teasing her. "It doesn't matter." Another time she might have joked about her outrageous behavior, but not tonight. Not while the longing for him still twisted inside her. She ducked out from under his arm. "I will return to the hotel and collect our things."

"I am not done with you."

Korvel turned her around, backing her up against the iron gate as his big hand slid down over her hip to the hem of her skirt. She forgot to breathe as she felt his fingers stroke up the outside of her thigh.

"Stockings." He pushed the skirt up out of his way, his fingers inching along the satin ribbon of her garter from the outside of her thigh to her waist. He then slid his hand around her and followed the small of her back down to the bare curve of her bottom.

"Captain."

He ignored her shocked whisper. "No knickers." With his other hand he tugged the edge of her bodice away from her body. "And no brassiere. I thought as much."

"The girl in the shop said they would show through the lace." She inhaled sharply as he shifted his hand back to the front of her hips. "If you want sex—"

"You are obsessed with sex." He worked his fingers through the thatch of her body hair, playing with the small curls. "Is it because of me, or have you always been this way?"

She went rigid. "I am not a whore."

"No, you're not. No whore offers such passion." One

finger parted her. "Feel how wet you are here, how hot you burn beneath my touch? A whore is hard and cold. You're softer than the silk you wear, Simone."

He was touching her as he had last night, but only because he felt sorry for her, because he wanted to appease her. It made her angry all over again. "I don't need you to pity me."

He stared at her. "Is that what you think this is?"

Korvel scooped her up into the cradle of his arm, snatching her off her feet and carrying her over to the fountain. Simone grabbed his shoulders, too startled to do more than hold on, and a moment later found herself on her back on the widest of the lounges beside the splashing water. The cushion under her sank as he straddled the lounge.

"Are you mad?"

"As it happens, I am." Korvel loomed over her, positioning her before he reached for the front of his trousers. "Look at me. *Look at me.*" When she did, he guided his penis to her, working the dome of it between her folds. "This is what I have for you. Only you." He pressed it, breaching her body. "This is why you wore that dress. For me. You want to tempt me, inflame me, have me on you like this."

Even flat on her back and pinned as she was by the weight of his body and the spike of his sex, Simone could think of a hundred ways to hurt him. All she could do was watch his eyes as he pushed into her, and feel the stretch and ache of her softness around his thick, hard shaft.

Korvel pushed her skirt up around her waist and looked down at the mesh of their bodies, holding himself deep inside her as he reached for her bodice and pulled it down to bare her breasts. His hands covered them, weighing and kneading before he pinched the tight tips.

It was too much, Simone thought, feeling the welling of some terrible emotion inside her. "Why now?"

"Because this is what I want." He slid his arms under her, lifting her up to give her a slow, deep kiss before he pressed her face to his throat and began to move. "I want to fuck you, Simone. And I think you want it too."

The delicious scent of his skin captivated her; she parted her lips so she could put her tongue against his cool skin. He stiffened as he felt the damp caress, and within her body she felt his penis surge.

Korvel draped her legs over his arms, spreading them wide as he forged deeper. "This time I want to feel you come all over me. You come on my cock."

Simone clenched around him, trying to hold him in the deepest part of her, but he dragged his shaft back, leaving behind a hot, wet emptiness. She almost shrieked until he stroked into her again, stabbing through the quivering ache and touching some part of her that sent a jolt through her belly and breasts.

"Yes," he said, watching her face as he did it again. "There you are."

With his hands and his mouth alternately ravishing her breasts, he worked in and out of her body, dragging the heavy thickness out before driving it back in again, over and over. Simone could feel the lounge shuddering beneath her, and heard the low, gasping sounds that escaped her lips and the liquid glide of his penis as he went deep into her core. Only some remnant of pride forced her to resist the delight that coiled inside her, begging to be released.

Simone could not bear it another moment. "Please."

He lifted his mouth from her nipple, his eyes glittering as he took her hand and brought it to the juncture of their bodies. Gripping her forefinger, he pressed the end into the top of her sex, rubbing the pad of her fingertip against the wet knot there.

Simone tried to pull her hand away, but he held on and whispered to her, words that made her cringe and pant and whimper. He told her how it felt to be inside her, to watch his cock push into her, to feel her body tightening around him, to see the bulge of her sex. As he spoke he made her stroke her clit faster, harder, matching the rhythm with his hips, until he brought her finger to his mouth and sucked on it.

Pleasure took her apart as her body convulsed under his. Korvel shoved deep into the heart of her delight, shuddering as his semen erupted in long, hard jets.

Chapter 11

Pájaro waited for nightfall before he entered Le Panier, Marseilles's oldest *quartier*. Once the refuge of whores, sailors, and other scum from the docks, the shameful ghetto had been gradually revitalized by a curious infusion of new blood.

Artisans, always in need of cheap lodgings, had first gravitated to the rough shantytown to rent rooms and studio space in its tall, squash-colored houses with their ladder-long white shutters. Of course, they had to peddle their wares as well, which ranged from decorative pots to hand-painted *santons,* tiny figurines used in traditional crèches to illustrate the Nativity scene. In time the stink of fish, liquor, and sex for sale had faded from the alleys, replaced by the pungent aromas of damp pots, gas kilns, and sunscreen-slathered tourists.

As he climbed the stone steps to a side street, Pájaro sensed someone coming up behind him. He glanced up at the washing-draped balconies, seeing only an amber cat with copper eyes staring down at him, before he turned to face his shadow.

Middle age and all its disappointments had soured the woman's triangular features, and just-freshened makeup failed to disguise the cobwebs of capillaries alcohol addiction had started to spread on either side of her hooked nose.

"Do you want something, mademoiselle?"

Her clumpy lashes fluttered with grotesque coyness as she assessed his clothes and the location of his pockets. "I'm just having a walk. Are you going to the Twelve Coins? They have live music." She shimmied around in an uneven circle to demonstrate her deplorable dancing skills.

"I don't drink or dance." He continued up the steps, knowing she would follow, listening for the second pair of footsteps as her partner tailed them. He changed direction, leading them to the back of a busy restaurant's kitchen, where he retreated to the shadows.

An overweight, burly man caught up with the barfly and yanked at her arm. "Where did he go?"

"I didn't see." When her companion went still, she made an impatient sound. "Come on, Porci, I haven't . . ." She darted out of the way as the man toppled over, and shrieked at the blade sticking out of his back.

"Shhhh." Pájaro clapped a hand over her mouth as he dragged her back behind some plastic crates of bottled water.

A short time later he emerged alone, and took two bottles from the crates to rinse the blood from his hands and his dagger. He yanked down a towel from a low-hanging balcony and used it to dry his hands before he dropped it in a rubbish container a block away.

Squeezed between a narrow gallery of *arts Africains* and a garden container shop, Pájaro found number eight Rue Méry, the current residence of Bonafacio Puget, formerly the department chair of medieval studies at a prestigious Paris university. The professor, who had retired to pursue his lifelong ambition of writing the definitive history of the French Church, was also the country's leading expert on the Knights Templar.

A man too young to be Puget answered the door, yawning as he asked, "Can't you read?"

Pájaro glanced at the faded red AUCUNE SOLLICITATION sign posted in corner of the front window. "I am not a salesman. Where is Professor Puget?"

"He's an old man; he's sleeping. Come back in the—*Hey!*" He recovered from being shoved aside and tried to get in front of Pájaro as he stepped inside. "You can't come in here."

"Yet I have." He caught the younger man's hand before he could touch him. "Who are you?"

"I am Puget's assistant, Alain. Let go, you—"

"Listen carefully, Puget's assistant." Pájaro applied enough pressure to his wrist bones to make him squawk like a chicken. "Take me to him, or you'll be picking your nose left-handed for life."

He kept hold of the boy as he shuffled down the corridor and into a room cluttered with old books, new computer equipment, and the stodgy decor of the lifelong academic. Hundreds of handwritten papers lay sticking out of books, protruded from folders and binders, and formed scattered piles over every horizontal surface. Near the fireplace an old man sat slumped in an overstuffed armchair, a fat tabby curled on his lap.

"Professor," Alain whimpered, startling the cat into jumping down and scampering away. "Wake up. *Professor.*"

Puget lifted a hand and swatted at the air. "Go home, boy. We will continue tomorrow."

"Puget." Pájaro waited until the old man's eyes blinked open. "I am in need of your expertise."

"What?" The professor hoisted himself into a more

upright position. "I don't cater to any *connard* who demands it. Are you not right in the head? Get out."

Pájaro put down his case, drew the blade from his forearm sheath, and yanked Alain back against him. The boy yelped until he felt the edge of the blade pressing against his windpipe.

"How do you feel about Alain continuing to breathe through his mouth?" As the old man grabbed for the phone beside his chair, Pájaro cut the boy enough to spill blood. "At this hour, it will take emergency services five minutes to arrive, by which time both of you will be quite brain-dead."

Puget slowly replaced the receiver. "What do you want?"

He released Alain, shoving him toward the professor's desk. "Clear off the top of that. Quickly."

Puget went to help the boy, who sobbed as he gathered up papers. The professor offered him a crumpled handkerchief before he shoved everything on the desk off one edge.

"Good." Pájaro picked up his case, carrying it over to the desk and opening it. He also swept out his leg to trip Alain as the boy tried to run past him for the door. With a back sweep of his boot, he knocked the boy unconscious. "Translate the contents of this scroll for me."

Puget glanced down at the case and drew in his lips. "I am not a linguist, monsieur."

"You have translated books written in several languages dating back to the twelfth century," Pájaro reminded him. "I know all about you, Professor. I ran your name through Google." He reached over and tugged back the cloth covering the scroll. "This was inscribed during the thirteenth century. For you, it should be like reading a menu from a chalkboard."

The luster of the gold worked its magic on the old man; he couldn't take his eyes off the treasure. "If I do this, if I give you what you want, will you go?"

"You have my word; I will go," Pájaro promised.

Puget removed a pair of white cloth gloves from a drawer, slipping them over his hands before he removed the scroll from the case. The weight of it caught him off guard, and he nearly dropped it before placing it to one side and moving the case out of his way.

Pájaro dragged one of the computer chairs over to the side of the desk, where he sat to watch as the professor examined the scroll. "There are clamps on either end."

"So I see." Puget made no move to release them, but turned over the two cylinders before he reached into his pocket for his reading glasses. "Where did you steal this from?"

He chuckled. "It belonged to my father."

"It belongs in a museum." Puget glanced at Alain's slack features before he released the clamps and rolled the larger cylinder apart from the smaller. He frowned, reaching to switch on the desk lamp before he bent close. "This is not paper or parchment. It is gold."

"That I already knew."

"It is woven from threads of solid gold and some other metal, then embossed by hand tools. I have never seen the like." His head bobbed as he examined the first row of symbols. "I cannot help you with this, monsieur."

"You care so little for Alain?"

"You misunderstand my meaning." Puget pointed to the script. "This is not a language. It is a code. A system of ancient pictographs invented and used by a small group of men. The key has never been found, and the code has never been deciphered. I know; I tried to crack it myself for thirty years without success."

He nodded. "Tell me about these men."

"Why?" Puget's upper lip curled. "They were disgraced Templars, and they are all dead."

Pájaro leaned forward. "How were they disgraced?"

"There have always been rumors about them. Nonsense, for the most part." The professor pushed his fingers under the lenses of his glasses to rub his eyes. "They were said to have traded their souls to Satan for his favors, and for such were cursed by God and cast out by their own brotherhood. One account claims that de Mornay himself had them excommunicated and driven out of France for their unholy practices. Some say they returned to the Holy Land and died there trying to redeem themselves. Others believe they fled to the Far East."

He might just have to let the old man live. "What were their names?"

"No one knows," Puget said. "Their names were removed from the temple rolls and obliterated from all histories of that time. No more than a handful of scholars in the world even acknowledge the possibility that these men ever existed."

Pájaro smiled. "What if I told you I can prove that the dark Kyn are not dead, Professor?" He noted the moment of stillness that came over the old man at the mention of their name. "But you already know that they still walk among us."

"I have no knowledge of devil worshipers who have lived for seven hundred years." The old man sniffed. "Of course, you would. You are a lunatic."

As the old man removed his glasses from the end of his nose, his unbuttoned cuff gaped, revealing the oval edge of an old tattoo.

Pájaro seized his arm, driving his dagger through Puget's palm to embed the tip in the top of the desk. As the old man released a hoarse cry of pain, Pájaro tore apart the sleeve to reveal the black cameo tattooed on Puget's forearm.

He grinned as he met the old man's eyes, now wide and glassy. "You wily old goat, speaking such lies about those you serve."

"I don't know what—" The professor grunted as his lip split beneath the impact of Pájaro's fist.

"We'll start over from the beginning," Pájaro said, "and this time you will tell me everything."

"Imbecile." Puget displayed his blood-covered teeth. "You stole from Helada. Even now he is coming for you." He took in a deep, shuddering breath, his gaze shifting to the unconscious Alain before he wrapped his hand around the hilt of the dagger. With a single jerk he pulled it out of his palm and brandished the blade.

Pájaro's brows rose. "Do you really believe you can kill me for him, old man?"

"I don't have to. You were dead from the moment you touched the scroll." Puget reversed the blade and plunged it into his own chest.

When Korvel let himself into the suite, he half expected Simone to be gone. Taking her had given him the most pleasure he had ever known, and as soon as he had removed himself from her body he had wanted to tell her that. But Simone had moved away from him, standing and tugging down the ripped skirt of her dress. She had looked down at the hand he held to her before she walked to the gate and out of the courtyard.

Korvel had thought she wanted nothing more to do with him. But no, there she was, fluffing the pillows and straightening the bed linens, as if she were a hotel maid. *She* is *a maid, and a* tresora, *and now my lover.* No escaping any of it, not with the smell of her all over him . . . and she was making the bed. His eyes strayed to the torn seams at the hem of her dress. The bed he had denied her their first time together. "Stop doing that."

"I am nearly finished." She tucked the coverlet under the bottom edge of the pillows before she straightened. "There." She regarded him without a glimmer of malice. "Are you ready to leave, Captain?"

"No."

She nodded. "Is there something you need?"

If she offered him blood or sex again he would put his fist through a wall. The momentary violence of his thoughts must have shown on his face, for she took a step back.

"I will not hurt you, Simone." Decency forced him to add, "What happened by the fountain was my doing, not yours."

Her mouth compressed. "I know what I did, Captain."

"You were not responsible for your actions," he said. "You may be immune to *l'attrait,* but no mortal can escape the effect of our particular talents."

"And what is yours?"

"I can compel any woman to desire me. None can resist or refuse. The passion you felt was not your own. I made you feel it." When she remained silent, he added, "If you wish I will make arrangements to return you immediately to the convent."

"We had sex, Korvel. We both wanted it, and we both enjoyed it. That had nothing to do with your talent." The bluntness of her words didn't match the curious sadness of her tone. "Excuse me." She retreated into the bath and closed the door.

For all its discomforts, celibacy had never reduced

Korvel to the level of a stricken, tongue-tied adolescent. He hadn't felt this plagued by emotion since his last confrontation with Alexandra at *le conseil supérieur,* when his master had forced him to try once more to bring her under his sway.

Alexandra had not been fooled for long, however. She had berated him for using his ability to make her attracted to him.

Korvel sat down at the desk and propped his head against his hands. For months after that unpleasant exchange with Alexandra, he had tortured himself, impaling his longing on the countless shards of his shame, writhing in silence on the innumerable racks of his regret. Bonding with Alexandra had no more been his choice than hers, but after her departure from Ireland the effects of being separated from her had been so maddening he would have done anything to have her. Had the bond between them been complete, or had she not so soundly rejected him, he might have descended completely into madness.

He lifted his head as he realized the significance of the night's events. He had not realized it until just this moment, but the reason no woman had appealed to him for so long was due to the damage inflicted by his unfulfilled bond with Alexandra. Losing her had rendered him incapable of touching another woman. Until tonight, with Simone.

I am free of her. Korvel closed his eyes. *At last.*

He knocked the chair over as he got up, catching and righting it before he leaped over the bed. But when he reached to remove the final obstacle between him and his salvation, a low sound came from behind the door. Gasps of breath, water splashing in a basin, the rasp of a towel against skin.

He pressed his hand against the wood. "Simone?"

Her reply came thin with strain. "Give me a moment, please, Captain."

Korvel slowly retreated, his thoughts snarling as he considered for the first time what she might be feeling. He'd taken her, used her for his pleasure, and yet had completely denied her the simple courtesies she deserved in return: tenderness, gentleness, and protection.

When Simone emerged a few minutes later, she had shed the ruins of her dress for her dark, sexless garments, and scrubbed her face clean of makeup. His eyes took in everything, from the black woolen cap covering her hair to the faint bulge of the ankle sheath about one thin-soled boot. "I liked the dress better."

"So did I." She picked up her case from the bed. "I've never worn silk. It's almost sinful how comfortable it is."

Thoroughly confused now, Korvel followed her out of the room to the lift. Once inside, the presence of another, mortal couple forced him into silence.

The concierge came from behind his station and hurried to them. "Monsieur, surely you are not leaving us so soon?"

"We are. Bring the car around at once." Korvel handed him the parking slip and glanced at Simone, who was staring at the screen of a television on the other side of the lobby. It was showing a late news broadcast and the photos of two men, one elderly and the other young. "Do you know them?"

"Not exactly." Simone walked over to the set, but by that time the program had switched to the weather forecast. She glanced at the couple sitting and watching it. "I beg your pardon, but can you tell me what was said about those two men in the photographs?"

"They were found dead earlier tonight," the woman

told her. "One of them was . . . tortured to death." She crossed herself.

"They think it was a murder-suicide," her male companion added. "The old man brutalized this student who worked for him until he died, and then he killed himself, the monster."

Simone thanked them and said nothing more about the news until she was alone in the car with Korvel. "That old man was a professor, and he had no reason to torture that boy. Although I think he might have killed himself."

"Why?"

"So he would not betray the Kyn. When I was a girl he served as a *tresora* in Paris." She looked out the window. "He was an expert in medieval literature and languages."

He grew thoughtful. "Perhaps the thief tried to force him to translate the scroll."

"He could not do it," she said at once. "No human can. The scroll is written *en le chiffre noir,* the night code, and only a *Nautonnier*—a navigator—can read it."

Hearing her use words that had not been uttered for seven centuries, even among the Kyn, stunned him. "Who told you these things?"

"My father." She took a map out of the glove compartment. "I would like to inspect the scene of the murders, but we must go to my apartment first. I have to contact—"

He took the map out of her hands and set it aside. "*Tresori* have no knowledge of the navigators or the night code. No human does. We made sure of it. How could you know about it?" When she didn't reply, he added, "Simone, we still use the night code. Anyone who has knowledge of it could use it against us. I must know the truth."

"One of my ancestors became Kyn," she admitted. "During his lifetime he remained close to his mortal family—my father's family. As *tresori* we have always served the Kyn, and we have always guarded his secrets."

Now Korvel understood why she had been chosen by the council to become a sentinel—she was a direct descendant of a Kyn lord. But to place such an enormous responsibility on such young shoulders...."Where is your father, Simone?"

"He's buried in an unmarked grave in Flavia's rose garden." All the emotion left her face. "He died of leukemia ten years ago."

She made it sound as if he had been murdered, and the body deliberately hidden. "Why was this done to him?"

"So that no one would know he was dead." Her voice went low. "Just before he died, my father and I made a bargain. He informed the council that he was taking the scroll out of the country to a safer, undisclosed location. I went to live with the sisters."

"Surely someone must have missed him."

"No one had seen my father since he was a boy," she admitted. "That made it simple to arrange for his steward to assume his identity. My father gave him most of his wealth and sent him away. The man pretending to be my father had instructions to contact me if his impersonation was ever discovered by anyone. I received that message the morning of the attack on the château. I was supposed to retrieve the scroll and take it with me out of the country. I promised my father that I would."

Korvel sensed she was once more giving him a tailored version of the truth. "Your father is the reason you gave up your life at the château to become a housemaid in a convent."

"I could not be what he wanted." She glanced at him. "Did your father expect you to become a warrior-priest?"

"I never knew my father." That was the most Korvel had ever said about him, and then he heard himself telling her the rest. "My mother was the only daughter of an important Saxon baron. One night raiders from the north attacked the keep and abducted my mother, holding her hostage in their country for many months. After my grandfather paid the ransom, she was brought back. The raiders had used her as a slave, and she was pregnant with me."

"Oh, no," she murmured.

"In my time bearing a bastard, even one conceived by rape, ruined a woman forever. My mother knew no man of her rank would marry her after that, but my grandfather still needed an heir to keep his lands from being escheated to the crown after his death. That is the only reason she didn't strangle me at birth."

"Was it your mother who left that mark on your neck?"

"No. That came much later, at the hands of mortals who wished me dead." He rubbed the scar on his throat. "Sometimes, when I was a boy, I did wish that she would put an end to me. My mortal life was not a happy one."

She slipped her hand into his. "Korvel, you were not to blame for what was done to her."

"I served as the daily reminder of it." Idly he rubbed his thumb across her knuckles. "She saw to it that I was fed and clothed and schooled, but she never spoke a gentle word to me; nor was I ever permitted to forget that I was a raider's bastard. If I did anything to anger her or my grandfather, she had me beaten. There were days when just looking upon my countenance could send her into a rage."

"So you became a Templar to escape them."

"My family was all I knew; given a choice I would never have left them," he admitted. "But my status changed in an unexpected fashion. My grandmother died of lung fever when I was fifteen, which left my grandfather free to remarry. He took a much younger woman to wife. I didn't understand why until he got her with child."

She caught her breath. "He had his legitimate heir."

He nodded. "As soon as my uncle was born, they no longer had any use for me. My grandfather allowed me to live at the keep until the night my mother died. Then he threw me out in the snow, with only the clothes on my back. When I would not leave, he had the servants drive me away."

"How could he do such a thing?" She sounded angry. "You were only a boy."

"Mortals did not live so long in my time," he reminded her. "Most could not expect more than thirty years. In the eyes of that world, I was a man, responsible for myself. I walked for three days to beg an audience with the king. Although my grandfather was his vassal, Richard could do nothing to restore me as heir. Just as I imagined myself joining the beggars at his gates, he offered me a place among his garrison. He had no reason to do so, but it was the first kindness I had ever known. For that, I swore to serve him until the end of my days."

Simone drew her hand from his. "You are a good man, Captain."

Her compliment pleased him, but at the same time he sensed her withdrawing from him. He also realized she had once again changed the subject to avoid talking about her own father. "Was your father an invalid?"

She made a small, choked sound. "No, Captain. Until he fell ill, he was in excellent health."

"You said that no one had seen him since he was a boy," he pointed out. "How did he manage that? Did he suffer from some phobia?"

Her mouth grew tight. "My father considered fear a weakness. He wasn't afraid of anything."

"Not even death?"

Her throat burned, and she pulled off to the side of the road, stopping the car and climbing out to run down to the brush, where she dropped to her knees.

"Simone." Korvel reached her in time to support her with his arms as she emptied her belly into the grass. "That idiot doctor promised me that the drugs would have worn off by now."

Once the spasms had passed, Simone straightened and accepted his handkerchief to wipe her mouth and blow her nose. "It's not the drugs."

He frowned. "Then this is my doing. I should not have reminded you of the loss of your father. I had not realized you were so close to him."

"I hated my father." She staggered to her feet. "The day I buried him in the garden was the happiest of my life."

The hatred in her voice matched the truth burning in her scent. "So he was your abuser."

"He never touched me. If he had, I would be the one in the ground." She started back toward the car.

A father whom she hated, who had never been seen, who could kill with a touch, and who had left her to guard the scroll. Korvel knew of only one man who could fit that description.

He got into the car, but when Simone reached for the key he put his hand over hers. "I must tell you something. I believe your father's pretense went far beyond concealing his death. The identity he used is very well-known among the Kyn. I cannot say why he deceived you, but in doing so he has made you believe certain things about him that could not possibly be true."

She turned to face him. "My father did many terrible things while he was alive, but he never lied to me."

"He convinced you that he was the guardian of the scroll," he reminded her. "As well as a killer who had never been seen. He told you that he was Helada, didn't he?"

She nodded.

"Simone, it couldn't be. Helada has been the scroll's guardian since the time it was made," Korvel continued. "One of the Kyn, called Cristophe, was a master smith before he was changed. After the Crusades he retreated to a Spanish monastery to live as a monk. When the Kyn broke with the Templars, the high lord called upon him to forge the scroll. It was Cristophe who chose the immortal master assassin Helada to be the scroll's guardian. That was more than seven hundred years ago." When she didn't react, he added, "The Kyn cannot sire or bear children. If your father were Helada, as he led you to believe, you would not exist."

"My father was Helada." She stared through the windshield at nothing. "Just as his uncle was Helada before him, as was his grandfather, and his grandfather's eldest brother, and their father before them. That is how Helada became an immortal, Captain. The legendary Helada is reborn in every generation of my family."

Chapter 12

In all the centuries Korvel had existed he had deceived many mortals, but never had he known any who had done the same to the Kyn. Humans were too simple in their motives, and constantly were made transparent by their actions; they never lived long enough to sustain their deceptions. That Simone and her family could perpetuate such a myth for so many generations staggered him.

He wanted to believe she was lying to him now, but her scent hadn't changed. "How could the men in your family do this without ever being discovered? The changes in age and appearance—"

"—were never noticed," Simone finished for him. "Why do you think my family spread the rumor that anyone who saw Helada would die?"

"So that no one would ever attempt to see him." He glanced at her. "Is that why your father allowed you to join the convent? Because the women there were all blind?"

"That is the reason he had me educated there," she said. "But I chose to go to the convent."

Korvel thought of how Richard Tremayne would react to learning the legendary Helada was a complete fabrication. "Do you know what the high lord would do if he knew only mortals were guarding the scroll?"

She nodded. "He would take it from my family. But my ancestor was determined that no immortal should possess the scroll, so they would not be tempted to use it to create immortal armies, or wipe out humanity altogether. That is why we never told the high lord."

He didn't know whether to laugh or groan. "If he knew, he would do much more than take it from you." The thought of his master punishing Simone for her part in the deception sobered him. "You can never tell anyone about this, Simone."

"I've told you."

So she had, and realizing how much trust that must have required made him feel a strange satisfaction. "I will keep your secret." He dragged a hand through his short hair. "You've lived among nuns, and yet you're the daughter of one of the most feared assassins of all time. Christ, I can hardly believe it."

"We believe what we want," was all she said.

Once they reached Marseilles, Simone left the car in a reserved lot a block away from the town house.

"You have been living at the convent for the last ten years," Korvel said as he took the case for her. "So how is it that you have a flat—and parking—in the city?"

"I am also a sentinel, and the council maintains a number of properties here." She reached into a side pocket of the case to retrieve the key to the door. "This one is used now primarily for storage purposes."

As they walked in and she turned on the lights, Korvel inspected the front room. "What do they store here? Air?"

"The illusion of vacancy is for the benefit of the

neighbors." She nodded toward the staircase. "Everything is kept on the second floor."

At the top of the stairs, he watched her input the code on the keypad to release the electronic locks. "Is there a self-destruct button on that?"

"No, but if you put in the wrong code, it sends a silent alarm to the council's security company. Just before it electrocutes you." She pulled open the steel door, which activated the lighting inside the flat. "We take safety measures very seriously."

"I see why."

She watched as Korvel made a circuit of the room, inspecting the racks of weapons and shelves of field supplies interspersed among the old apartment's shabby furnishings. "If you need blood, fresh supplies are stored in the kitchen. The satellite phones will need charging before we can use them, but the landline in the bedroom is safeguarded."

He picked up a small book from the window seat. "They store children here as well?"

"Oh, that belonged to me." The sight of the old storybook made her heart twist. "My father used this property as a flat when I was young."

"He brought you *here?*"

"It was the safest place in the city." Feeling awkward now, she added, "I'm going to wash up. Please make yourself at home."

Simone retreated to the adjoining room, where she opened the doors to the large walk-in closet. On one side a long rack of fashionable garments in a variety of styles hung grouped by sizes ranging from petite to giant; on the other, stacks of body armor and other protective gear had been shelved. She chose from the clothing a pair of black leather leggings and a matching long-sleeved cashmere pullover. After she retrieved black lingerie from the drawers beneath the rack, she carried the stack of fresh clothing into the bath so she could change.

Simone turned on the sink taps to warm the water before she stripped out of her trousers, stopping only when she smelled a faint vanilla fragrance.

Larkspur.

She looked over her shoulder, but saw no sign of Korvel. As she pulled the shirt over her head the scent grew stronger, until she realized it was coming from her own body.

Of course she still smelled of him. He had been all over her, inside her. She would have to scrub every inch of her body to be rid of him.

Slowly Simone turned off the taps.

At the hotel she had behaved out of anger and jealousy, and she still didn't understand from where it had come. Why had seeing him with those women enraged her? Korvel had to use mortals for blood. She knew that. What he'd done was nothing out of the ordinary. If anything he'd been clever about it.

Why had it felt so different when she'd seen him with those women?

Simone had known from the moment she'd begun to flirt with the man at the bar that Korvel would see her as well. She'd made certain of it, even choosing the Spaniard because he was within the captain's line of sight. She'd also known Korvel would recognize her, even dressed and made up as she had been. And when she had left the hotel with that whiskey-soaked fumbler, she had known Korvel would follow. That was why she had taken the Spaniard's keys out of the ignition, and fended off his clumsy embraces. She had only wanted to show the captain that she could be just as beautiful and desirable as the women he had gathered to him in the club.

All of it simply so he would see her.

From there everything had raced out of control, so fast and so far the rest of the world had faded away. He had been so angry, but so had she, and they had somehow become mirrors of each other, with their furious tempers exploding into outrageous passion. Her own behavior had shamed her into leaving him, but he had followed her again, and cornered her, gently urging her to face what burned between them. And then he had her under him, the pleasure had come over her, and nothing more mattered than giving the same to him.

Time had melted into Dalí's pocket watch as she lost herself in his hands, in the exquisite invasion, his flesh into hers. She remembered the splintering sensation of her orgasm, the hard urgency of his, and how, for the briefest moment, it had merged them into one. It had frightened her to feel so destroyed and utterly remade by him.

Even more shameful, Simone wanted to feel it again. Her desire for him was stronger than ever.

She removed the last of her clothing before she walked out into the bedroom, unsure of what she meant to do. Somewhere in the city Pájaro had hidden with the scroll as bait for a dead man. In Italy the council waited for word that Simone had successfully retrieved it. In Ireland, the high lord expected Korvel to return and deliver it into his hands. Men, good men who had devoted their entire lives to preserving the peace between the mortal and immortal worlds, had been tortured and murdered.

In the next few hours, the future of the Darkyn and humanity might be forever altered, even obliterated.

Simone knew the weight of it, the massive, crushing responsibility of it, was a burden she had to carry alone.

"This I would take as an invitation." Korvel's hands curved over her shoulders. "If I thought it was for me that you were standing here, naked in the dark."

As his thumbs followed the outer curves of her breasts, an unnerving heat flared up in her. He had only to touch her and she was his. Just as all women were. "Who is Alexandra?"

His hands stilled. "How do you know that name?"

"You called for her just after you collapsed in the greenhouse." She turned around. "Who is she? Your *sygkenis?* Your *tresora* in Ireland?"

His hands fell away from her. "She is no one of consequence."

The small changes in his musculature made her heart clench. "You're lying to me." When he went toward the door, she darted in front of him. "If she means nothing to you, then why can't you talk about her?"

His expression turned to stone. "I have no *tresora* or *sygkenis,* and Lady Alexandra is not your concern. You should get dressed now."

The soft way with which he said the other woman's name made her stand her ground. "Do you love her?"

"Simone."

"Yes or no?"

"She belonged to another man, and I tried to take her from him. She would not have me." Regret echoed behind the words, but he also sounded strangely relieved.

The truth made less sense than his lie. "I thought no woman could resist you."

"Alexandra is different," he admitted. "She was the first mortal in five hundred years to survive being made Kyn."

Of course, the woman he loved would be one of his own kind. There were few females among the Darkyn, but Flavia had described how strong and beautiful they were. Nothing like Simone, with her human imperfections and scarred body.

"Thank you for telling me." She went to the bathroom and began to dress.

Korvel appeared in the doorway. "Why did you ask me about Alexandra, Simone?"

"*Tresori* are not permitted to violate the boundaries of a Kyn bond." She reached behind her back to fasten her bra. "If this Lady Alexandra were your *sygkenis,* she would be within her rights to kill me for having sex with you."

He studied her face. "Now *you* lie."

"When you were in pain, you called out for her." She glared at him. "I was right there, saving you, dragging you to a horse, and you wanted another woman." Aware of how ridiculous she sounded, she shook her head. "It doesn't matter. Tomorrow you will be on your way back to Ireland, and I will return to the convent, and we will forget each other."

"Will we?"

"We have to." He wasn't listening to her; he was staring at her bottom. "Captain." She saw his pupils had turned to splinters. "*Captain.* You need blood."

His eyes shifted to hers. "I need many things."

So did she, but the night would not last forever. "My contact is waiting down at the docks."

Reluctantly he withdrew, and she finished dressing. Knowing she would be searched at the docks, she didn't bother arming herself when she rejoined Korvel.

"I'm leaving now," she told him. "I'll be back in an hour."

He frowned. "Where are you going?"

"I have to meet my contact alone. He agreed to help me only because he owed a debt to my father." As Korvel scowled, she added, "He will not give me any information in front of you."

"You are not going there alone." When she began to protest, he said, "I will wait in the car."

Korvel was a good man. He would never allow her to go unguarded into a dangerous situation. But once she obtained the information from Lechance, she would know the location of the scroll. Once the scroll was in their possession, her orders were to destroy it and kill Korvel.

"If you insist." She checked her watch. "I have to call Rome before we leave. It should be only a few minutes."

She returned to the bedroom, crossing quickly to open the back window and climb out onto the fire escape landing. Knowing the ladder would rattle, she swung herself over the edge and dropped.

As soon as her feet touched the ground, Simone ran.

While he waited for Simone, Korvel made use of the bagged blood stored in the refrigerator. With no wine to mask the unpleasant taste of the thick, chilly stuff, he drank only enough to take the edge off his hunger. Having Simone naked in his arms had again aroused the beast inside him, and too much blood would compromise his self-control. She deserved more from him than another mindless, frantic coupling.

She deserved pampering, and Paris, and a hundred silk dresses. Korvel imagined taking Simone to one of the city's most exclusive hotels, where she would have her own personal maid, and dine on fine cuisine, and bathe in Chanel-scented water. She would love the fashion district, with its chic designers and elegant couture, the magnificence of the Louvre and its endless treasures of the ages, the quiet spots on the banks of the Seine where Renoir and Monet had once painted their masterpieces side by side.

From Paris they could travel to London, where he could show her his side of the channel, and the many jewels of the past hidden within the bustling metropolis: Shakespeare's Globe Theatre, with its wooden benches and immortal plays; the quiet peace of evensong at St. Paul's Cathedral; the breathtaking views from the London Eye. They could walk the same path William I had ridden almost a thousand years before, when he had conquered the Saxons and claimed the throne. Korvel had always had a soft spot for the conqueror, who like him had been a bastard.

Once she had sated herself on shopping at Harrods and gorged on the best of the city's fish and chips, he would take her north to Lancashire. They could spend a week soaking up the sea and sun at Blackpool. He could even take her back to his family's lands, which now belonged to the crown as part of Bowland Fells, and show her the moors he had so loved as a boy.

As Korvel went to the window to look down at the deserted streets, he realized how long it had been since he had seen the place of his childhood. He had never gone back, not once since Richard had offered him sanctuary, but with Simone at his side it would be different.

His eyes drifted down to the storybook she had said belonged to her, an artifact from her childhood. She had never said why her father had come to Marseilles, or why she had been left alone in such a dreadful place for a child. Korvel had confided to her the most painful and intimate details of his mortal life. Not even Richard knew all of it. Yet Simone had told him almost nothing about herself.

Korvel glanced over at the bedroom, and then the digital clock in the kitchen. Twenty minutes had passed — too long for a single phone call.

"Simone?"

When she didn't reply he went into the bedroom to find it empty, and followed her scent to the open window. Seeing the fresh boot marks in the soil below made his hand clench on the marble sill until the stone cracked in half.

He vaulted through the window and dropped to the ground. The dampness of the frigid air had preserved the scent of her passage, and when he followed it to the front of the town house he found it veered away from the car still sitting in the lot across the street. Wherever she had arranged to meet her contact, she had gone there on foot.

Few mortals understood how the Kyn had become such effective trackers. Unlike humans, with their limited senses, the Kyn could detect even the faintest trace of scent left behind by a living creature. The more moisture the air contained, the greater the concentration of scent it absorbed from anything that passed through it. Simone may have intended to elude him, but here in this city by the sea she had left behind what amounted to a virtual map to her location.

Korvel sensed the first man following him a mile from the town house, and confirmed the existence of his shadow when he diverted into a small park and doubled back. As he came up behind the mortal man following him, he noted the dark clothing as well as the weapons concealed under it. He took cover as a second man converged on the first, and they spoke briefly in hushed voices.

"Where is he?"

"He made you before you entered the park." The second man nodded in Korvel's general direction. "I think he went that way."

"Monsieur?"

Korvel turned around to see a gendarme standing just behind him. "Officer." He glanced at the younger man's utility belt. "May I borrow your nightstick?"

"No, you may not." As Korvel moved closer, the gendarme's stern features relaxed, and he hefted the baton, waving it with enthusiasm. "You wish me to bash someone over the head for you, monsieur?"

"I thank you, no." Korvel gently took the nightstick from him. "You should forget about this and return to your rounds, Officer."

As soon as the smiling gendarme wandered off, Korvel tucked the baton in his sleeve and emerged from behind the tree, pretending to fasten the front of his trousers before he walked with a casual gait toward the two men.

One began to hurry away, at which point Korvel took out the baton and hurled it. It made a loud thunk as it connected with the back of the other man's head, and he sank to the ground.

His companion's eyes went wide before he turned and broke into a flat run for the nearest building. He crossed ten yards before Korvel seized his collar and lifted him off the ground, tossing him to land atop his unconscious friend.

Korvel heard the snap of a bone but not the usual accompanying howl. When he moved to stand over the two men, the one who was still conscious flipped over and tried to crawl away.

"Be still." When the man didn't obey him, Korvel

grabbed the ankle of his functioning leg and dragged him back, taking hold of his head by the hair and jerking it back. Once he removed the clear pronged nose plug from the man's nostrils, the resistance ceased. "Why were you following me?"

"You were with her at the house." The man grinned. "He said to kill you if you came after her."

"Who said this?"

"The guild master." The man's eyes rolled back in his head, and he went limp.

A search of both men's garments produced only pistols fitted with silencers; neither of the assassins carried any form of identification or any clue as to who had sent them. Attempting to rouse either of them for further interrogation would cost too much precious time.

He had to find Simone, now.

Korvel used the men's belts to bind them to a street sign before he returned to the block where he had last detected Simone's scent. It led him out of the residential area and into the narrow streets of an industrial section, where prefabricated buildings sat quietly rusting, their windows boarded up or broken. Here and there he saw the faded and battered signs of cargo handlers, importers, and storage facilities, but from the lack of lighting and activity he guessed it had been years since any of them had been in business.

Simone's scent ended in front of the unmarked bay of an enormous warehouse. Korvel didn't detect any light or sound coming from within, but he could smell a large group of mortals—at least twenty. He walked around to the side door of the building, which stood ajar. Through the gap he saw the outlines of crates and shelving filled with plastic-wrapped pallets of goods.

He avoided the door, going to the service ladder at

the back of the building to climb to the roof. A clouded skylight afford him a better view of the interior, and when he lifted one of the fiberglass panels out, he spotted a man standing just inside the side door. The mortal held daggers in both hands and appeared poised to attack anyone who came through the door.

Korvel jumped down through the skylight, landing lightly behind the man, whom he knocked out with a blow to the back of the head. As he stepped back, he heard the clink of metal and a rushing sound, and looked up to see a wide net falling atop him. He lunged, but not soon enough to avoid the heavy net. As he struggled to free himself, his skin began to burn wherever the net touched him.

"Bring him to me," an amused voice said, the words echoing in the stillness.

Two more men came, one kicking Korvel off his feet before they both gathered up the ends of the net and dragged him across the concrete floor. Overhead lights flickered on, and more mortals came into sight. Only when Korvel saw Simone's pale, taut features and the gun being held to her head did he stop clawing at the net.

"Have they hurt you?" Korvel demanded. When she shook her head, he scanned the faces around her. "You have me now. Let the girl go."

An older man approached the net. "Why do you think we want you, vampire?"

Chapter 13

Nick eyed a bunch of mixed-race kids hanging out in front of one of the countless anonymous concrete apartment buildings they had passed since leaving the motorway. "What do they call this part of Marseilles? *Les projects?*"

"This is Noailles," Gabriel said. "The *banlieues* here were built to accommodate those who fled Algeria after the war." He glanced at her. "I thought you had seen all of my country."

"Nothing ever brought me this far south." She thought for a moment. "Well, not counting that time I did the Riviera."

He frowned. "What did you do to the Riviera?"

"Nothing. It's still there." She avoided talking about the years she had spent stealing back Kyn treasures from France's wealthiest collectors, many of whom had lived in the disgustingly celebrity- and McMansion-riddled Cap Ferrat and other private gold-pot communities along the Riviera. "Once we reach this safe house and unload, I'd like to hit the street." She watched a string of soccer flags flutter as the wind swept in from the harbor, and felt a funny pang in her chest. "He's here."

"The thief?"

"No, Korvel." She rolled down the window, breathing in the air, but smelled only car exhaust and fish. "Where is this safe house, anyway?"

"A few miles to the south." Gabriel gestured ahead toward a white church standing atop a hill.

Nick's radar told her they were heading in the right direction, but without a scent to track she couldn't assume the Kyn whose presence she felt was Korvel. "Are there any other fangsters living here?"

"Richard ordered all Kyn to leave France months ago," he said. "There is always the possibility someone has defied him or gone rogue, but it is unlikely."

"Okay." She settled against the seat, forcing back the anxiety that always accompanied the triggering of her talent. "We should split up. I'll go after Korvel, and you can chase down the vampire king's priceless scroll."

"We track together, Nicola."

He sounded hurt, and he probably was, but for once she didn't feel like catering to their bond. "I know you have to follow Richard's orders and go after the scroll. Fortunately, I don't. We can cover more ground this way."

Gabriel didn't say anything else until they reached the safe house. "Nicola, please wait," he said as she reached for the door handle. "You have not been yourself since we searched the château."

She closed her eyes. "Can we not talk about that and just say we did?"

"Helada is not the cruel, conniving wife of a completely clueless king," he said, deliberately using one of her many sarcastic references for Elizabeth Tremayne. "That girl in the video is not you."

He knew her better than anyone, and for a moment

she hated him for it. "Baby, everything is not about me and that sadistic fucking evil bitch. In case you haven't noticed, I'm still here; she's not, end of story."

He inclined his head. "While I am no longer blind or helpless."

"Yep." She pretended to shake a pair of pom-poms. "Yay for both of us."

"Is it the end of our story?" Gabriel asked softly.

Nick got out of the car and stalked up to the front door of the safe house. She could smell Korvel all around her, and while she knew he wasn't inside she could track him from here. She needed to get started, to find him, but her legs wouldn't move and her arms wouldn't work. She was going to spend the rest of eternity waiting at this fucking door like a stubborn Girl Scout with a wagonload of cookies to sell.

Gabriel reached past her, using the key Benetta had given them to unlock the door before he ushered her inside. He breathed in deeply, frowning as he sorted out the scents. "Korvel was here. So was one of the mortal females from the convent."

Nick took in the empty rooms. "No blood or bodies." She started up the stairs, and on the second-floor landing input the code to open the door.

What Korvel and his female companion had left behind in the apartment told Nick little about why they had been there, or where they had gone. At least until she found the pile of clothes the woman had left in the bath.

"Uh-oh. He's using the nun for sex." She handed the pullover to Gabriel. "Good thing he's immortal. I'm pretty sure you go straight to hell for that."

"Korvel would not . . ." He paused as he breathed in the mingled scents from the garment. "Perhaps she is not a nun."

Nick sorted through a traveling case and pulled out a gray head veil and habit to show him. "Think again, pal." She dropped the clothes and followed Korvel's and the nun's scents to the window left open in the bedroom. "They both went out this way." She leaned out to study the footprints left on the ground below, where a wider man's tread overlay the smaller, narrow impressions. "Looks like she left first." Gabriel came to stand beside her, but he seemed more interested in her face. "Problem?"

"You're thinking of leaving me," he said, stunning her. "You have been for months."

Nick prided herself on being a practiced, accomplished liar. She had conned the world into believing she was still human for ten years. Not even Gabriel had known the truth, at least not until Elizabeth's pet serial killer had attacked her. She could deal with this. "I'm not going to leave you."

"Not now," he agreed. "You're waiting until Richard gives me Ireland and I assemble my household. Once I'm settled, once I'm safe, then you'll go."

So he knew. Maybe it was for the best. "I'm not doing the *jardin* thing. I love you, and I know how important this is to you, but . . . no."

He nodded. "I will tell Richard that he must choose someone else."

"Don't do that." Nick lifted her hands to her head and then dropped them. "Don't placate me. My issues are not yours, and they never were."

"I cannot agree," he said gravely. "You are my *sygkenis.*"

"Yeah, the bond thing, I know. I'm going to talk to Alex." She started to pace around the room. "She's a doctor, and she's already been through it herself. She'll know what to do for you. I mean, she figured out how to tranquilize the Kyn. I'm sure she can come up with another miracle drug to treat you for bond withdrawal. Like some kind of antipsychotic. It's not that different from a human having a nervous breakdown, is it?"

"I do not believe that when mortals have a breakdown they lose control of their abilities, descend into insanity, or try to kill anything that moves. But the doctor was able to help the high lord from succumbing to changeling madness; perhaps she can save me as well." He sat down on the bed. "While Alexandra attends to me, what happens to you, Nicola?"

"Nothing. Nothing happens to me. I go back to my old life, stealing and hoarding medieval shit, and messing with the holy freaks, and rescuing the occasional crucified vamp, and you're not buying this at all, are you?" When he shook his head, she sighed and dropped down beside him. "Okay. When it gets bad for me, I'll come and visit. We'll spend the weekend in bed."

"I fear the occasional booty call will not be adequate." He regarded her solemnly. "The only reason Alexandra survived being separated from Michael during her captivity in Ireland is because Korvel bonded her to him."

Nick almost fell off the bed. "He *what?*"

"It was not intentional," Gabriel said. "For a time after her reunion with Michael, Alex was torn between the two bonds. Eventually she freed herself of Korvel's influence, but the captain has never been the same." He picked up the nun's pullover. "That is why I find this so odd. Richard has said that Korvel has not touched a woman since Alexandra left Ireland."

Nick chuffed out some air. "The vampire king keeps tabs on who his captain is boinking?"

"Korvel's ability makes any mortal female desire

him," Gabriel told her. "His prowess with women is the stuff of legends. Believe me, *everyone* has noticed."

"But that means two Kyn breaking up isn't automatically instant madness and destruction and death." She felt a little better. "Good to know."

"Korvel and Alex never consummated their bond." He picked up her hand. "You and I, however, have been lovers from the first time we met." He traced the spaces between her fingers. "Perhaps that was when we bonded as well."

"You didn't know I had fangs, and by the time you did it was already a done deal." A surge of shame made her add, "Back then I knew what was happening between us. I mean, I didn't get a Kyn instruction manual with my fangs, so I didn't know how serious it was, but I could feel it. It's why I tried to dump you in London."

"You came back for me," he reminded her. "Do you know, you are the only soul in the world who has never abandoned me?" He brought her fist to his lips. "That is why you are first in my life. I love you. Richard can go hang himself."

He was going to turn her into a big puddle of goo. "Gabriel."

"Now come." He kissed her lips. "We will track Korvel together."

Simone tried not to look at Korvel, but even in the murky light she could see the contact burns on his face, and the bloody lacerations he'd received from trying to tear his way out of the net. "You agreed to meet with me, Lechance, and on your word I came here unarmed. Is this how you intend to repay your debt to my father?"

"I would certainly never do this to your father, but he is still traveling abroad, isn't he? Or perhaps not."

Rellen Lechance went over to the net and crouched down to peer at Korvel. "Incredible. I had been told several tales of how dangerous copper is to these creatures, but I thought them somewhat exaggerated. Yet here is proof that it was all true. Does it actually burn you, vampire?"

"You have made a mistake," Korvel said, rising to his feet and flooding the air with his scent. "Release me and the girl. At once."

"Now I'll wager that you are giving off that pretty scent you bastards use to turn humans into mindless slaves." The guild master tapped the clear nose plug he and all the men were wearing. "Won't work here, I'm afraid. Can you do anything else? If we toss you off the roof, will you sprout wings and fly?"

"Oh, yes. All vampires can." Korvel bared his *dents acérées*. "Remove the net and I'll give you a ride on my back."

Lechance chuckled. "I like you. Captain, is it? Simone, please introduce me to your new friend."

She gritted her teeth. "This is Monsieur Rellen Lechance, Master of the Assassin's Guild."

Korvel's eyes became slits. "Brethren?"

"Ex-Mafia, as it happens," Lechance told him before she could answer. "Once our employers packed up their operations here in Marseilles and moved down the coast, many of us decided we should form an organization of our own. Contract killings, for the most part, but we occasionally pick up a political assassination or a divorce-case settlement. I find it astonishing how many extremely wealthy men neglect to secure a proper prenuptial agreement before they wed themselves to cocktail waitresses and strippers."

"You said you didn't want him," Simone said, trying

to fight back against the panic. "You have me, and you know what I am worth."

"True, but these creatures are quite valuable, too," the guild master said. "The Italians who pose as priests have kept a massive bounty on them for years. A scientist from the States has offered to pay a million American dollars for a specimen, as will several unsavory governments. For the scientist, we do not even have to deliver him breathing."

Simone saw the way he was looking at her. "What do you want, Guild Master?"

Lechance removed two fighting blades, walking them over his knuckles before he threw them at her. They struck the dirt by her feet, their hilts bobbing. "Fight for him, win, and I will free you both."

She did not move. "I am not my father."

He shrugged. "Then die for him."

Ten of the guildsmen came toward her, each taking a position in an unseen circle. The black cloth covering their heads from crown to neck prevented Simone from seeing their faces, and from their formation she had no doubt the guild master had taught them to strike as one. Their movements, however, shouted who they had once been: soldiers, martial artists, street fighters.

Training begins in childhood, so that you may learn, her father told each boy brought to the château. *An adult cannot be trained; what they bring to the circle can never be unlearned.*

Simone saw the guildsmen in her head as she looked down at the blades by her feet. The three soldiers would be first to attack, then the street fighters, and finally the martial artists. She felt the tension of their muscles as they gathered themselves; she heard the soft movements of their gloves as they exchanged subtle hand signals.

Four of them had begun to sweat; one licked it from his lips.

"Simone," she heard Korvel call. "Run."

She looked over at the copper net and the bleeding fingers tearing at it. "I'm sorry I never told you, Korvel."

The first charged at her from behind as two flanking her ran a cross pattern. As soldiers, they had been trained to fight upright, falling prone only to take cover or to change position, and expected the enemy to do the same. Simone dropped, seizing the blades and diving between the legs of her first attacker, cutting his hamstrings. She rolled over in time to parry the man on her left as he struck down, grabbing his shoulder and using his momentum to throw him into the third soldier, who collapsed in a tangle with him.

Back on her feet, she moved to the scaffolding, using a running jump to pull herself up to the first level and turning to drive her boot into the face of the guildsman who pursued her; she leaped over the one who followed him and swept her arm back, slamming her elbow into the base of his skull.

She regarded the five who were left, and how they rearranged themselves. These were the watchful ones, the martial artists with their black belts and their clever techniques. They would be strong, practiced, and deceptive, but they had been trained to read the body of the enemy to anticipate his or her actions.

Simone remained still, holding her arms to shield her upper body while she shifted her eyes from one chest to another. Two of the men danced back and forth as they approached, feinting strikes at her head before they lashed out with their feet at her legs. She fell before they could touch her, jerking the legs they stood on out from beneath them.

Both fell back, one striking the back of his head and going still, the other managing to partially break his fall with an arm. The snap of his ulna sounded like a brittle branch as Simone wrapped an arm around his neck and dragged him up, heaving his body toward two more guildsmen.

That left one standing only a few feet from her, and he stepped forward, keeping his eyes on her face as he bobbed in a shallow bow. He raised his arms, his hands cupped, his legs slightly bent at the knees, prepared for any move she intended to make.

Except this one, Simone thought, raising the .22 she had taken from one of the soldiers and shooting the last guildsmen in the knee.

Handlers rushed in to help up the wounded and drag away the unconscious as Lechance clapped his hands together, once, twice, three times.

"Your father would be proud, Simone, although I am surprised you were trained to handle a gun," the guild master said. "As I remember, he was all about the blade."

"The only thing my father cared about was the kill." Simone bent, reaching under the shelving unit to retrieve the rifle the unconscious guard had dropped.

He tilted his head. "A pity he didn't live long enough to see this. Before you ask, I knew that he died ten years ago. I provided the documents he needed for his steward to assume his identity, and swore never to tell anyone of his death or how he had concealed it. As you see, I kept my word."

"Thank you." She chambered the next round with a snap of her wrist, aiming for Lechance's heart. "Release him."

The guild master nodded to his guards, who grabbed the pulley ropes and raised the copper net. Korvel staggered to his feet.

"Captain," Simone said, not taking her eyes from Lechance. "Please go. I will join you outside in a few moments."

"Not without you."

As he walked over to her, her mouth tightened. Their chances of getting out of here alive were dwindling by the second, but she had to know. To Lechance, she said, "You gave Pájaro sanctuary when he ran away. You helped him fake his death as well." When Lechance inclined his head, she asked, "Why?"

He folded his hands. "I couldn't resist the boy's offer. He gave ten years of service in exchange for my protection and instruction. He might have failed to meet your father's impossible standards, but by the time he had finished his service to me, he had over four hundred clean kills. Almost twice as many as my next-best man."

She almost pulled the trigger. "You know where he is now. Tell me."

Lechance smiled. "I will do even better. I will take you to him. Pájaro wants both of you. Alive."

An air rifle fired, and Korvel lunged in front of her. He turned, still protecting her with his body, and she looked down to see the dart sticking from his chest. He sagged, and as she grabbed him she felt a sharp pain in her neck.

Korvel remained on his feet, but he was swaying like a tree in a high wind. As the guild master came to them, he turned his head. "Why did you make her fight?"

"It's simple, vampire," Lechance said. "I promised her father that I would."

Chapter 14

Rellen Lechance watched his men struggle to lift the vampire's heavy body. "You know, with a blood sample and a few days, I could convince the Americans to double their offer."

"Yes, and if he escapes them, he will know precisely where to find you." Pájaro eyed the wounded still littering the floor of the warehouse. "Why didn't you shoot him as soon as he arrived?"

"There was no warning." The guild master gestured overhead. "He jumped through the skylight."

"I warned you that they were clever, Rellen." Pájaro used his first name with a certain relish before he rubbed the end of his nose and sniffed. "You should take more precautions with your security, before you end up being loaded into a trunk yourself."

"Good advice." The guild master made brief eye contact with his bodyguard, who shifted his position and drew a pistol. "When can I expect payment for my services?"

"Don't be greedy. I'll contact you when the old man is dead." Pájaro strode off.

The guild master made a subtle hand signal, and three

men scattered in different directions. His bodyguard followed him into his office, and stood watching through the window as Lechance sat down and placed a call to Rome.

"He has them," he told the man on the other end of the line. He described the events of the night before and said, "My men will continue surveillance until yours arrive."

"Does he have the scroll?"

"Oh, yes," Lechance said. "And the Spaniard is already showing the first signs."

"Keep me informed."

Lechance ended the call and sat back to brood. In all the years he had known Simone Derien and her father, he had always wondered whether the legends were true. From what he had observed over his long and violent lifetime, women were not fashioned for fighting. While they could be vicious, particularly when defending their young, they lacked the killing instinct.

Simone had cut through his men without hesitation or the slightest degree of difficulty; seeing her fight had been alternately thrilling and dismaying. He had witnessed power and precision beyond his comprehension; he knew he would never have it at his command. In fact, if events played out as the men in Rome had orchestrated, Simone Derien would not live to fight again.

Lechance saw his bodyguard's back muscles tense. "What is it?"

"Two intruders. A man and a woman." The bodyguard stiffened and drew his pistol. "They are not human."

"Put that away." The guild master walked out into the warehouse, where a tall, white-haired female and her handsome companion were making short work of his men. "*Arrête.*" Once the few remaining men who were still mobile hobbled back, Lechance regarded the couple. "*Vous désirez?* Can I help you?"

"Personally I'd like a nap," the woman said in American-accented English as she stepped over a limp body. "These late nights totally wreck me. So be a nice guy and tell us where you have them stashed."

"You have come to the wrong address, mademoiselle." Lechance took in a sharp breath as she moved in a blur to stand in front of him. "There is no one stashed anywhere here."

"I can smell big fat lies, you moron." She whipped out her arm, sending his bodyguard flying. "Where did you take them?"

"I did not take anyone," Lechance said, grimacing slightly as the blond man circled around to stand behind him. He felt cool breath on his neck, and something crawling up his legs under his trousers. When he glanced down he saw dozens of wasps that commonly nested in the rafters alighting on his shoes, and felt sweat break out all over his body.

"Do you know how many times a wasp can sting you before it uses up all of its venom?" the man murmured as Lechance felt something crawl inside his briefs. "Would you care to find out? Perhaps with your testicles."

"My client collected the vampire and the nun," he said. "He took them south, toward the docks. That is all I know."

"Who is your client, and why did he want them?" the man asked.

Lechance held perfectly still. "I was hired to capture them, monsieur. My client did not give me his name or explain his reasons to me."

"I always thought guys would do anything to protect the package." The woman looked past him. "Guess I was wrong, baby."

"Wait." A drop of sweat ran down his nose to hang from the tip of it. "His name is Pájaro. He's worked for me as an assassin for hire." He gave them an accurate description of his former pupil. "He took the man so he could translate an old scroll. That is all he said about him; I swear it."

"Yeah?" The woman leaned close. "Then why did he take the nun, too?"

Lechance closed his eye as a wasp crawled across the lid. "She is his sister."

Korvel opened his eyes to see Simone carrying a light through a darkened room. She had on a long gown made of plain muslin, and her feet were bare. She placed the candle in a window and sat beside it, looking out at the darkness.

When he was able to speak, his voice came out in a harsh rasp. "Where are we?"

"I don't know, Captain." She pressed her hand to the window. "I think we're somewhere out there."

Gradually he saw that they were back at the *tresoran* safe house. Metal clattered as the weapons began to fall off the shelves around them, disappearing as soon as they touched the floor. The racks and shelving followed, melting into nothingness. When the furnishings shifted and grew brighter, he realized at last where they were.

"Simone, we are in the nightlands," he said. "We're having the same dream. Can you wake up?"

She picked up the storybook and opened it on her lap. "I don't want to."

"Try."

Around them the flat began to fade, the colors and shapes flattening into an ashen gray. Just as suddenly it brightened and shifted around again, until all of the furnishings and carpet looked new.

Simone touched her neck. "I can feel myself out there, but I can't find my body."

Korvel closed his eyes, willing himself to wake, but a silver-blue haze drove him back from the void. "The drugs will wear off eventually. We will have to keep trying."

"Do we have to?" When he looked at her, she picked up her book and held it against her breast. "We could stay. This is a good place now."

"If we do not return to our bodies, you will die and I will go mad." He focused on gaining control of his limbs, and when his body was steady he rose out of the chair. Since the dream was hers, everything around them would be governed by her subconscious. He knew little of the nightlands, except that they could be very dangerous. "Is this how the flat looked when you were a child?"

She nodded. "He needed a place to leave me, and he didn't like hotels. At first I liked it because I was always warm here." Simone smiled at the old radiator. "I didn't really know what a home was. The château was always so cold and silent, and my brothers and I could talk only in whispers when they weren't watching."

He didn't want her to shift the dream to the château and send them into a nightmare. "What did you do when your father left you here alone?"

"I would pretend that I was a grown-up lady who lived here with my husband, like the other ladies I saw from the windows." She walked over to the table near the kitchen, and before Korvel's eyes it set itself with plain white china and stainless-steel utensils. Three emergency candles in glass jars appeared in the center, and flames flickered from their wicks. "I would put on a pretty dress, set the table, and cook dinner. I'd always light the candles while I waited for him to come home from work."

Korvel watched the glow of the flames chasing itself through the weave of her braids. The light loved her, gilding the tips of her eyelashes and gleaming along the curve of her bottom lip. "What was he like, this imaginary husband?"

"He was handsome and smiling." She adjusted a fork and smoothed a napkin. "When it grew dark outside I pretended he was late because he stopped to buy flowers from the little stand at the corner. Sometimes tiger lilies, or hyacinth, or white roses with just a touch of orange on the tips of the petals."

Korvel heard footsteps coming up the stairs. "What happened when he came home, Simone?"

"He would hide the bouquet behind his back and show them to me only after I kissed him." She opened the door and stood there looking out at nothing before she closed it. "No one ever came, of course, but it seemed so real that I would fall asleep listening for him."

The thought of Simone being touched by some mortal man—even one loneliness had conjured—sank like a copper dagger into Korvel's belly. Yet even that stab of jealousy could not keep him from speaking the truth. "You can still have that life."

"I'm scarred and barren." She drifted past him to return to the window. "What decent man would have me?"

"You are right." He saw her shoulders go rigid. "I forget what fools modern mortal men are in their desires." He walked to stand behind her and began removing the pins holding her braids in their coil. "Among my kind, every warrior who set eyes on you would fight for the chance to claim you."

A small shudder passed through her before she leaned back against him. "I am so tired of fighting, Korvel."

"You can always choose another path." As her braids fell out of the coil, he began unraveling each one. "When this is over, come with me on mine."

The flat vanished, and Korvel found himself tumbling through the darkness, falling into an oval room with mirrored walls. The icy temperature of the air and the bleak expression on Simone's face told him they were somewhere inside Château Niege.

"How would the high lord have me serve him?" she asked, her voice bleak. "As an assassin?" Her gown shrank onto her body, turning into a gray sparring uniform. "Or a housemaid?" The sparring uniform spilled out into her nun's habit.

Frost began to swirl across the walls of mirrors, racing and curling into bizarre shapes as it crystallized on the glass. In each panel Korvel saw a ghostly silhouette of a little girl performing some task, but none of them made sense. In one she herded goats; in the next she crossed swords with a grown man. The ice child picked flowers, threw daggers, hung clothes on a line, and straddled a fallen opponent.

The last panel showed the little girl making a rosary out of her own frozen tears. She looked back at him with her snow white eyes and suddenly moved, crackling as she hurled the rosary at him.

Korvel brought up his arm to protect his face and felt the teardrop crystals stab into his flesh. As he lowered his arm, the panel began to crack, and the ice child knelt down, wrapping her arms around herself until, like the mirror, she fell into pieces on the floor.

"Look at this mess I've made." Simone brought a broom and dustpan over and began to sweep up the child's remains. "You should go now, Captain. Severance is about to begin."

He took the broom from her and set it aside. "Simone, come with me. We'll go back to the flat."

Her face paled as she looked past him. "It's too late."

A faceless ice giant came into the room, his fists hefting two impossibly long swords. "Quatorze," he whispered, his voice splintering like cracked glass. "You are worthy."

Korvel tasted death in the air. "Who is that?"

"Helada." Simone stepped in front of him and spoke to the monster. "You've taken everyone I loved from me, Father. You can't have him."

The giant flung one of the swords at them, but Korvel grabbed her and spun out of the way. It crashed into the mirrored wall, shattering the panel.

"He's not real." Korvel put his arms around Simone and turned her to face him as the giant came rushing at them, raising the ice blade over their heads. "He can't hurt you unless you want him to."

The sword stopped in midair and dropped out of the giant's hand, splashing the floor as a wide swath of water.

"I never wanted this," Simone whispered. "Any of this."

"Then let it go." Korvel removed her head veil and threaded his fingers through the bright tresses, drawing them over her shoulders. "Forget your father and this place. Be with me."

"I'm not fit to serve you."

Behind her the giant loomed, his body spreading and absorbing the room itself, stretching high above them as he became a towering mountain of ice and snow. He roared without words, and the world disappeared in a blizzard of fury.

Korvel held on to her. "I don't need a servant," he shouted over the screaming wind. "I need you. I want *you,* Simone."

The giant bellowed, showering them with needles of ice, but his body shook as several sharp cracks pierced the air. One leg and then the other collapsed beneath the crumbling weight of his torso. One mighty hand reached out, clawing at Simone, only to fall short as the arm attached to it came apart. Dark water began to pour around them in a cold, rushing flood, and Korvel lifted Simone off her feet, holding her above the rising waters as he looked into her frightened eyes.

"I can't stop it," she said. "We're going to die."

"No, love." Korvel put his lips to her brow. "We're going to live."

As the water closed over his head, he drew up the iron will that had never failed him, and reached for the void, dragging Simone with him, until the nightlands receded and he felt her limp body being moved away from his.

Korvel came back to consciousness in a complete killing rage, ripping out of the ropes binding him and grabbing the first throat within reach. As his eyes adjusted to the glaring light in his face, he inspected the mortal choking beneath his grip and the four other men flanking a metal hatch. "Where is she?"

"Are you looking for your little whore?" someone asked in a pleasant tenor. "She's here."

Korvel dropped the now-unconscious mortal and turned to see a smiling priest sitting beside a pallet to which Simone had been tied. The priest held a straight razor poised at Simone's throat, and when Korvel took a step forward, he pressed the edge into her skin, causing a trickle of bright blood to stain the blade.

"Stay where you are," the priest advised him, "and I won't slice through the artery." He studied Korvel for a moment. "I'm assuming you want her back in one piece. Or if you'd rather I relieve you of this burden—"

"Who are you, and what do you want?"

"You may call me Helada."

Korvel sneered. "You are not Helada."

"Oh, but I will be, as soon as you give me what I need. A translation of the Scroll of Falkonera." The priest nodded to one side of Korvel. "It's right there on the table, next to the notepad and pen."

He glanced at the two gleaming gold cylinders of the scroll. "I am not a linguist."

"The last man who said that to me killed himself. Shortly thereafter I tortured his assistant, who provided a surprising amount of information. I think his employer grossly underestimated the boy's powers of observation." The priest scratched the back of his head in a lazy gesture, frowning at some strands of dark hair it left on his fingers before shaking them off. "I know who and what you are, Captain, and how your kind used the night code to communicate with other Darkyn after the fall of the Templars. You will sit down and translate the contents of the scroll for me."

Korvel could feel the motion of water beneath his feet, and from the dank smell of the compartment he guessed they had been brought to a ship's hold. He also saw that the priest and his men were wearing nose plugs. "I will do nothing for you until the girl is set free."

"Then while we wait, we will have to amuse ourselves." The priest nodded to one of the men, who picked up a long-handled bolt cutter and approached the pallet. "Caesar, start with the toes rather than the fingers. If she survives, she can cover up the stumps with her shoes."

Korvel knew he could reach either Caesar or the priest before they could hurt Simone, but not both. "Leave her here with me, and I will translate the scroll." As the priest frowned, he added, "The sun is up. If I am to stay conscious, I have to feed. On her."

"Very well," the priest said as he removed the blade from Simone's throat. "You have until noon."

Simone waited until the last man had left the compartment and the sound of his footsteps faded before she opened her eyes. Korvel stood beside the pallet, his hands tearing a strip of fabric from the end of his shirt. Dried blood still stained his fingers, but the wounds from the copper net were only dark pink lines on his skin. "You can't translate the scroll for him."

"I don't care about the bloody damn scroll." He folded the torn fabric into a square and knelt down to press it against the wound Pájaro had left on her neck, blotting it carefully before he bent close to examine it. When she tried to work her hands free he said, "Be still. Pretend I am shouting at you for walking into an ambush."

"I didn't know Lechance had settled his debt to my father." She shook her head. "You shouldn't have followed me. I can take care of myself."

He sat back on his heels. "Yes, I can see that." He

lifted his wrist to his mouth, biting into it before he held it against her wound. "The cut is deep. This will help it close."

A cool, tingling sensation erased the burning pain. "Thank you, Captain." She wriggled one hand loose and went to work on the knot binding the other while she scanned the compartment. "No portholes. Have you tried the door?"

"It's barricaded from the outside. He will have men standing guard in the corridor as well." He removed the rope tying her ankles and helped her sit up. "This priest—Pájaro—he is calling himself Helada. Why?"

"He believes he is, or that he will be, as soon as he kills my father. He doesn't know he's already dead." Light-headed, she gripped the edge of the pallet to steady herself. "My father trained Pájaro. He deceived him into believing that he would become Helada by assassination."

Korvel lifted a hand for silence and went to listen at the door. After someone walked past the compartment, he asked in a low voice, "Why did he deceive him?"

"So he would fight me." She held out her arm, turning it to expose a long scar, until she saw how he was looking at her. "I fought him, and all my brothers, and grown men, and anyone else my father told me to. Every day of my childhood I fought for my life, until I went to live with the sisters." Shame as well as the dizziness and nausea made her curl over onto the pallet. She knew vomiting would only make her weaker, so she breathed through it until it passed.

Korvel found a dark woolen blanket and draped it over her, tucking it in around her shivering limbs before he brushed the hair back from her face. "We have a few hours before they return. Rest now. I will keep you safe."

"Don't translate the scroll for him, Captain." She wrapped her hand around his wrist. "Please. There is no elixir, and once he knows the location, he'll kill us both and go after it."

"After what?"

She closed her eyes. "I can't tell you."

Chapter 15

"Looks like two on the ramp and three guarding the access points to the hold," Nicola murmured as she lowered the binoculars. "No sign of Korvel or the traitorous little bitch."

"We do not know for a fact that she is a traitor." Gabriel handed her a pair of dark sunglasses before putting on his own. "Korvel may be using her to find the scroll."

"She's a nun who's having sex with him, and she lured him into an ambush, and she's the sister of the guy who grabbed them." Nicola shook her head. "You're right. I'm being too quick to judge. When we're done with the mission we should invite her over one night to play Pictionary."

"Be nice." He went back to the car and opened the boot, removing a colorful tote bag before he returned. "Do you want to wear the red beret or the Mickey Mouse ears?"

She scowled and held out her hand. "Give me the ears."

Once they were ready, Gabriel walked with her to the pier, where Nicola began to tow him by the arm toward the ship.

"Get a picture of those barnacles, honey," she said in a loud voice as she started up the ramp. As Gabriel pretended to use the oversize camera hanging from the strap around his neck, she fluttered her hand at the men standing above them.

"Yoo-hoo. Fellas. Has the tour started?" She frowned as she pulled out a phrase book. "Um, I mean, lay tour co-men-say?"

The men looked at each other before one of them said, "Madame, this is a private vessel."

"Oh, you speak English, thank goodness." She heaved a sigh. "I failed French in high school. Twice."

"Madame, I must ask you—"

"Right, right, you need our tickets for the tour." Nicola opened the tote bag and began searching through it as she pushed between them to step onto the deck. "Honey, did you put them in the pocket this morning like I told you?"

"Sure did, darlin'." Gabriel took advantage of the distraction to move past the men and slip up behind another guarding the entrance to the hold. He covered the man's mouth as he plucked the clear plug out of his nose, and the scent of evergreen grew thick and hot.

"Madame," one of the men said, "there is no tour."

"Just a sec, sweetie, I've got them right here somewhere." She lifted her head and gave Gabriel a wink before he went around the corner to deal with the other two guards. "I can't believe how authentic everything looks," Gabriel heard her say. "You're even wearing guns, like real scumbags."

By the time he had knocked out and secured the other guards, the two by Nicola were growing visibly agitated. "You must leave," one of them told her. "Now."

"You're not our tour guide, are you? No offense, but

I'd like someone a little friendlier." She reached out and plucked the nine-millimeter from one of the guards' shoulder holster. "Wow, this is really heavy." Before he could react, she relieved the other guard of his Glock. "I think I like this one better. It's shinier."

One of the men grabbed at her, dislodging the Mickey Mouse ears off her head. The wind caught the hat and sent it sailing over the side.

"Hey." Nicola glanced over the railing before she scowled at the guard. "You drowned my ears. You *douche*." She straightened, then flipped the guns in her hands, holding the barrels as she used them to pistol-whip both guards at the same time. "I loved those ears." As the men crumpled to the deck, she tossed one of the guns to Gabriel before she leaned over the unconscious guard. "I ought to shoot you in the head, you heartless Mickey Mouse–hating bastard."

Once they had dragged the bodies out of sight, Gabriel listened at the entrance to the hold. "Several down below. Korvel?"

She turned around slowly, her eyes glittering before she stopped and pointed at a spot on the starboard side of the ship. "Two decks, maybe three. He's not alone. 'Clueless Tourists' isn't going to work down there." Nicola stripped the dark windbreaker and wool hat from one of the guards, and handed them to Gabriel. "By the way, why do *I* always have to be 'Helpless Hostage'?"

"You're the girl." He exchanged his beret for the wool hat, using it to cover his hair, and shrugged into the jacket.

"So?"

He took the gun from her hand and tucked it into the back of her belt. "When do we ever raid a place with girl guards?"

She sighed heavily as she placed her arms behind her back and leaned up against him. "Well, if we ever do, *you* have to be 'Helpless Hostage.'"

"Agreed." He pressed his gun against her temple and walked down the stairs into the hold.

Gabriel opened his mind to the insect life infesting the ship, using their eyes to navigate through the narrow, dark passages between decks. Nicola walked naturally until they encountered the first crewman, and then her gait changed to a cringing stumble as Gabriel marched her past the man, who didn't give them a second glance.

"These boys are hard-core," she murmured, tugging Gabriel around a corner and pausing there to focus on their surroundings. "We're close, but there are a couple guys near them." She shook her head slightly. "The scroll is there, too."

He heard the odd note in her voice. "Is something wrong with Korvel?"

"Not him. The scroll." She brought one of her hands to her temple. "The treasures and stuff you guys made always call to me, but something about this thing has my radar all fucked-up."

"Fucked-up how?"

"It feels good to find stuff, you know, like scratching an itch. But this time, it's not itching." She tapped the heel of her hand against her head. "It's screaming."

Gabriel didn't understand the other side of her gift, but he had learned to trust her instincts. "Could it be a forgery? Bait for another ambush?"

"No. This is definitely Kyn. Old, scary Kyn." She gripped his hand with hers. "Come on. Korvel is right on top of the thing."

Gabriel reached out to the minds of the Many, but none inhabited the deck where Korvel was being held.

When he tried to compel a swarm of fruit flies to abandon a crate of rotting lemons in the galley and fly down to the second level, they would go only as far as the stairwell. While he could force them to carry out his commands, Gabriel instead released them. The only time insects resisted his control was when their survival instincts were aroused. The fruit flies, the least discriminating of all winged insects, knew something on the deck would kill them.

When he and Nicola reached the bottom of the stairs, Gabriel breathed in. Along with the scents of the three mortals guarding the corridor came a sickly-sweet smell of a very specific decay: blood rot. The three men shared the same disease.

And all three men were dying of it.

At the turn of the passage Gabriel held Nicola back. "Walk ahead of me to the compartment. Do not engage the men. Leave them to me."

"Don't worry; I can smell it, too." She took a quick glance around the corner and then stepped out into plain view. When he reached for her, she shook her head and walked into the corridor.

The three mortals Gabriel had sensed sat unconscious in slumped positions against the walls, their weapons where they had dropped them, their clothes soiled with vomit and blood. Nicola eyed the nearest man, breathing in his scent before she pressed two fingers against his wrist.

"He barely has a pulse." She scanned the corridor. "What the hell did this?"

Gabriel pressed the side of his finger to his lips, and went to the door of the compartment in the center of the corridor. On the other side he could hear a mortal speaking.

Nicola came and put her hand against the door, and then held up three fingers before she took the gun out of her belt and chambered a round.

Gabriel put his hand on the latch, nodding to her just before he wrenched the door open. They stepped in together, guns ready.

Korvel, whose hair was oddly short and copper-colored, stood by a table, a notepad and a golden scroll in his hands. On the other side of the room a man dressed as a priest held a pale-faced woman in front of him. He had lodged the tip of a stiletto in her ribs, and held it at the correct angle to thrust it into her heart. In his left hand he held a pistol trained on Korvel.

Nicola focused on the weapon. "Copper rounds," she murmured to Gabriel, before she said in a louder voice, "Nice haircut, Captain. Can't say I love the color, though."

"Put down the guns," the priest said, "or I will kill him."

"No." The woman's green eyes fixed on Gabriel. "Shoot me."

"No one is going to shoot anyone." Korvel kept his eyes on Pájaro. "Your men are dead, and you can't escape. Give her to me, and I will let you live."

"You're not a fool. You will do no such thing." The priest sniffed several times before he suddenly changed his aim and fired, striking Nicola in the upper arm.

She dropped her gun and reeled back into the wall, almost falling before Gabriel caught her in his arms. She clapped a hand over the bloody hole in her jacket. "You son of a bitch."

Gabriel eased her to the floor. When he straightened his eyes began to glow with an eerie coldness. To Pájaro, he said, "Now you die."

The priest fired again as Gabriel came at him, grazing his head. It took two more rounds, one in each leg, to bring him to his knees.

"Enough." Korvel stepped in front of Gabriel to shield him, and flung the notepad at the priest's feet. "Take it and go."

Instead of grabbing the translation, he lifted Simone. "Where is he? I left a trail even an idiot like you could follow."

"He's not coming for you," she said, her head recoiling as he backhanded her. "He's never coming. He's dead."

"Lying bitch." He raised his fist.

"She speaks the truth," Korvel told him. "Her father has been dead for ten years."

Simone reached into the collar of her shirt and pulled out the cross. "Do you recognize this?"

Pájaro jerked the chain from her neck. "The old man's cross. He never took it off." He tightened his fist around it and laughed with delight. "I don't even have to fight him." He shoved Simone down on her knees. "Pick up the translation."

When Simone had Korvel's notes in her hands, Pájaro dragged her back to her feet and hauled her around the two wounded Kyn to the door. He took the notepad out of her hands before he raised the pistol over the back of her head and clubbed her.

Korvel picked up Nicola's gun and shot the priest four times in the chest.

Pájaro staggered back, then looked down at the holes in his cassock. Flattened slugs began dropping to the deck as he patted a bulky vest under his garment. "You can't kill me, vampire. I am Helada now, and the scroll will make me Helada forever." He stepped out into the corridor, slamming the door and barricading it from the outside.

Korvel knelt down to check Simone, who was unconscious. Once he carried her back to the pallet, he charged the door, ramming against it with his full weight. Steel buckled, and a large dent appeared in the surface, but the door held.

"Captain." Nicola hobbled over to Gabriel, who was trying and failing to get to his feet. "Give me that stiletto, will you?"

He picked up the blade and brought it to her. "What are you doing here, Nick?"

"Oh, rescuing your ass. Aren't we doing a bang-up job?" She glanced at Gabriel's face. "No. You are not going after him."

His *dents acérées* glittered as he snarled, "He shot you."

"He shot you more. We've got Korvel; we've got the scroll; we're done." She pushed him onto his back. "Fucking priests, I swear to God, I should just shoot them on sight."

"He's not a priest." Korvel tore the bullet holes in Gabriel's trousers wider before he looked at the Kyn lord. "This will be painful."

"I spent several years being tortured daily, Captain. I believe I can endure a few minutes of discomfort." Gabriel closed his eyes.

Korvel gently inserted the tip of the stiletto into the bullet wound, pressing in until he felt the slug. With a quick twist he forced it up and out of the wound.

Nicola bit her wrist and held the wound so that her blood dripped onto the bullet hole. "So how have you been, Captain? Get a chance to see the sights while you were here, or have you been too busy doing the nasty with Little Miss I Might Not Actually Be a Nun?"

"Simone isn't a nun. She is *tresori*. A sentinel. We have been working together." Korvel went to work on the other leg. "Did Richard send you after me?"

"Uh-huh. Vampire king really wants that scroll. You, maybe not so much." As Gabriel grimaced, Nicola took his hand in hers. "Hang on, baby. He's almost got it out." She touched the graze the first bullet had left on the side of his head. "What were you thinking? That asshole could have put one in your heart."

"I was not thinking at all," Gabriel admitted.

A low moan made Nicola turn her head toward the pallet. "Not much of a *tresora*, is she? What's the sentinel thing? Is that like one that still has training wheels?"

"Simone serves the *tresoran* council." Korvel gave Gabriel's *sygkenis* a direct look. "She was trying to protect us."

"She asked Gabriel to shoot her," she reminded him. "How, exactly, was her dead body going to protect us?"

Korvel's jaw tightened. "She did not wish to be used as a hostage."

"I believe I know what she intended," Gabriel said, his voice weary now. "At that range, the bullet I fired would have passed through her flesh and into the priest's body." When Nicola made a scoffing sound, he said, "I saw it in her eyes, *ma belle amie.* She did not care what the priest did to her." He regarded Korvel. "She was afraid he would kill you, Captain."

Once he had the other slug out, Korvel used his blood to seal Gabriel's second wound. "Let me see your arm, Nicola."

"It's a through-and-through. I'm fine." She stood and helped Gabriel to his feet, putting her good arm around his waist. The sound of metal scraping over the deck from outside the compartment made her scowl. "He's coming back. Give me one of those guns."

Korvel glanced past her. "Why would he return?"

"I don't know. He forgot to let me kill him?" she suggested.

Warped as it was, the hatch opened only partway, and Benetta frowned as he edged inside. "My lords. My lady." The smell of strong cologne filled the air in the compartment as he set down the heavy metal case he was carrying. "Are you in need of assistance?"

"Duh," Nicola said.

"Forgive me, my lady. It is a matter of form to ask." He inspected the room until he spotted the scroll. "You have found it."

"I wouldn't touch that if I were you," Nicola said as the *tresora* went over to pick it up. "There are three nearly dead guys out in the corridor who probably wish they hadn't."

"Yes, of course. Thank you for the warning." Benetta retrieved his case, opening it and placing it on the desk. "My lord Korvel, if you would be so kind."

Korvel grabbed the scroll and tossed it into the case before he moved over to the pallet. "How did you know we were here, Benetta?"

"Last night the sentinel informed the council that she was meeting with Lechance, my lord. When she did not report back, my men and I were sent to interrogate the guild master." The *tresora* closed the case and after a brief hesitation offered it to Korvel. "Are you in need of transportation?"

"No," Nicola said before Korvel could answer. "I think we're good."

"You are in no condition to drive, my lady," Benetta said. "My men and I were sent to Marseilles to provide—"

"That reminds me," she said, cutting him off. "Where exactly are your men, *tresora?* Don't say out on the dock, because if they were, I'd sense it."

Benetta's smile slipped. "You are mistaken, my lady. Perhaps the loss of blood has weakened you."

"Wearing all that cologne so we couldn't smell you lying wasn't bad, but your research?" She made a chiding sound. "Sloppy, sloppy."

"Who sent you?" Korvel demanded. "Ramas?"

"Ramas is an old fool. Eternity is my master," he said in old, flawless Latin. "Soon you and your kind will be dust beneath his feet." He lifted a hand, clenching it into a fist that he touched to the center of his chest. "So have we sworn."

"Your master has sent you to your death," Korvel told him. "Give me his name, and I will spare you."

"I will tell you who he is." The animation left Benetta's features and his eyes went flat as he reached into his jacket. Under the placket a weapon bulged. "When I see you in hell."

"No." Nicola lunged over Gabriel, trying to shield him with her body.

Korvel put himself between Simone and Benetta as gunfire shattered the air. The Italian collapsed, his legs twitching several times before they stilled. His face went slack as blood slowly seeped out from under his body.

Korvel bent down to check for a pulse and then rolled the dead man over onto his side. The gun Benetta had turned on himself had blown a fist-size exit wound through his back; the remains of his heart lay spattered across the wall behind him.

"Jesus Christ," Nicola said, staring at the corpse. "What kind of oath of loyalty do you make these guys take, anyway?"

"He did not serve the Kyn," Gabriel said.

Korvel searched through the dead man's pockets, but all he produced was a money clip stuffed with euros and an extra clip for the weapon. "He came knowing he might die. He may have been an infiltrator."

Gabriel braced himself against the desk. "Why would the council send one of their assassins after us?"

"Not us," Nicola said. "The scroll. He even brought a carrying case for it."

"He does not serve the council, or Ramas." Simone pushed herself off the pallet and staggered toward Korvel, bracing herself against him as he caught her.

Nicola's expression turned skeptical. "And you know this how?"

"His nose. Inside. Look." She rested her head against Korvel's chest.

He smelled blood, and found a wet patch of it on the back of her head. "You're bleeding." He swung her up into his arms.

"I have to go after him. The translation." She gripped the front of his shirt. "You don't understand. He will lead them to the cross."

"Lead who?" When she didn't answer, he said, "I translated the scroll, Simone. Cristophe inscribed it only with some psalms from the Bible, nothing more. What is this cross, and how can a few prayers be used to find it?"

"Benetta won't be the only one. When Pájaro leaves the country, they'll follow him to it." She struggled to focus on his face. "Korvel, please. It's why they ordered me to kill you. So Tremayne wouldn't find it."

Nicola sat up. "What did she just say?"

"She's delirious." He carried her back to the pallet, placing her with her back to him so he could examine her head wound. The gash on her scalp was wide enough to be bleeding freely, and he reopened the wound on his wrist.

She flinched as she felt his blood against her skin. "Couldn't hurt you," she murmured, her voice indistinct. "Never kill . . ."

"I know, love." He pulled the blanket over her and waited until she drifted off before he went back to Benetta's body. He tipped back the dead man's head and peered into his nostrils. "He has metal plugs embedded in each nasal passage."

"I thought *tresori* didn't have to worry about being zonked by *l'attrait*," Nicola said.

"Most of them don't." Korvel pulled back Benetta's sleeve to reveal a black cameo tattoo. Unlike the council pin he wore on his lapel, the center of the inked cameo did not contain a rose. Only recessed scar tissue filled its center, as if the image of the rose had been hacked out of his flesh. "Lord Seran, have you ever seen a *tresora* mutilated like this?"

"No." Gabriel gave him a troubled look. "Never."

Chapter 16

Dreams came to Simone, thin ghost worlds of what had been, but she hid from them until they passed. On some level she felt the waking world around her, her body being carried, cradled, cared for by strong hands with the gentlest touch.

Korvel.

She wanted to wake, to tell him how sorry she was, but her failure chained her to the darkness, hiding her from him.

Something pressed in, a presence unfamiliar to her. It moved easily, parting the curtains of her misery and peering in at her. Simone caught a glimpse of white curls, and realized it was someone from the ship, the one with the sharp tongue. She wore leather as if it were silk, and stood with her hands tucked in her back pockets as she inspected the nothingness.

"I know this place. I used to waste months here." She regarded Simone. "Nice fetal position. You doing okay there, sis?"

She curled up tighter. "I'm not your sister."

"We'll tell everyone that you were adopted." She sat down beside her and held out a hand. "During all that shooting we didn't get a chance for introductions. I'm Nick, or Nick's subconscious, or whatever."

Simone buried her face in her arms. "Please leave me alone."

"Haven't you had enough of that?" Nick scooted around in front of her. "Tell you what. Give me five minutes, and then I'll get out of your hair and you can sulk for the rest of eternity."

Anger jerked her upright. "I'm not sulking."

"That's better." Bright eyes studied her. "I know you. This is something the awake me won't process right away, mainly because my guy is hurt and I blame you for that, and for saying you were supposed to kill Korvel, et cetera. I've also got my own shit to deal with shortly. But on this level I know who you are. Here we're cool."

Nick snapped her fingers, and a television screen with a fuzzy picture appeared behind her. On it Simone watched herself dueling with an older boy.

"No." When Nick didn't listen, Simone jammed her fists against her eyes. "Turn it *off.*"

"Want to see mine?" She snapped her fingers again, and a second television screen appeared. "We'll keep it on mute. You'll thank me later."

On this one Simone saw a naked blond woman with a terrible wound across her face tearing into Nick's throat with her teeth.

"Wait for it." Nick glanced over her shoulder, and the screen changed to show her hands clawing away at the dirt as she dug her way out of the ground. "Bingo."

Simone cringed, but she couldn't stop watching the image of Nick sobbing as she dragged herself out of the shallow grave to stumble toward a farmhouse.

"By that point I was screaming," Nick told her. "I

locked myself in my bedroom and I crawled under the bed and I kept screaming. All. Night."

"How did you survive that?" Simone whispered.

"I decided to get me some well-earned revenge. I went to find the evil bitch who did that to me and rip her fucking heart out." Nick cocked her head. "You, on the other hand, became a nun. How's that working for you?"

"I'm not a nun." She hunched her shoulders. "I don't want revenge."

"Sweetie, we're women. We love revenge. It's the Y we didn't get in the chromosomes." She gave her a nudge with her elbow. "Come on, be honest. All those years of training and practicing and fighting for your life every goddamn day? You knew that the worst thing you could do to Daddy Dearest was walk up that hill and play housemaid for those nice old blind ladies."

Simone stared blankly at her hands. "I was supposed to kill the boys he made me fight. I could never do it. I don't know why. When I was little I wanted to—I knew I had to—but when the moment came?" She shook her head. "It all ends with me now. I made sure of it."

Nick reached out and took hold of her hand. "What happened to your brothers?"

"When they failed and I would not kill them, my father had them taken away. I never saw any of them again." She took a deep breath. "I think he murdered them. Pájaro was the only one who escaped."

Nick stood up, bringing Simone to her feet. "You're not a killer, but you're not a quitter. Like you said, it all ends with you. You have to finish this."

"I can't."

"Yeah, but you will anyway. For him." Nick gave her a rough hug. "See you in the real world, sister."

Nick winked out of existence, leaving Simone alone

again in the dark. The shame that had trapped her had gone as well, and while she could still feel it, lurking somewhere close, it had lost the power to keep her here.

Simone reached out with her thoughts and her hand and touched cool, hard muscle. "Korvel."

"I'm here, love."

Simone opened her eyes to see the sun setting over the city. She sat on Korvel's lap on the window bench, a soft coverlet swaddled around her.

His blue-purple eyes searched her face. "How does your head feel?"

"It doesn't hurt." She touched the back of it before she looked around the flat, expecting to see Nick scowling at her. "Where are the others?"

"They will return in a few hours." When she shifted away he kept his arms around her. "I know the scroll is a hoax. I translated the code into six psalms, all of which can be read from virtually any copy of the Bible in the world. What I don't understand is why. Why create the myth about the elixir?"

Simone had hoped that Korvel knew more than how to translate the code, but it seemed Cristophe had kept his word. "My father said the scroll was a test of loyalty." More like a cruel joke.

"Yet you have repeatedly risked your life to protect it. You even asked Gabriel to kill you. And while we were on the ship, you told me that it led to a cross. Just before you said you'd been ordered to kill me."

"You should hate mortals. We've hurt you so much." She touched the strange green mark on his throat. "My father believed that scars are the reminders of our failures, but you never try to hide yours."

"It has marked me for centuries," he admitted. "But I am not ashamed of it. I hung from those gallows for weeks, first fearing that I would die again, and then terrified that I would not. The scar reminds me that whatever is done to me, I can survive it." He folded her hand in his. "Simone, isn't it time you told me everything?"

Her heart died a little. "You have the scroll. Your mission is completed."

"Yours isn't. Even now, I can feel the tension in you. As if the moment I let go of you, you'll run out of here." Before she could reply, he touched his fingertips to her lips. "When you're ready, you'll tell me the rest."

No, she wouldn't. "Are you leaving tonight for Ireland?"

"That depends on you." He ran his hand up the length of her arm before he caressed her cheek. "I want you to come back with me. Come and be my *kyara*. My mortal wife."

Joy and despair tore at her insides. "I'm not fit to be a wife to any man."

"Not even the man who has shared your dreams?" He smiled a little. "Do you remember what you told me in the nightlands? About the game you played here in the flat? You could have that life with me."

"That was a child's pretense."

"We could make it real," he said as he stood up and set her on her feet. "I have just come home from my work."

"You don't have any flowers," she said, feeling a little desperate now.

"The stand closed early." He leaned back against the door. "I still want a kiss from my lady. Come here."

Simone caught her bottom lip with the edge of her teeth as she crossed the distance between them and put her hands on his shoulders. "This is foolish."

"No, love," he said as he bent his head to hers. "All

night I've thought of nothing but you. I've counted the hours until this moment, when we could be alone together and I could take you in my arms." He pulled her closer, but held his mouth a whisper away from hers. "I will show you what I have for you, and I think you will like it more than flowers, but you must kiss me first."

She slid her hand to the side of his neck as she balanced on tiptoe to put her lips against his. An instant later she moved back to separate their mouths.

Korvel kept hold of her. "Why do you stop?"

"I can't." She pressed her brow against his chest. I don't know. . . . The man in my dreams was never real. He never came home."

"*I'm* here. *I'm* real." Korvel pulled open his shirt and put her hand against his chest. "Kiss *me.*"

"I can have sex with you, but I don't know how to kiss." She moved her palm until it lay over the slow throb of his heart. "I wasn't trained to do that."

He drew back. "Trained?"

She nodded. "When I was old enough, my father sent one of the handlers to my room each night for a week."

Fury blazed over his features. "He did *what?*"

"It was part of my training. I didn't like it," she admitted, "but the man was not rough, and after the first time it didn't hurt. Kissing was not demonstrated or required."

His arms tightened, and he held her close for several moments before he spoke again. "Tell mc that your father suffered a vast deal before he died in agony." He cradled her head with his hand. "Please, God."

She wouldn't tell him that her father had been ill only a few weeks, or that he had killed himself the night his steward left the country. "He died knowing I took back my life from him." She thought of what Nick had told her in the dream. "There is no better revenge than that."

"You know what this means?" When she glanced up at him, he smiled. "I am the only man who has ever kissed you."

He sounded inordinately pleased, as if she'd given him a gift. "You're the only man who ever wanted to."

"You have been living with nuns." He smiled as he brought her lips to his, allowing her to feel the barest press of his mouth before he lifted his head. "Live with me, Simone, and I will kiss you every night."

Simone knew Pájaro had already left Marseilles, and where he had gone, and what she had to do. But now she also understood how wrong her father had been about her. The years of brutal training, the deliberate and systematic destruction of her childhood, her oath of loyalty to the council, even the wretched bargain her father had forced on her, no longer held any power over her. She would keep her word, but out of love for Korvel, and for all that might have been.

The first kiss Simone gave to Korvel landed slightly off center, and the edge of her teeth grazed his lower lip. She clasped her hands to his face, moving her mouth against his until his cool breath rushed out and his arms came up around her, pulling her in. With the second she used her tongue, awkwardly, timidly, until she found his, and he used it to draw her in and take it deeper. A frantic heartbeat later she fused their mouths together, no longer testing or tasting but stroking and suckling, as if their mouths were starved and the kiss had become a decadent feast.

She broke away, panting as the heat of the kiss drenched her body in a shivering, aching delight. She felt his hands clenching against her back, saw the hard line of his jaw, and inched closer, the slight curve of her belly pillowing the rigid length of his erection.

I will have this much for myself.

"Do that again," Korvel said, his voice deep and soft. "A thousand times again."

Simone drew back. "What if I want to kiss more than your mouth?" She drew her finger down the vault of his chest, tracing the faint depression of his navel through his shirt. "I want to kiss you here. Is that customary?"

His eyelids drooped. "It is now."

She hid a smile as she bent, unfastening the button at his waist before she pressed her lips to his belly, licking the tight dent.

"Christ Jesus," he muttered. "Your mouth should be a sin."

"Hmmmm." She went down on her knees, clasping his hips with her hands as she rubbed her cheek against the long bulge under his trousers. "Is it still kissing if I do it here?"

"Oh, yes, love." His hand came up to splay across the back of her head. "That is the one every man wants."

"You're the only man I've ever kissed," she reminded him as she slowly unfastened his trousers and worked them down the muscular columns of his legs. As he stepped out of them, she ran her hands from his ankles over his calves, putting her lips to one knee and then the other before she kissed her way up one massive thigh, lingering to taste the smoothness of his cool skin.

"Simone." His fingers tightened in her hair, urging her higher.

She drew back to admire the heavy thickness of his shaft and the tight bulge at its broad base. Unlike most modern men he had never been circumcised, and his velvety foreskin fascinated her, as did the gleaming knob that had emerged from it. "You are so splendidly made." She traced one of the veins popping up under his skin with her fingertip before she glanced up at him. "I have to kiss you here." She watched his face as she put her lips against the flared edge of his glans.

He gripped his shaft in his fist as she kissed the slick head, rubbing it back and forth on her lips. "Will you open your mouth for me?" When she did he lodged himself between her lips and stared down at her. "Damn me, but I love seeing my cock in your mouth."

She drew back a little. "Then give me more, Korvel." She parted her lips, letting her breath touch him before she licked a pearl of semen from the tiny slit in his dome.

He pressed in gently, guiding her with a shaking hand, his head falling back and his eyes closing as she rubbed her tongue along the barrel of his shaft. "Yes, love, suck me. Just that way. Oh, God. You're so beautiful like this."

Simone took every stroke he gave her, relishing the power that came with the helplessness of her position, and when she found the rhythm she sucked his penis with avid delight, feeling as if she had been given a gift now with this most intimate of kisses. The ache between her thighs swelled, jealous of the pleasure that glided between her lips, and she moaned around him, unwilling to stop, shaking with her own need.

"Simone." Korvel drew himself from her mouth and then lifted her up into his arms, carrying her into the bedroom and placing her on the coverlet as if she were something precious. His hands blurred as he tore at her clothes, stripping her to her skin before he loomed over her, guiding his penis between her thighs and working it into the clenching folds.

"Korvel." She clutched at him, lifting her hips as she tried to draw him in. "I need you."

"I know, love." He bent down to nuzzle her ear as he pressed in. "Feel me coming into you? Oh, yes. You're drenching me, you're so wet. I'll make it better now, Simone." He went deeper, working his head along the quivering tissues until she felt him nudge against the soft cup of her cervix. "There we are."

The first time with him she had felt impaled, invaded; now he filled every desperate space inside her with each heavy thrust. She wrapped her legs around his as he fucked her, her heart pounding and her blood screaming, until he drove her past all thought and reason and the pleasure rocketed through her.

"Kiss me again," he muttered against her mouth, and when she did he ravished her with his tongue, groaning into her mouth as his muscles coiled and he shoved deep, holding himself as his cool, thick cream pulsed into her body. The feel of it flooding her felt like a spiritual baptism, relieving her of the last of the sins of her father.

Korvel eased over onto his side, his penis still planted deep within her, and he cradled her close, stroking her back with a soothing caress. "I don't want you kissing any other men. You're too good at it."

"Don't worry." She tucked her face against his neck. "I never will."

Gabriel glanced up at the window of the town house where they had left Korvel and Simone, and caught his lover's arm before she reached for the door. "We should take a walk around the block."

"Let's not and say we did." She looked down at his hand. "Baby, I'm tired, I'm cranky, and my arm is covered with itchy dried blood. Anyone who gets between me and a shower is going to regret it. Deeply."

"It is a beautiful night," he said. "Look at these houses. They were built in the seventeenth century."

"It's freezing and architecture bores me." She didn't budge. "P.S., you suck at lying, so just tell me what it is."

Knowing Nick's dislike of Simone, he chose his words carefully. "I think Korvel and his lady need a little time alone."

"She's his lady now?" Nicola made a rude sound. "Please. She admitted she was under orders to kill him." She gave him a suspicious look. "How do you know what they're doing? He could be calling Richard. She could be polishing her crucifix."

Gabriel took her arm. "I know because the beetle clinging to the bedroom window has an excellent view of the bed."

"No wonder you never rent porn." She sighed and started down the steps. "All right. Come on and show me more fascinating architecture."

While they walked Gabriel pointed out several interesting features of the old town houses, but his lover appeared lost in her own thoughts. Their bond permitted him to gauge her emotions, but since boarding the ship she had been withdrawing into herself and locking away her feelings, as if she needed to hide them.

"During the revolution, some of the local aristocrats jumped from those balconies," he said, pointing up. "The people caught them in large nets, freed them, and then painted their faces with rainbows and unicorns."

"How cool." Nicola kept walking.

Gabriel came around and blocked her path. "If you do not tell me what is wrong, I will tickle you. Unmercifully. Until you wake up the entire neighborhood."

"I'm sorry. Balconies, right?" She gave the town houses a wan look. "Fuck the balconies."

"Nick." He bent down and pressed his brow to hers. "Talk to me."

"You're going to think it's stupid," she warned. When he shook his head, she shoved her hands in her pockets. "Korvel was in love with Alex, right? So why he is up there making the French connection?"

Gabriel felt more rather than less confused. "Korvel cannot have Alexandra. She does not want him."

"But you said that they were bonded. As in, he couldn't resist her. He had to have her. She was his life companion; no one could ever come between them, and he was going to love her forever." She flung a hand in the general direction of the safe house. "If that's true, why is that happening? And don't give me that crap about an incomplete bond. Alex may have been torn between two lovers, but does this mean a Kyn lord can survive a broken bond and rebond, or what?"

Gabriel heard the bleakness behind the anger in her voice. "Are you upset with Korvel for breaking his bond with a woman who doesn't want him, or afraid that I will find someone else to love if we are separated?"

"I just need to know that if anything happens to me you'll be okay. I mean, you've been through enough pain, baby." She shook her head. "Forget it. I need to get our stuff from the car."

"I am not going to forget it." Gabriel followed her to where they had parked the car. Once he unlocked the trunk, she began searching through a bag. "Nicola, I will not let anything come between us. As for Korvel, what he did to Alex was wrong, but it was not deliberate or malicious, and he has paid for it many times over. I think he deserves some happiness."

"We all do, baby. Just not with a woman ordered to kill him." She opened the case containing the scroll, checking it before she closed the lid and set it on the ground. "Where did you put the shampoo and stuff?"

"In the black bag." Gabriel watched her for another moment before he finally understood. "You think I would violate our bond. That is why you're angry with Korvel. Because he has freed himself from Alexandra, you believe I will do the same with you. I have told you—"

"You love me. You'll never leave me. I got it." She bent down and picked up the scroll case. "We shouldn't leave this in the car. Do you think they're finished by now, or should we go find a hotel room?"

Before Gabriel could reply, the latches she had left open on the case came loose and opened, and the scroll dropped to the ground.

"Damn it." Nicola reached down and picked up the artifact. "This thing is such a pain in the ass." An expression he didn't recognize crossed her face as she shook her head, putting the artifact back in the case and closing it before she handed it to him. When she spoke again, her voice sounded hollow. "Gabriel, don't touch this thing. Ever. Promise me."

"I have no desire to," he assured her.

"Don't let Richard have it, either." Nicola removed from her jacket one of the guns they had taken from the men on the ship. "He doesn't understand. None of you do."

"Nick?"

"I'm sorry." Before Gabriel could snatch the weapon away, she pressed the barrel to the front of her throat and pulled the trigger.

Chapter 17

Korvel left Simone sleeping peacefully in the bedroom, closing the door so the sound of his voice wouldn't disturb her. He was almost sure he had convinced her to return to Ireland with him, but there was still a chance that she would refuse. For that reason, and several others, he had to talk to his master.

He used one of the satellite phones to place the call to Ireland, which was answered by Éliane Selvais.

"The high lord has been expecting your call, Captain." A faint note of relief colored her cool voice. "He will be pleased to know that you are well."

Korvel doubted that. "Thank you, Éliane."

After a few moments of silence the line clicked and Richard's voice said, "Where are you?"

"Marseilles, my lord," he said. "We have recovered the scroll." He related a brief version of the events that had occurred since he had arrived at Château Niege. "The thief escaped, but since the scroll is a hoax, he has nothing of value but a few prayers."

"Prayers? Richard echoed. "You translated the code? He knows what the scroll contains?"

"Yes, my lord." As Richard swore, Korvel held the

phone away from his ear. Once his master had fallen silent, he said, "All that was written in the scroll were a half dozen psalms from the Bible. The same as could be read in any hotel room."

"Which psalms did he use?"

"You wish me to recite scripture for you?" Korvel asked politely.

"Tell me which psalms." Richard's voice lashed across the line like a copper-barbed whip. "*Now,* Captain."

Korvel looked up as Gabriel burst through the door to the flat. He carried Nicola, who was covered in blood, in his arms. "I will have to call you back, my lord." He switched off the phone and dropped it as he hurried to help Gabriel with his wounded *sygkenis.* "What happened to her?"

"She shot herself in the throat." Gabriel laid her down on the table by the kitchen. "I can't stop the bleeding."

Korvel saw the pattern of the black powder on her neck, and reached under her neck to feel for the exit wound. "The bullet is still inside her."

"She used one of the guns from the ship." Gabriel's hand shook as he wiped a streak of blood from her face.

Korvel gently turned Nicola onto her side and brushed back the white curls from her neck. He saw an angry, mottled red flush spreading beneath her pale flesh, and as he moved his fingers over her skin he found the telltale bulge of the round. He slowly straightened. "Gabriel. It is copper, and it is lodged in her spine."

The Kyn lord shook his head. "You are mistaken. She would be dead."

Korvel glanced down at Nicola's still features. Since the Brethren had begun using copper rounds in their weapons, the Kyn had learned only too well the devastating effect they had on immortal flesh. The copper began to poison the victim from the moment it entered the body; it also burned any tissue surrounding it. Because it was embedded in her neck bones, the bullet would quickly go to work on her spinal cord. Even if she could resist the effects of the poison, once the copper had burned through the cord Nicola would die.

"We must cut it out of her." Gabriel left the table and began tearing through the shelves of weapons. "Where are the daggers?" He looked back at Korvel. "Don't just stand there. Help me."

"I have seen such wounds before, my lord," he told him. "To remove it is delicate work, and requires skill that neither of us possess."

"No." Gabriel pulled over the shelf, smashing it on the floor. "I will not have it. We have to try." He fell to his knees. "I cannot lose her. Not like this."

"We are not surgeons." Korvel moved to help him up, and then stopped and changed direction, grabbing the satellite phone he had dropped and dialing a number he had sworn never to call.

When Alexandra Keller had become the first human to make the change from mortal to Darkyn in five centuries, she had also brought with her the science, technology, and training of the modern era. Using it, she had relentlessly pursued the original cause of the change in order to create a cure. She believed that the curse was actually a strange form of plague, one that altered rather than killed.

Korvel had not been inclined to believe something so simple could be responsible, not until the American doctor had found the means with which to reverse the high lord's condition. Richard, who had been forced to live on feline blood for decades, had been turned into an animalistic changeling. Now, thanks to Alexandra, his monstrous feline appearance was gradually transforming back into that of a man.

As soon as Phillipe of Navarre answered, Korvel said, "I need to speak with Dr. Keller immediately."

"Forgive me, Captain," Navarre said, "but my mistress does not wish to speak to you. At least, not until hell freezes over entirely."

"Nicola Jefferson has been shot with copper. I need Alex to tell me how to get it out of her spine." When the seneschal didn't reply, Korvel said, "There is no time for games, Navarre. Nick is dying."

After a short pause, Phillipe said, "Wait."

Korvel carried the phone over to the table and put it on speaker as he retrieved a copper dagger from Simone's bag.

"What the hell is this?" Alexandra Keller's voice suddenly demanded. "Someone shot Nick?"

"Yes." Korvel repeated what had happened, leaving out the fact that the shot had been self-inflicted. "None of her arteries were severed, but I can feel the bullet wedged between two of the neck bones. The skin on her nape is dark red."

"That's copper poisoning," Alex confirmed. "How long has it been since she was shot?"

"Only a few minutes." Korvel touched Nicola's throat. "Her heart has already stopped beating."

"Jesus Christ. All right. You're going to do a modified anterior cervical decompression. Put her on her back on a hard surface and immobilize her head."

Korvel picked up the phone and switched it to talk. "Alex, the bullet is in the back of her neck."

"The surgical pathway is less complicated if you go in from the front," she told him. "You'll only have to cut one vestigial muscle and follow the anatomical planes to get at her spine. Tell me you have a copper-coated scalpel."

"I don't."

She muttered under her breath. "Then use sharpest, thinnest copper blade you can find."

Gabriel came to the table as Korvel turned Nicola, and held her head between his hands.

Korvel switched the phone back on speaker and gripped the blade in his hand. "We're ready, Doctor." He swatted at a large black beetle that flew at his head.

"All right, you're going to make an incision on the right side —"

"Wait." Gabriel held out his hand, and the beetle landed on his palm. "Alex, it is Gabriel. I know how to take the bullet out of her without cutting into her throat."

A sigh came over the speaker. "You only have a minute or two, Gabriel. Whatever it is, do it fast."

He placed the beetle on Nicola's collarbone, and the insect disappeared into the entry wound. As Gabriel focused on his *sygkenis*, Korvel picked up the phone and quietly described what was happening.

"If this works, she's going to need at least two units of blood to dilute the poison," Alex told him. "Don't give her more than three or you could send her into thrall. After the bullet's out, you'll also have to clean and close that entry wound."

The front of Nicola's throat bulged, and slowly a misshapen slug pushed out of the wound. As Gabriel pulled it free, the blood-covered beetle emerged and trundled across a collarbone, fluttering its wings before it flew off into the bedroom.

"The bullet is out." Korvel took Nicola's wrist between his fingers. "Her heart has begun beating again. Thank you for your assistance, Doctor."

"Gabriel and the bug did all the grunt work. Call me if for any reason her condition takes a dive." She hesitated before she asked, "You all right?"

A year ago her gruff question would have brought him to his knees. Now he felt only a vague regret for all the trouble he had caused her.

"I am now. Good-bye, Alexandra." Korvel glanced at the bedroom. The tremendous noise Gabriel had made tearing apart the shelving had been enough to wake the dead, and still Simone had slept through it. He walked over to look in at her, and the sight of her still body made guilt gnaw at him. Their lovemaking must have exhausted her.

"Cristophe did this," Gabriel said as soon as Korvel came back to the table. "Him and his wretched curse."

"I don't believe in curses, my lord." He went to the kitchen to retrieve the blood she would need to heal. "Did your lady say or do anything before she turned the gun on herself?"

"She touched the scroll," Gabriel said. "She held it in her hand, and then she begged me to destroy it, just before she shot herself."

"I know Nicola is sensitive to objects belonging to the Kyn, but gold is harmless to us. Besides that, I handled the scroll myself, and nothing happened to me." Korvel didn't want to upset Gabriel any more than he was, but Nicola's love-hate relationship with their kind might drive her to attempt suicide again. "I think perhaps your lady acted on impulse. It may be that the scroll reminded her of the treasure that led to her being made Kyn."

Gabriel's expression turned to disgust. "The Golden Madonna." A low sound came from Nicola, whose eyes

were open and watching the two of them, and he rushed
to the table. "Nicola? I'm here."

Korvel joined him and looked down at Nicola's
throat. The wound had closed on its own, and within a
few seconds the pale pink scar left behind smoothed out
and disappeared. "How is she healing so fast?"

"I do not know; nor do I care." Gabriel pressed a kiss
to her brow, her nose, and her lips before he murmured,
"Don't ever do that to me again. Not unless you shoot
me in the heart first."

Nicola's expression softened. She opened her mouth,
frowned, and then swallowed a few times before she
spoke in a rough whisper. "Sorry." Her eyes shifted to
Korvel. "The scroll isn't cursed. It's a map."

"To what, my lady?"

"I don't know. I saw where it was. There was a beach,
and water, and for a second, something else. Something
green. As soon as I saw it I could feel it in my head. Then
I was taking the gun out of my jacket." She touched her
throat. "I couldn't stop myself."

"Don't think about it." Gabriel picked her up in his
arms and carried her over to the big armchair, where he
sat down with her. "Captain, is there an extra blanket?"

"Of course." Korvel went into the bedroom, glancing
at the still form on the bed before he went into the
closet. Seeing how close Gabriel had come to losing Nicola made him go over to the bed to tug back the coverlet
and give his lady a quick kiss.

All he found were crumpled garments, carefully
shaped and arranged to mimic the contours of a sleeping woman.

Although he seldom spent a full night in his bed, Rellen
Lechance never had trouble sleeping. He attributed this

to his mother, the French mistress of a Salerno hit man, who had let him share her bed whenever his father was not in town. She had slept with a blade under her pillow and a gun tucked under the mattress, and taught him to wake at the slightest sound.

"Your father will kill *me* if he finds you in here," she would always say.

What brought Lechance fully awake was not a sound, but another memory: that of collecting some rosemary from his mother's tiny garden. He kept his eyes closed as he rolled onto his side and reached for the gun under his pillow, finding only smooth sheets.

"It's not there."

The sound of Simone Derien's voice came as no surprise; nor did the sight of her sitting on the end of his bed. Death, like his hit man father, often came in the night. "*Coucou, ma petite amie.*"

"Your guards are unconscious. One will need his arm cast when he wakes." She popped the clip from his gun and began thumbing the rounds out of it. "Which member of the council do you serve?"

"I serve no one but myself, Simone," he chided.

"By tomorrow Pájaro will be dead." She produced his blade and tested the edge with her thumb. "But the men who are following him will not die for many days."

"They are not my men," he said honestly.

"That I know." She stood up, and tossed a cordless phone into his lap. "Call your master. I will speak to him myself."

"I have no master." He waited for her to attack, and when she didn't, he sighed. "Go back to your village, child. Wash your blind women's sheets and herd their goats. You don't have the stomach for this."

She moved then, the blade flashing, and before he

could evade her she straddled him. He froze as she put the tip of the blade at the corner of his right eye.

"Make the call, Rellen," she said, "or the next thing you will be master of is a white cane."

He dialed the number by touch and lifted the phone to his face. "I have been compromised. The girl is here, and she wishes to speak to you."

Simone took the phone from him. "There is a traitor among the council, Padrone Ramas, and his operatives are failed *tresori* who are using your name, probably to frame you and create chaos among the council. The traitor orchestrated all of this in order to obtain the location of the cross." As she listened, she removed the blade from Lechance's eye. "I will retrieve it if I can, but you must advise the high lord directly."

Once she ended the call, Lechance looked up at her. "You know that Tremayne wants the cross for himself."

She climbed off the bed. "He will not have it, and neither will the council. I need your car keys and money."

"Of course." He retrieved the cash from his wall safe, and brought it to her with the keys to his sedan. As she pocketed the money, he said, "I can provide you with an appropriate escort."

"No, you can't." She pocketed the cash. "Before I came here I contacted Interpol. They already have most of your men in custody, and should be arriving here in a few minutes to arrest you. Good-bye, Guild Master." She went to the door.

"Simone." When she looked back at him, he said, "You already knew I serve Ramas." As she nodded, he gestured at his face. "Then why go through the pretense?"

She looked at him, and for a moment he saw her father in her eyes. "I wanted to watch you squirm." She walked out.

* * *

Simone parked Lechance's car in a short-term lot at the airport, and at the international counter purchased her plane ticket with some of his money. Before going through security she detoured to the lavatory, donning the clothes of a casual traveler and slipping her passport into her pocket before she took the bag to the luggage claim office.

"Hello," she said to the clerk, and placed the bag on the counter. "Someone left this in the restroom."

"You are the honest one." The clerk looked over the outside of the bag. "No tag. Ah, well, I'll give it to the security people to check. *Merci,* mademoiselle."

At the security station a bored guard had her walk through the metal detector before he checked her passport. "No carry-on today?"

"I checked it." She covered a phony yawn with her hand. "I don't need anything on the plane but a few hours of sleep."

The guard eyed a woman and a shrieking toddler at the opposite station. "*Bonne chance.*"

Most of the expensive seats in the first-class section were unoccupied. Once the tourists and businesspeople had been packed into the back of the plane, a smiling flight attendant told Simone she could sit wherever she wished.

She chose a window seat in the corner and, once the flight attendant had finished her presentation of the emergency procedures, looked out at the glass-fronted terminal, where some friends and family of the passengers stood outside the entrance to the passenger gates, where they watched and waved at the plane. Among them stood a tall, broad-shouldered man with fair hair who held a little girl in his arms, and while he looked nothing like Korvel, the sight of him with the child gave her a strange sense of reassurance.

By tomorrow it would be done. Korvel and his people would be safe, and no father or child would ever again have to waste his or her life bearing the burden of Cristophe's legacy.

The sunlight made her tired eyes burn, and Simone pulled down the window shade and settled back in the seat.

"Mademoiselle?" The attendant offered her a light blanket and a small pillow. "We will be landing in ten hours. Do you wish me to wake you for your meals?"

"Please." Simone reached up to switch off the seat light.

Chapter 18

The water in the sink had turned red by the time Nick had finished washing up. She stared down at it as she reached and touched the back of her neck. "Man. I never thought I'd drink the Kool-Aid."

"You are not drinking at all." Gabriel turned her to face him and dried off her throat and face. "You refused the bloodwine Korvel offered. Is it your throat? Does it still pain you?"

"My neck is fine. I didn't need the blood." She saw the way he looked at her. "Baby, I haven't felt this good since the last time we were naked together. It feels like having great sex—well, sex is always great with you—but more like the after part. You know, when you want to cuddle and tell me how hot I am and I get all girlie."

"Generally shooting yourself does not produce such feelings." He pulled her close and held her tightly. "Korvel can track down his lady. You and I need to get away. As far from here as we can go."

"Simone was the little girl in the videos." Like most of the things that had been popping into her head for the last half hour, she didn't know how she knew that. "We can't walk away from this, baby. I can't. Not until I get some closure. It's what I need."

After they both changed into clean clothes, Nick went out to help herself to some of the weapons. Korvel, who stood listening to the satellite phone, looked ready to rip off someone's head. When he spoke, he said something in a version of English Nick didn't understand. Her lover did, however, from the riveted look he gave the captain.

"What's his deal?" she asked.

"I believe the high lord has recalled Korvel to Ireland." Gabriel winced as the captain threw the phone through the window. "And it seems he has refused."

"Forgive my show of temper, my lord," Korvel said as he joined them. "You should know that I have broken faith with my master."

"That means you told him to fuck off, right?" Nick grinned. "God, I wish I could have seen the look on his furry face." She bumped her fist against his shoulder. "Way to go, big guy."

"Nicola." Gabriel gave her a disapproving glance. To Korvel he said, "When it comes to acts of malice, Richard has few equals. He will not allow your disobedience to go unpunished, Captain."

"I have no intention of rejoining his household," Korvel said. "Once I find Simone, I will retract my oath to Richard and offer my services elsewhere."

"None of the sig-lords will touch you," Nick guessed. "Everyone else is a big step down. Unless you're open to something a little less conventional." She nudged Gabriel with her elbow. "This would be when the unconventional lord in the room makes a job offer."

"I have no territory or household," Gabriel admitted.

"No seneschal or *tresora*. My garrison consists of my *sygkenis,* who never obeys orders and seldom even follows my suggestions. Our work is always dangerous."

"Honey." Nick poked him. "We want him to *take* the job, not run away from it screaming into the night."

"I would not run, my lady. My lord." Korvel gave them each a deep bow of respect. "You honor me."

"Likewise." Nick knew Richard and his captain would have to make things official in person, but at least now Korvel knew he had somewhere to go. "So where do you think sis went?"

"Simone paid a visit to Rellen Lechance at his home," Korvel said, and related the details of the call a council member had made to Richard. "According to Ramas, shortly after Simone left, Lechance was arrested by Interpol and taken to police headquarters for processing and questioning. Ramas believes Simone is responsible, but he doesn't know where she has gone."

Nick checked the time. "Do we have people in Interpol?"

"We have people everywhere," Gabriel said.

Less than thirty minutes later they were shown into a private visiting room at police headquarters, where Rellen Lechance was brought in wearing a prisoner's jumpsuit, chains, and handcuffs. As soon as he saw Gabriel he took a step back and lowered his hands in front of his crotch.

Nick smirked. "Awww. Look, honey. He remembers us."

Lechance quickly recovered his poise and sat down at the desk while Korvel took the seat opposite it. The pane of safety glass that divided the entire room ran across the center of the visitor's table, but a tinny intercom allowed the two men to talk.

"We will have to keep this brief," Lechance said. "My attorney is waiting to have me released on a technical-ity—"

"Where is she?" Korvel demanded.

"Do you mean our friend Simone?" Lechance shrugged. "I would imagine she went back to her village. She never really liked the city, and, of course, the goats at the convent are still waiting to be milked."

This time Gabriel looked at the agent, who inclined her head and left the room.

"I can't watch this." Nick turned and walked over to a map hanging on the wall, which showed the entire planet flattened and divided by longitude and latitude.

"Tell me where she went," Korvel said.

"Why do you think she would tell me?" Lechance countered.

Nick idly rubbed the back of her neck. The grid lines on the map made the Earth appear like a giant's game board. *Maybe that's all we are. God's latest chess game. Richard the king, Gabriel the knight, Korvel the rook.*

What was happening in the room faded as the sound of water rushed inside Nick's ears, and a green darkness filled her eyes.

What will you be, little thief? a deep voice asked. *A queen, or a pawn?*

Nick felt a touch of the same madness that had made her put a hole in her own throat. The thing was back in her head, and while it wasn't trying to take her over this time, she still came out swinging. *You get out of my mind, you son of a bitch. I don't play games.*

You will, little thief. The alien presence winked out, like the flame of a candle being snuffed.

"Why did she come to you?" she heard Korvel say.

"She did not confide her motives to me, vampire." He smiled. "Perhaps she tired of your company."

Nick jumped as Korvel punched his fist through the glass and grabbed the assassin by the collar, hauling him across the desk. The scent of larkspur on fire flooded the room. "You will tell me what I wish to know."

Lechance's eyes lost their focus. "Simone came to me for my car and money so she could pursue Pájaro. She also humiliated me into betraying my master, but she already knew he was Padrone Ramas. They spoke on the phone." He sighed. "He is going to be very angry with me."

"Repeat exactly what Simone said to Ramas." Korvel listened carefully to every word Lechance said before he demanded, "Where is this cross?"

"No one knows but Pájaro and Helada." He frowned. "Why didn't she blind me? Her father would have, if he let me live. Which he would not have done. He was quite ruthless about such things—"

"Shut up." Korvel released him.

Nick looked over at the world map hanging on the wall. "Korvel, hang on." She went over and took down the frame, removing the back and taking out the map. The flimsy print was nothing but a cheap reproduction, but along the margins of the map each grid line ended at a number.

Nick carried it over to the desk, brushing off the shattered glass before she laid it out. "Korvel, look at this. What if the scroll isn't a map, but directions on a map? Like a GPS, but with longitude and latitude?"

"How could it be, my lady?"

"Psalms are numbered," she reminded him. "Six psalms would equal two sets of map coordinates."

"I think that is unlikely, my lady," Korvel said. "At the

time Cristophe forged the scroll, the modern world's methods of mapping were unknown."

"That is not precisely true." Gabriel came over and pointed to the numbers in the margins. "After we broke with the Templars, the high lord began assigning territories. First he had to divide up the world, and he used a system created by Babylonian astronomers, who used number systems of sixty."

Korvel looked outraged. "Why was I never informed of this? I am a *Nautonnier*."

"The high lord shared it only with the seigneurs who governed the territories. This was to prevent the Brethren from discovering how to locate our strongholds," Gabriel said. "Much later, when mortals began searching for a more accurate method of mapping, Richard changed his mind, and made certain that they used his. I cannot say why."

Nick rolled her eyes. "I can. His ego. He knew humans were going to be mapping everything, and now every time he looks at one, it's laid out the way he wanted." To Korvel, she said, "Tell me the numbers of the psalms in the order they appeared on the scroll." As he did, she wrote them on the margin of the map. "All right, this only shows degrees, so we use the first and fourth numbers, right?" When Gabriel nodded, she studied the margins. "Psalm eighteen by psalm seventy-seven. Some compass headings would be nice."

"There are only two possibilities. The center of India." Korvel studied the map. "Or Jamaica."

"It's Jamaica," Nicola said at once. "I know it is. That beach I saw could not possibly be in the middle of India."

"I will contact our people at the airport and have them prepare a jet," Gabriel said, taking out his mobile. "We should leave as soon as possible." He glanced at

Lechance before he said to Korvel, "This man can never go free, Captain. Not with what he knows about us."

"We are not killing him," Nick said flatly.

"That will not be necessary, my lady." Korvel sat down in front of Lechance. "When I leave this room," he told the guild master, "you will give the Interpol agents a complete confession for every murder you have committed. You will also inform them of the names of the clients who hired you to carry out the killings."

"Confess. Murder. Clients." He nodded.

"You knew Simone's father was Helada, and that he died ten years ago," Korvel continued. "Who took his place, and where is he?"

Confusion passed over the guild master's face. "But you know where she is, vampire."

"I am not talking about Simone." He put his hand on the other man's neck. "She said she had many brothers. Which one of them became Helada?"

"They were not her brothers," Lechance said. "They were orphans her father adopted from different countries. He brought nearly seventy of them to the château, but Simone was the only natural child he ever sired."

Korvel stalked out of the room, and when Nick caught up with him she saw how angry he was. "Captain, what was all that about? What has Simone got to do with Helada?"

"Everything," he told her. "Simone *is* Helada."

Spending ten hours feigning sleep didn't trouble Simone. As a child she had been taught surveillance tactics that required her to remain unmoving and alert for an entire night. Until the plane landed she had nothing to do but sit alone and think, so she closed her eyes and thought of Korvel.

The high lord would expect his captain to bring the scroll to Ireland immediately, so Korvel was likely on a plane himself right now. He might even be thinking of her, although she doubted it was with any pleasure. He had asked her to be his human wife, and for a Kyn warrior of his rank that was no minor honor to extend to a *tresora*. Flavia had told her that such relationships happened only rarely, and from the beginning were doomed to end in tragedy, for a human wife always died a human death.

Live with me, Simone, and I will kiss you every night.

If her life had been her own, Simone knew she would have gone with Korvel to Ireland. She would have learned to be a good wife to him, and devoted the rest of her days to seeing to his pleasure and comfort. Long after she died, he would remember how much she had loved him.

How much I love him.

How that had come to be, Simone didn't know. Love had never been part of her life. Her father had not been interested in or capable of any emotion. Flavia and the sisters had been affectionate, and had allowed Simone to regard them as her surrogate family, but their hearts belonged to their duty and their God. For all his pride and reserve, only Korvel had shown any real love for her. A very physical love, perhaps, but given time it would have grown. Simone felt sure of that. Just as she knew she was on this plane because she loved him.

He will never know. But that, too, was as it should be.

The flight attendant gently touched her shoulder twice during the flight, and Simone ate the food she was served without tasting it, but the airline's bland dishes didn't agree with her. An hour away from Kingston she finally went to the lavatory, where she emptied her stomach as quietly as she could.

After she rinsed out her mouth, Simone studied her reflection. Thoughts of her father and the bargain she had made with him always made her feel sick, but this was different—as if she had picked up some sort of bug.

In a few hours it won't matter. She washed and dried her face.

"You are feeling unwell, mademoiselle?" the attendant asked as Simone passed her in the aisle. "You look very pale."

"Just a little airsickness." As she continued toward her seat, she noticed two men sitting on opposite sides of the first-class section; both looked out their windows at the same time.

Simone made note of their unremarkable clothing before she turned around and walked back to the attendant. "Excuse me, but may I have a soft drink?" She pressed her hand to her waist. "It may help with the nausea."

The attendant nodded. "I'll bring it to your seat right away."

Once Simone sat down she checked the interior of the cabin, measuring the open areas as well as the obstacles around her. The attendant promptly delivered the small can of soda along with an ice-filled plastic tumbler and a packet of crackers, which she suggested might also help calm her stomach.

While she munched on a cracker, Simone placed the sealed can in her pocket. By the time the plane began to descend for landing, Simone handed the empty tumbler back to the attendant, who by that time was hurrying to clear all the tray tables, and didn't notice the absence of the can.

The landing occurred without incident, and over the intercom the pilot welcomed the passengers to the island, and thanked them for flying the airline. The moment the seat belt sign switched off, passengers began rising and crowding the aisles, but Simone remained in her seat, waiting and watching every man who passed by her. The two men who had been so interested in the view from their windows did not exit with the others.

Two other attendants walked up from the rear of the cabin; both stopped by Simone's seat as one said, "We have arrived, mademoiselle. Do you need a wheelchair?"

"No, thank you. I can walk." Simone got up and moved quickly out of the plane, eyeing the empty ramp in front of her before she ran for the gate.

Two sets of footsteps thudded rapidly behind her as the men hurried to catch up.

She turned to stop on one side of the gate entrance and looked around, listening to the running steps until they were only a few strides from the end of the ramp. She turned the corner and ran at them, striking both in the rib cage with the heels of her hands, snapping bones. As they doubled over she struck a second time, snapping up her fists into their jaws and knocking them flat on their backs.

She took the can of soda from her pocket, opened it, and removed the tab ring in such a way that a small triangle of the thin metal from the top of the can came with it. She poured the soda onto the bottoms of their shoes and the floor in front of their feet before she dropped the can.

"Monsieurs," she said in a loud, horrified voice as she bent over one of the gasping men. Quickly she jabbed the sharp end of the tab ring on her finger into his hairline. "*Mon Dieu,* you are hurt." She turned to the other and inflicted the same injury before she turned and called, "Can someone help, please?"

Two security guards promptly arrived and surveyed the men. "What happened, miss?"

"I don't know. I heard a terrible crashing sound and found them like this." She watched as the guards pulled the men into sitting positions, at which point blood from the scalp wounds she had inflicted streamed down their faces.

One of the men tried to speak, but fell silent as his companion glared at him.

"There's a puddle here on the floor," the second guard said to the first before he noticed the empty can nearby. "Someone dropped a soda. They must have slipped in it." He took his handheld radio and called for medical assistance before he said, "Thank you for helping, miss."

"Oh, it was nothing." She made eye contact with the man who had not spoken. "Such a bad way to fall, but I think it could have been much worse."

The silent one inclined his head.

Simone took advantage of the gathering crowd of terminal employees and onlookers to slip through customs and change her money at the international exchange counter. From there she walked outside, squinting in the powerful sunlight as she studied the long line of taxis and hotel shuttles. She ran the gauntlet of hawkers and down the line of vehicles until she found an empty, ramshackle white van with a bored-looking young black man sitting behind the wheel. He had on a Bob Marley T-shirt, but the tinny radio in the van played Debussy.

She ducked her head to look in the open passenger window. "Excuse me, but do you know how to get to Runaway Bay?"

"Your travel agent book you there, lady? That's on the other side of the island. I don't go that far." He nodded at a bus. "Shuttle to Ocho Rios get you there in about an hour, and it won't cost you two hundred dollars."

"Money is not a problem." His British accent made Simone smile a little as she produced enough cash to make the young man gape. "Would this help change your mind?"

He hooted and reached over for the door handle, and then sat back and sighed. "Ah, I still can't do it. My sister needs me to pick up her girls from school. If I take you, I won't get back in time."

"I can wait until after you take your nieces home," she assured him.

"Then, beautiful lady, I take you anywhere you want to go on the island." He grinned and opened the door for her. "Half price."

Once she had her seat belt on, the driver held up a scratched CD. "You want to listen to Bob Marley's greatest hits?"

Simone glanced at name on the operator's license hanging from one of the A/C vents. "If you don't mind, Jamar, I prefer Debussy."

"So do I." He tucked the CD into his sun visor, and eased into the stream of cars driving by the loading zone.

Jamar's nieces turned out to be three very polite little girls who sat together on the bench seat behind Simone and told their uncle about their day at school. As Simone listened to the children, she watched the side-view mirror, but saw no one following them.

Jamar stopped in front of a small house, where the girls' mother was waiting at the curb. She gave Simone a curious look as she helped her daughters out of the van and then herded them inside.

Simone felt better as she watched the girls disappear into their home. *You will be safe, too, little ones.*

"So where are you staying in Runaway Bay, lady?" Jamar asked once they were back on the road. "The SuperFun, the Gran Bahia, or Club Ambiance?"

"I'm going to Winter Cove."

"You really need to fire this travel agent, lady." He shook his head. "Winter Cove isn't a hotel. It's a big ugly old house back in the woods."

"I know what it is."

Jamar didn't seem to hear her. "My cousin Denisha, she drives a shuttle for the SuperFun, and she go past the road to that house ten, fifteen times every day. Nobody ever stays there. She heard that as soon as he built it, the owner left the island and never came back." He reached over and patted her hand. "I'll take you to the SuperFun. Denisha can get you a nice room for a good rate."

"Thank you, Jamar, but I don't need a room," she told him. "I'll be staying at the big, ugly old house."

He gave her a startled look. "You know who owns the place, lady?"

She nodded. "Yes. I own it."

Chapter 19

Once the excavation equipment had been unloaded, the men Pájaro had hired to transport it gathered in a circle on the beach to share a blunt. He watched them as he injected himself with the last of the morphine. It barely took the edge off his pounding migraine; he should have taken all the vials from the drug dealer he'd killed thirty minutes after landing in Montego Bay. At least he'd had the sense to search the dealer's car, which had provided him with three fully loaded machine guns.

Another lung spasm gripped him, and as he coughed the needle slipped from his hand and rolled under the seat.

His driver glanced back over the partition. "You don't look too good, boss. You want to go to your hotel now?"

"Later." He wiped the bloody mucus from his mouth and pocketed the handkerchief before he picked up the GPS unit. "Call the surveyor again. Tell him if he's not here in fifteen minutes he's a dead man."

The driver looked uneasy. "You mean he's fired, right, boss?"

To keep from blowing the man's brains out sooner than would be convenient, Pájaro climbed out of the limo. At once clammy, salt-riddled heat engulfed him, adding a layer of briny sweat atop his chilled flesh. Whatever infection had invaded his system seemed to be sinking into his bones; his very limbs felt like they were grinding into his joints.

The illness aggravated him, but he knew it was only a temporary annoyance. He had taken back from the old man's brat the legacy that belonged to him. Once he unearthed the Trinity cross, the sickness would vanish along with all the other mortal weaknesses that plagued him. He would never again have to endure a single moment of suffering.

Pájaro walked down to the edge of the beach and surveyed the snowy white sands. That the old man's family had managed to retain ownership of three miles of pristine shoreline for all this time impressed him. Now that it was to be his, he would build his first palace here. Perhaps he would have the old man's brat brought here to serve as some entertainment. With all the time and power and wealth in the world at his disposal, he could make her suffer for decades.

"Mr. Helada?"

He turned to see a nervous-looking man carrying a leather case. "Are you the surveyor?"

"Yes, sir." He put down the case and took out a note from his pocket. "I checked the information you gave me, and I'm afraid I can't help you."

"Why not?"

"Sir, whatever you're trying to locate isn't on this island." He gestured toward the sea. "According to the coordinates you provided, it's about halfway between here and the island of Cuba."

Pájaro glanced out at the vivid turquoise water. "There is nothing between here and Cuba."

"There is the Cayman Trough, sir," the surveyor said. "If these numbers are correct, that is your site." He offered a feeble smile. "It's the deepest point in the Caribbean. Whatever you're looking for is three miles under the ocean."

The man's nervous chatter had at last exposed the true reason for his anxiety. "Why do you believe that I'm looking for anything?"

"Oh, I don't," the surveyor said quickly. "I just assumed you were."

"Don't concern yourself. It was only a small error." He walked over and put his arm around the man's thin shoulders to guide him into the trees. "I'm certain whoever bribed you to lie to me will still pay whatever he promised, as long as I allow you to live to collect it. Keep walking."

"I'm sorry, sir, but you're wrong." The surveyor stopped and tried to shrug off Pájaro's arm. "I have to get back to my office."

"And so you will." He released him and took out his straight razor, turning it to catch a beam of sunlight. "Tell me where it is, and I will let you go. Lie to me again, and you lose an eye."

"Why ya be taking dis mon back in da trees?" a friendly voice asked.

Pájaro eyed the light-skinned laborer whose dreadlocks obscured most of his face. "Go back with the others and wait."

"I take dis good brudda with me." The laborer walked in front of Pájaro and clapped the surveyor on the shoulder. "De spot to dig, you show us, yeah?"

"Yes." The trembling man sounded dazed. "I'll show you."

Pájaro looked into the laborer's bloodshot gray eyes,

but saw only the haze of drugs and ignorance. The reek of cannabis coming from the man turned his stomach. "Good." He tucked the razor back into his sleeve. "Make it quick."

The laborer grinned. "It will be, boss."

Gabriel emerged from the back cabin and sat across from Korvel, placing a bottle of bloodwine and two glasses on the table between them. "You've not rested since we left Marseilles."

"I can sleep when it's done." He glanced up from the financial records he was reading. "How is your lady?"

"She seems fully recovered, but I sense that something still plagues her." He filled both glasses and handed one to Korvel. "I want to know who did this to her, Captain."

The Kyn lord's wording made him frown. "You believe that one of us used talent against her?"

"I don't know what to think." Gabriel stared down at his glass. "Nicola's sensitivity to the Kyn is profound. If an enemy can use her ability as a conduit into her mind, as a means to control her, she will never be safe."

"Most Kyn don't possess abilities that allow them to exercise influence over other Kyn. Richard, Lucan, and some of the modern mortal women who were changed are the only exceptions." He thought of the reports Cyprien had sent to Richard after his initial meeting with the Kyndred in New York. "These mortals whom the Brethren meddled with are powerful, and they were engineered to be our adversaries. We know a few, like the brother of Valentin's lady, were taken and trained by the order to serve as field operatives. It could be one of them."

"It's not the Kyndred," Nicola said as she joined

them. "Whatever got in my head felt like the Kyn, but I don't think it was one of us or them. It felt strange. Older. Ancient."

Gabriel leveled a direct look at Korvel. "I want that fucking scroll destroyed."

"Baby." Nicola put a hand to her cheek. "Such language."

The attendant came out of the front cabin to inform them that they would be landing in a few minutes.

Korvel reached to switch off his laptop when he saw the new e-mail icon flashing, and accessed his in-box. The new message came from an unknown sender, but the subject line read, *Derien Estate Winter Cove Runaway Bay Jamaica.* As soon as he opened the e-mail, code began scrolling across the screen, which abruptly went blank as the computer shut down. When he restarted it, the laptop remained inert.

"Let me have a look at it." Nicola turned the laptop toward her and tapped on a few keys before she rested her hand on top of them. "You just got hit with the mother of all viruses. Your hard drive is completely fried."

Korvel told them about the strange e-mail. "Why would someone send me the exact information I needed and then destroy my computer immediately after I read it?"

"He doesn't want you to trace it back to him. Seems like someone wants to help, but doesn't want us to know who he is, where he is, or why he's doing it." Nicola went to retrieve the in-flight phone and dialed a number. "Benny? *C'est moi.* Yeah, well, I'm between countries at the moment. I need you to pull up a property listing in Jamaica."

Korvel paced the cabin as Nicola spoke to her contact, stopping only when she ended the call. "What is it?"

"Winter Cove is listed as a private residence. There's a house, a couple acres of woods, and three miles of beach." When he started to speak, she held up a hand. "One more thing. It's not the Derien estate. It's owned by a Christopher Black. I'll give you three guesses what his name is in French."

Korvel didn't have to guess. "Cristophe Noir."

Simone tucked Jamar's business card in her pocket and waved to him before she went to the security gates and input the date of her birth on the keypad. The locks grated as they disengaged and the gates opened.

She didn't stop walking toward the house until she spotted the first of five sedans parked around the fountain. Her father had never explained the arrangements he had made to safeguard his house on the island, so it was possible the cars belonged to his security guards. Only the prominent rental company stickers suggested otherwise.

Before she came within sight of the windows she circled around the house, noting the lights that shone in the kitchen and several of the second-floor rooms. She drew closer, moving behind a row of azaleas to glance inside an open window.

"You tromp like a cow, Quatorze." The man who stood just inside folded his arms. "We could hear you as soon as you stepped off the drive."

Simone stared into the twinkling brown eyes of the man inside her house. He had a Swiss accent, and his face was unfamiliar, but the eyes . . . "Seize?"

He glanced over his shoulder. "Good news. She can still count." In one fluid move he jumped through the window and landed beside her. "I have been waiting to do this for fifteen years."

Simone found herself in a tight hug. "How are you here? But you . . . I thought he—"

"Killed me?" Seize drew back. "No. Although while I was at the damned château he certainly made me wish I was dead." He took her hand. "Come inside. The others are waiting."

"Others?" she echoed weakly as she followed him to the back door.

"Not all of us could come," he admitted. "Dix's wife is ready to give birth any second, and Trente broke his leg last month on the slopes. I told him slalom skiing is only for the mentally ill, but does he listen to me? No."

She understood when she stepped inside and saw the seven men sitting around a table piled with weapons. One who was covered in tattoos and wore his white-blond hair spiked pitched a throwing blade at her, which she caught reflexively before she spotted the crescent scar dividing his right eyebrow. "Vingt?"

The Dutchman grinned. "I told you she wouldn't forget the important things. Fuck, you grew up gorgeous, too."

Simone handed the blade to Seize before she went to Vingt. His grin faded as he looked up at her face.

"I'm not a ghost, beautiful," he said gently. "Stop looking at me like I am."

"I thought you were . . ." She stopped and reached out, almost touching the scar above his eye before pressing her hand to her mouth. She looked at all the faces around her, every one invoking memories she had tried so hard to bury deep. Overwhelmed, she started shaking her head. "No. Not all of you. I thought . . . He made me think . . ."

"We're real." Vingt stood and folded her into his arms. "Now don't faint," he murmured, "or everyone will think you're a girl."

That made her laugh instead of weep. "I *am* a girl."

"Yeah, but you're not a pussy." To the man standing by the stove, he said, "Told you she'd be a goddess, Quarante. You owe me twenty."

The burly man arranging cups on the counter sniffed. "Then you'll have to make your own damn tea, Metal Head."

"Quiet." The oldest man among them, a tall, dignified Belgian with the beginnings of silver showing at his temples, slapped Vingt in the back of the head before he stood and came to her. "You need a haircut, little sister."

"Cinq." Of all the boys she had trained with, only he had come close to defeating her in the sparring room. He had also been her best friend and closest confidant. Once more she scanned the faces of the other men. "How did you know I would be here? Why are you here?"

"We all received the same message: 'The frost has ended, and so the harvest must begin,'" Cinq said. "Your father made us promise that when it did, we would gather here."

"I was in the middle of an American tour when the telegram arrived," Vingt grumbled. "I thought my manager would have a fucking stroke."

"My wedding is in three weeks," Seize told him. "Assuming my fiancée hasn't called it off by now."

"Oh, stop whining," Quarante said as he went over to turn off the whistling teakettle. "I had to quit my job. How many companies do you know that are hiring aerodynamic engineers?"

Simone's head began to whirl. "But all these years— why didn't any of you come back? Why didn't you let me know you were alive?"

"The old bastard sent us off to boarding schools,"

Vingt told her. "Of course, after spending a year at the château having my ass kicked by you, little girl, it felt like an extended vacation."

Seize touched her shoulder. "We all remained friends over the years, but your father made each of us promise never to return to France in order to see you or contact you. He said if we tried, he would kill us."

Cinq nodded at her wide-eyed look. "In return for our promise to stay away, he paid for all of us to go to university and set us up with new lives." His mouth curled. "Believe it or not, I'm an investment banker."

"I play lead guitar for Icepick," Vingt put in. "I brought a copy of our latest album for you."

"Don't listen to it." Quarante brought her a cup of tea. "Unless you want go deaf in one sitting. It's heavy metal."

"I think sitting is a good idea." Cinq ushered her over to the table, where Simone sat down and numbly sipped the hot, sweet tea. "What did he tell you about us?"

"Nothing. After we fought in the trials, he had me beaten and locked me up. The next day you were gone." She looked at each man's face. "I thought he had killed you because I wouldn't."

"Derien's dead, isn't he? That's why we received the summons. Why you came in his place." When she nodded, Vingt released a long breath. "Fuck me. Now I have to go back to church."

"What have you been doing all these years, Quatorze?" Cinq asked. "Surely not still training."

"My father died ten years ago," she said. "Since his death I have been working as a housemaid in a convent."

Vingt looked horrified. "Oh, when this is over you are *definitely* coming back to America with me."

Simone smiled at him before she looked at Cinq. "Why did my father make you promise to come here?"

"We're here because we belong to you, Quatorze," he said. "We're your garrison."

At that moment four men came into the kitchen, led by a massive German with a bald head and a black goatee.

Simone recognized him by the lobe missing from his left ear. "Neuf."

"Look who is all grown-up now." He bent to give her a quick affectionate hug before he spoke to Cinq. "Some men are down on the beach. A Spaniard with a bad temper has them digging. He's calling himself Helada, but his voice reminds me of that little bastard Pájaro. You remember, the one who tried to hurt Quatorze before he ran away from the château."

"Huh. The old man always said the cowardly shit drowned himself." Vingt picked up a blade from the table and tested the edge before he patted Simone's hand. "Don't worry, sweetheart. I'll take him for another swim."

"I'm afraid this is my fight, brother." She examined the weapons on the table before she selected two fighting knives. "There will be others coming," she told the men. "I need you in three squads to form a perimeter around the dig. Stay out of sight, keep watch, and don't let anyone interfere. Seize, Neuf, Vingt, you will lead the squads. Cinq, you're to shadow me."

"I never thought I'd get the chance to see you fight again." Vingt grinned as he stood. "This is going to be fucking amazing."

The men dispersed from the kitchen, leaving Cinq and Simone alone.

"I am glad your father is dead," he said quietly. "What he did to you was unforgivable."

"Allowing me to believe that all of you were dead was the worst of it. But now . . . I don't know what to think." Simone carried her cup over to the sink. "I fought the handlers all night after your trial, Cinq. They finally had to drug me to take me down."

"You thought I was dead," he suggested. "You needed to mourn."

"I wanted to die with you." She leaned back against the counter. "I wouldn't go back to training after he took you away. I wouldn't eat or even get out of bed. So to persuade me to return to training, my father began bringing the boys to my room and having them beaten in front of me. That was how Neuf lost this." She touched her left earlobe. "The handler's whip severed it."

"He never speaks of it," Cinq said. "But I know he doesn't blame you for it. None of us do. We all carry scars of the past, but now most of us are quite happy."

"How can you be, after what my father did to you?"

"We chose to be, sister," Cinq said gently. "When I'm not shuffling funds for my clients, my wife and I grow roses. Vingt likes to scream at crowded arenas and chase skirts all over the world. Neuf is a pediatrician in Hamburg." He nodded at the startled look she gave him. "Oh, yes. I've visited his clinic. His little patients adore him."

Simone couldn't forgive her father for the heartless brutality he had inflicted, but knowing what he had done for her brothers made the burden of his legacy a little easier for her to bear. At least they had normal lives. "I'm glad you've given up fighting."

"We haven't." His expression grew wry. "We maintain our own workout routines at home, but all of us meet twice a year to train together as a garrison."

"You're not a garrison. You're my family." She pressed

her lips together and blinked. "I can't believe you're all still alive. I've missed you so much."

He came over and put his arm around her shoulders. "Now you should tell me the rest."

"Pájaro stole the Scroll of Falkonera from my father's château." She gave him a brief description of the events that had led to her coming to Jamaica before she added, "He had the scroll in his possession until he left France yesterday. I think he must have handled it several times."

Cinq, who had witnessed what had happened to one of the handlers who had tried to steal the scroll, shook his head. "You don't have to fight him, Quatorze. From what Neuf described, he's already dying."

"I'm not here to fight Pájaro." She turned and sorted through one of the drawers until she produced a pair of scissors. "I came just as you did. Because in exchange for my freedom, I swore that I would."

"I know we are here to defend you," Cinq said. "What did he demand of you?"

"I promised him that Helada would never die," she said as she handed him the scissors. "Now, if you would, brother, please cut off my hair."

Chapter 20

Korvel got out of the car and walked up to the gates of Winter Cove. He could smell Simone in the air everywhere here, as if the tropics had made her bloom. He tried the intercom first, and then opened the gates by wrenching them apart and pushing them aside.

"She's close," Nicola told him when he got back into the car. "So are a bunch of other humans, and something that feels like the scroll."

"You are not to touch anything," Gabriel told her. "In fact, you are to stay in the car. With the doors locked."

"In case you forgot"—she turned around and braced her arms on the top of the seat—"you need me to find her. No, Captain," she said to Korvel. "Not the house. Other way. She's near the water."

Korvel drove as far as he could in the car, and then stopped it when they reached an impassible grove of palm trees interlaced with enormous backlit cobwebs. Beyond the glinting threads he could see shadows moving and torches burning.

Nicola leaned forward. "Holy cow. Some of those webs are like ten feet tall."

"You should remain in the car," Korvel said as he and Gabriel got out. "My lord, I will scout ahead."

"We work together, Captain." Gabriel eyed his *sygkenis* as she joined them. "What happened to your aversion to spiders?"

"I got over it. Plus, three Kyn are better than two, baby." She focused on the area ahead of them. "About thirty guys are hiding in the trees and the brush. There's another group of humans headed our way, maybe a dozen, but they won't be here for a while. They're on foot, about four miles west."

Korvel assessed their options. "We'll have to go around."

"Wait." Gabriel's eyes began to glow. "I can clear out the mortals in the grove."

"And who's going to help you do that?" Nicola eyed the webs overhead. "The spiders?"

"No." He smiled a little. "The sand fleas."

Korvel watched as the speck-size insects began hopping up through the grass toward the hidden men. "They are harmless."

"Yeah, but their bites itch like a bad Brazilian wax," Nicola told him.

Within a few seconds men began dancing in and out of the trees, scratching at their arms and legs. Korvel advanced along with Gabriel as the Kyn lord created an open corridor through the swarming fleas, and made it through the grove unscathed.

Down on the beach a woman walked toward the deep pit that had been excavated in the sand. At first Korvel didn't recognize her with her hair shorn so close to her scalp, but as she stepped into the torchlight he saw the serene, pale features and the tilt of her eyes.

"Simone."

Gabriel caught his arm as Korvel surged forward. "The men are coming out of the grove. They are heavily armed, and they are surrounding her."

"I will go to defend her back," he told Gabriel. "Will you and your lady flank me?"

"Um, I think that's what they're doing, big guy." Nicola nodded toward the beach. "Look."

The men who came up around and behind Simone fell into formation, daggers ready. As for his lady, she drew two fighting knives as she strode forward toward the pit.

"Please," a frightened voice called from inside. "My legs are broken. Don't hurt me."

Machine-gun fire erupted as a front-loader came roaring out of the brush, Pájaro with one hand on the controls and the other firing on Simone and her defenders. As the men were cut down, Simone dived into the pit.

Korvel started running as soon as he heard the first shot, but something came flipping through the air and slammed into his knees, throwing him to the ground.

As he struggled to his feet, Korvel saw Pájaro lower the front-loader's shovel and push the pile of excavated sand back into the pit, burying Simone and the man inside.

The roar of outrage rising inside Korvel never made it past his lips; something came over him and held him, trapping him in his own body like an insect caught in amber. As Gabriel and Nicola appeared beside them, they also stopped moving.

You must not interfere.

Korvel saw a distorted shadow step between him and the beach, and sensed that the power paralyzing him was coming from it. He fought wildly to free himself so he could attack, but while he could think, his body had been turned into stone. *Release me.*

In due time. As the shadow moved closer, the presence in Korvel's mind picked through his thoughts until it retrieved a memory of his mother shrieking at him. *Your sire was not among the men who took her, warrior. She gave herself willingly to another slave.*

Korvel saw a memory not his own: that of his mother in rags, coupling with a large, naked, fair-haired man. Both wore slave collars. *I don't care what that bitch did. Get out of my head.*

So that you may go to your woman and rescue her again? A rusty chuckle echoed inside his skull. *I cannot permit that. This time she must save herself.*

Simone is mortal. He buried her alive. She will die.

Yes, warrior, she will, the ancient voice agreed, and the shadowy figure retreated into the woods. *She must.*

Simone barely had an instant to hold her breath and close her eyes as the mountain of wet sand fell atop her, pushing her facedown deep into the pit. Beneath her she felt the feeble shifting of the wounded man, and tried to work her hand down to reach for him, but he was buried too far below her. Her other hand was pinned in front of her face, and she turned her arm back and forth, loosening the sand around her face.

Have to get to the air before I smother.

Once she had made a small pocket, she jabbed her elbow backward, pounding it into the sand over her. Repeating the motion over and over shifted enough of the layer atop her to allow her to turn her body, until at last she liberated an arm and used it to pull her head and shoulders free.

She coughed and spit sand before she could drag in the

first cool, sweet breath, cut short by a dousing of warm seawater over her head. Although it choked her, it also washed the sand from her face and allowed her to open her eyes. She blinked away the blurriness and the sting as she focused on the swaying form standing over her.

"You should be dead," Pájaro ranted, his voice thick with phlegm. "Did Lechance tell you? Did he give you the antidote? Is that why you're still alive?"

Simone saw how badly he was shaking. "I don't know what you mean."

"You don't? Then what is this?" He pulled at his hair, which came off his scalp in a clump, and threw it at her face. Blood trickled from his nose and ears as he coughed and spit bright red sputum onto the sand. "What did you do to me?"

"My father told you," she reminded him. "Never touch the scroll."

"Lying bitch." Pájaro lifted a heavy, sand-encrusted object, and Simone saw a tiny glitter of green just before he clouted her with it. Through the roar of pain she heard him shout, "Where are the emeralds? What did you do with them?"

Simone grimly held on to consciousness as warm wetness seeped down the side of her face. She looked at the cross in his fist and saw the gold shining plainly through the sand, but that was all. The three large ovals that formed a triangle in the center of the cross held nothing but sand. The jewels that had once adorned the cross had been removed, probably before it had been buried. Since Simone knew it was the emeralds that bestowed immortality, the cross was useless.

Cristophe, it seemed, had trusted no one. Not even his own kin.

She had kept the bargain she had made with her father without sacrificing her own humanity. That should have made death seem like a blessing, but she didn't want to die now. She wanted to be with Korvel. A strange green darkness crowded in on her vision, making her wonder whether she would pass out before he killed her. "I don't know where the emeralds are, Pájaro."

"You have to know." He coughed into his fist, which came away red and wet. "He told you everything. Tell me or I'll crush your skull like an empty egg."

"The emeralds are gone. It's over." She looked up at him, at the death blow he was prepared to deliver, and summoned an image of the last thing she wanted to see on this earth: Korvel smiling at her.

"You little bastard."

Out of the corner of her eye Simone saw Neuf push himself up from the sand. He threw a dagger at Pájaro's hand, piercing the palm and making him drop the cross.

"Never could fight fair." That was Vingt, somewhere behind her, and Simone saw his blade bury itself in Pájaro's crotch. "Fucking cowardly shit."

As Pájaro dropped to the sand, clapping his hands to his groin and screeching, Cinq appeared beside the pit. Bullet holes riddled his shirt, and through them Simone caught a glimpse of the bullets lodged in the protective vest he wore underneath.

"Cinq."

"I told you, little sister. We don't take any chances." He walked over to Pájaro, who lay in a ball, and reached down, grasping the front of his priest's cassock as he pulled the blade out of his groin.

"I have to find the emeralds," Pájaro groaned, and two teeth fell out of his mouth. "I am Helada. I have earned immortality."

Cinq crouched down over him and said over his babbling, "You don't even deserve this, you murdering scum."

Through the shadowy green haze clouding her eyes Simone saw Cinq drive Vingt's knife into Pájaro's thigh, severing the femoral artery and causing a gush of blood to soak into the sand. As Vingt and Seize began to pull her out of the pit, Pájaro's voice grew weak and then fell silent.

And then it was over, and she was free.

"Just like a girl to lie around on the beach while the men do all the work," Vingt said as he supported her with one of his tattooed arms.

Seize gently touched her scalp. "Neuf, she's bleeding a lot."

The big German joined them and checked the wound. "She'll need sutures for this. My bag is back at the house, but we should take her to hospital and have X-rays taken."

"That won't be necessary," a deep, beloved voice said as a tall man walked toward them. "She has a hard head, or so I've been told."

"Who the fuck are you?" Vingt demanded.

"Korvel." Simone stumbled away from her brothers and into his arms, holding on to him with tight hands. "Oh, God. I never thought I'd see you again." Her knees buckled. "I'm going to fall down now."

"I think not." He swung her up into his arms. "But perhaps you should tell your brothers who I am before they draw the wrong conclusions."

Simone looked at Cinq. "This is Korvel. He's the man I love. I haven't told him that yet, but now he knows. Oh, and he calls me Simone."

"Does he know you work in a convent?" Vingt asked.

The darkness crowding in on her was not like any she

had ever known, and suddenly Simone understood what was happening to her.

"He knows." Her eyelids wanted to close, but she refused to stop looking at him. "He's taking me back to Ireland with him."

"Tonight," Korvel promised.

As Gabriel and Nicola appeared at the edge of the sand, Korvel regarded the oldest of the men, the one Simone had called Cinq. "My friends and I will take her back to the house. There are men moving in from the west. Can you deal with them?"

He nodded. "Neuf will meet you there. He's a physician." He picked up the cross. "What should we do with this thing?"

"I don't care," Korvel said. "Whatever you like. Toss it in the ocean."

"No," Nicola said, and walked down to the edge of the pit. "Bury it again. Bury it deep."

Cinq nodded, and turned to speak to his men. Korvel carried Simone, who was drifting in and out of consciousness, up to the car, and held her as Nicola drove back to the house.

"Did either of you recognize the Kyn who turned us into spectators?" Nicola asked.

Gabriel exchanged a look with Korvel before he said, "It was not Kyn."

She nodded. "Told you so, told you so. Now that we've established that I'm not losing it and that there is something out there that can get into our heads and control us, anyone want to guess what it is?"

"I have seen the high lord enrapture a thousand mortals using but a few words," Korvel said. "Evidently this being can do the same to us with only a thought."

"It reminded me of Richard as well," Gabriel said. "The strangeness of his animal side. The nonhuman ways in which he behaves."

Nicola nodded. "That's it. Mortal or otherwise, that thing is not all human. Could it be some kind of severely fucked-up version of Richard?"

"I don't know," Gabriel said. "Captain, you have more experience with changed Kyn. What is your opinion?"

"If it is a changeling, it is unlike any I have ever encountered." Korvel glanced down at the pale face of the woman in his arms. "Whatever it is, it wanted Simone to die. If I ever find it, I will *end* it."

The big German with the goatee stood waiting for them at the door to the house, and led them into a sitting room. As Korvel gently placed Simone on a chaise longue by the windows, Nicola and Gabriel left to check the rest of the house.

Neuf opened the leather case he had carried in and took out pads, which he placed over the wound. "Hold these in place for me," he said to Korvel. "Keep steady pressure; it will help slow the bleeding. How did you become involved with our sister?"

"I met her during a trip to France," Korvel said. "I'm a businessman from England."

"Then I am the new chancellor of Germany." Neuf spared him a glance. "You move like one of us, but you are not. You are stronger, faster. That you smell like a pretty flower also troubles me, for obvious reasons."

He suppressed a smile. "Most men don't care for my cologne."

"We are not most men," the German said as he prepared a suture needle. "We are her garrison. And if that swine Derien sent you to meddle with her, I will introduce you to your entrails."

That Neuf considered himself and his companions Simone's garrison—a term rarely used by the modern world, even among its many militaries—puzzled Korvel. "I thought her father trained you and the others to serve him."

"We took the oath he demanded, but it was to serve Quatorze. I often wondered why, until my final year of residency, when he came to me in Hamburg. He had me diagnose his blood disease. You can remove the pad now." Neuf soaked some gauze with antiseptic and gently cleaned Simone's wound. "Derien would never admit it, but he must have known he was unworthy. If he hadn't, he would never have taken her from her mother, or used us to train her. He made sure that she never lost a battle, so that she would be judged worthy."

"Worthy of what?" Korvel caressed her cheek. "Why did she come to this place? She wanted nothing from her father. She turned her back on everything he might have given her."

"Not exactly." Neuf began to sew the edges of the wound closed. "Derien knew that above all she wanted to live with the sisters. It was his way to dangle our heart's desires as an incentive to get what he wanted out of us. She was no different."

Korvel still didn't understand. As the German tied off the last suture, he asked, "What did her father want from her? He must have known she would never become an assassin."

"He wanted me to be Helada," Simone murmured. Her eyes fluttered open and she shifted her gaze from Neuf to Korvel. "I agreed that when his death was discovered, I would come here and use the Trinity cross to become an immortal, so that I could spend the rest of eternity guarding it." She sighed. "I promised my father that Helada would never die."

"A cross cannot make you immortal, love," Korvel said gently. "Much as I wish it could."

Her lips curved. "You would want me to live forever?"

"You said I was the man you love," he reminded her. "What I know is, I never want to be parted from you again."

"Don't say that. I'm mortal, and someday death will part us. When it does, you have to go on. You have to live for both of us." She sounded desperate. "Promise me you will, Korvel."

"I promise, love."

She started to say something, but Neuf interrupted with, "You may badger him later, Quatorze. For now you must rest. I am going to give you something for the pain." He took out a syringe, uncapping it and tapping the side with his finger before he prepared to inject her.

With a startlingly quick move, Simone seized his wrist. "No drugs, brother. Please."

"Very well." He put the needle aside.

She relaxed and closed her eyes. "I'm sorry I keep leaving you, Captain. I wish I could . . ."

"I'll be right here when you wake up, my angel." He kissed her brow, which felt cooler than his own flesh. "She needs a blanket."

Neuf frowned and rested a palm on her forehead, and then checked her pulse. "Quatorze, why don't you tell me about the convent. What were the sisters like?"

Simone didn't respond, even when Neuf patted her cheek.

"Let her sleep," Korvel suggested. "She is exhausted."

"No, she's not," Neuf said. "Her body temperature is dropping and her pulse is weak. She's going into shock."

Nicola and Gabriel came into the sitting room, followed by a petite woman with her chestnut curls caught back in a ponytail.

"Okay, so I'm here. Where's the patient?" Dr. Alexandra Keller stopped as soon as she saw Korvel. "Christ. *You're* the reason Richard had me fly through the freaking Bermuda Triangle?"

"I cannot say, my lady." Korvel turned his back on her to watch Neuf work on Simone. "I no longer serve the high lord."

"You no longer . . . Wait." She held up her hands. "Don't tell me; I don't want to know." She turned to Nicola. "Can you give me a ride back to the airport? I need to fly to Ireland to kick me some furry immortal ass."

"Scheiße." Neuf drew back from Simone as the wound in her head began to glow with a faint green light. "What is this?"

Alexandra nudged him aside. "Korvel, you want to tell me why this girl is looking like a Lite-Brite?"

"She was struck with a Kyn artifact. A cross." Korvel held Simone's hand tightly between his. "It must have transferred something into the wound."

As abruptly as it began the glow faded, and Simone began to convulse.

Alexandra held her head as she began issuing orders. "Nick, bring me my bag. Gabriel, call the airport and tell my pilot to keep the jet engines running." To Simone she said, "It's okay, honey. Hold on."

The convulsions abruptly stopped, and Simone went limp.

As soon as Nick brought the bag, Alexandra reached in and took out a pair of suture scissors. "Did you clean out the wound before you stitched her up?" she asked Neuf.

"I did, thoroughly." He frowned as she cut through the sutures and deftly plucked them out of Simone's scalp. "What are you doing? She's lost too much blood already."

"She's not bleeding," Alexandra snapped. "Look at the wound. It's been cauterized." She leaned close. "From the inside."

Korvel watched as Alexandra checked Simone's pulse and used her stethoscope to listen to her heart and lungs. Once she had completed the physical assessment, she put her nose next to the wound and breathed in deeply, closing her eyes for several seconds before she straightened.

"All right, folks," she said. "I need to know exactly what happened to this girl. Somebody start talking."

"I will tell you everything I know," Korvel promised. "Only answer me this: Is she making the change from mortal to Kyn?"

"No, Captain." Something like pity came into Alexandra's eyes. "She's not changing into anything. Her organs are beginning to fail. She's dying."

Nick sent Gabriel to the upstairs bedroom where Alexandra had Korvel carry Simone. "I'll look after the humans. If you need anything, just yell."

"Will you tell them?" When she nodded, he kissed her. "I love you."

"Back at you, baby." She walked back to the sitting room, now packed with all of the men Simone had called her brothers. "Hey."

The Dutchman with the foul mouth and the tattoos stopped whirling the knife in his hand. "Is she awake?"

"No." Nick shoved her hands in her pockets. "Alex—Dr. Keller—is with her, and she's making her as comfortable as possible. I need to, uh, talk to you guys about the situation."

"We know the situation," Tattoo Guy snarled. "She's fucked all to hell. What are you doing about it? Why are you keeping her here when she could be in a hospital?"

The oldest man, the one Simone called Cinq, stepped forward and put a hand on Vingt's shoulder. "She's not going to wake up again, is she?"

There was no kind way to do this, so Nick went with direct. "Your sister is in a coma. Someone poisoned her, probably before she left France."

The man with the laughing brown eyes looked ready to kill something. "Pájaro did this." He glanced at Cinq. "You heard what he said on the beach." He turned back to Nick. "What about an antidote?"

"She's too far gone for that now." She looked at the faces all around her. "The truth is, she's not going to make it through the night. I'm so sorry, guys."

"You're sorry? That's it? We should have taken her to a real doctor. You *let* her die, you fucking snow-haired bitch." Vingt lunged at her, coming up short when Cinq grabbed him from behind. "Let go of me. Let . . . go . . ." He sagged, and covered his face with his hands.

Cinq turned him around and held on to him. Over the spiked blond head he said, "Thank you for telling us."

"If you guys want to start going up to say good-bye to her," she said, "Alex said it'd be okay."

Sensing that they needed a little privacy, Nick went to the kitchen. There she found the big German brewing tea. "Got any wine?"

"In the fridge. There's a case of some piss water the locals call beer, too." He carried a cup of tea to the table and pulled out a chair.

Nick grabbed a bottle that had already been opened

and an empty mug off the counter, and sat down with him. "Alex fill you in on what's happening upstairs?"

"She did." He stirred a spoonful of honey into his tea. "I should have realized what was happening. I have dealt with some accidental poisonings among children. The head wound distracted me."

"There was nothing you could have done for her." She uncorked the bottle, filled the mug halfway, and took a sip, grimacing at the undiluted taste of it.

"Here." Neuf took out a penknife and began to roll up his sleeve.

"I'm good." Nick watched him pull her mug across the table before he made a small incision in his wrist. "What are you doing?"

"Making your drink more palatable." As he held his dripping wrist over her mug, he gave her a wry look. "If the green-eyed man were not with you I would permit you to bite me, but I think he would object to finding us having sex on the kitchen floor."

She didn't know whether to laugh or slap him. "Maybe I'm not that easy."

"Well, I am." He handed her the mug before he pressed a napkin to the wrist wound. "We know what you and your friends are, lady, and you can trust us."

"I'd rather do that than brain-wipe you." She toasted him with the mug before she sipped the mixture of blood and wine. "Thanks for the donation."

"My pleasure." He sampled his tea. "You want to know why Simone and the rest of us came here."

She moved a shoulder. "Would be nice to fill in the blanks."

"We were trying to protect a cross that Simone's ancestor buried on this island a very long time ago," he said. "It was said to contain three flawless, priceless jewels set in the gold. Her father called them the Emeralds of Eternity. It's the gems themselves that are said to bestow immortal life, but I don't know precisely how. Only Helada is entrusted with that secret."

"Explain something to me: Why do they always name priceless treasure something like that?" Nick asked. "I mean, if you want to keep them safe, why not call them the Worthless Fakes or Three Big Hunks of Cheap Glass? The Emeralds of Eternity. Please." She made a rude sound.

"I wish we had found them." He looked up at the ceiling. "They might have saved her life."

"Emeralds don't do anything but look great on red-haired chicks, my man. Doesn't matter what you call them." Nick heard a crashing sound from upstairs, as if large pieces of furniture were being thrown against walls. "What's the German word for *shit?*"

Neuf got to his feet. *"Scheiße."*

"Stay here and keep your brothers out of the way." Nick ran upstairs to the bedroom door, ducking as part of a chair came flying through it.

"Korvel, calm down." That was Alexandra, and she sounded pissed.

Nick stepped inside and saw her lover and the captain grappling on the floor. Gabriel came up on top, but not for long. Korvel threw him aside, rolling to his feet and going to the bed, where he picked up Alex's case and shoved it in her hands.

"Do it, Alexandra," he said. "It will save her. Do it, you heartless bitch, or I swear I'll make you suffer."

"Take your best shot." Alex dropped the case on the bed and folded her arms. "Because I'm not doing it."

"Whoa. Time-out." Nick stepped into the room and helped Gabriel up from the floor. "Alex?"

"He wants me to inject her with my blood. Because Lucan used my blood to change Sam, the idiot thinks it will save this girl." Her expression turned murderous. "But as I've explained to him—twice now—she's not Kyndred. She's a normal, garden-variety human. The minute I inject her, my blood will attack hers, eat it, and kill her."

"You don't know that," Korvel bellowed.

"Okay, okay." Nick stepped between them and pointed a finger at Korvel. "You. Stop tearing the place apart." She turned to Alex. "Simone is dying. There's no hope. No coming back from this. Are you sure about this?"

"She'll be dead in an hour," Alex said through her teeth.

"So inject her with your blood." As Alex glared at her, she added, "If you're right, it won't make any difference."

"Yes, it will, Nick. It'll make a difference to me. I'll be murdering her." She took a deep breath and released it. "I'm a doctor. We take an oath to do no harm. I can't inject her with toxic blood."

"Can't, or won't?" Nick studied her face. "What if Korvel's right, and she changes? You'll save her."

"You had the change forced on you," Alex reminded her. "You want to go thank Elizabeth for it? Oh, wait, I remember now. She's dead. You had Richard kill her for doing this to you."

"You finished?" Nick asked. When Alex looked away, she said, "Don't use me and my shit to justify yours. My guess is you don't want to inject her because you're afraid it *will* work. If that happens, and the vampire king finds out? Your ass *and* your blood will be his."

"Alexandra, we swear never to tell," Gabriel said. "All of us."

Korvel nodded. "I will take Simone away with me. Richard will never know."

"Like I'd throw you under the bus, Alex," Nick said.

Alex walked up to Korvel. "If she lives, are you planning to bond with her? Make her your *sygkenis?* After everything you did to separate me from Michael, why should I hand her over to you?"

"If you don't want me to have her, then you can take her back to America with you." He looked past her at Simone. "You can tell her I'm dead, or whatever you like. I will never try to see her again. Only save her, Alexandra. Please."

Alex picked up the syringe, stabbing it into her arm and filling it with her blood. "This should go to work within a few minutes. Gabriel, I assume you know the difference between a human beginning the transition to Kyn and one who dies from Kyn blood poisoning."

"I have witnessed both many times, Doctor," he said.

She went to sit on the side of the bed by Simone and prepare her arm for the injection. "After I do this, I'm leaving. I don't want to know what happens to this girl. Ever." She slid the needle in and pressed the plunger down slowly.

When it was done, Alex stood and gathered up her things, stuffing them in the case.

As Alex passed her, Nick touched her arm. "Thank you for giving her a chance."

"Is that what I did?" She stalked out of the room.

Korvel took Alex's place beside Simone and focused on her face, while Nick joined Gabriel at the foot of the bed.

She curled her hand around his. "Alex was right. I couldn't ever thank Elizabeth for what she did. She murdered my parents."

He tucked her against his side. "Alex spoke without thinking."

"If it had been different, if she changed only me, and somehow I still found you, then maybe I could thank her." She squeezed his hand. "After I kicked her ass."

As Alex had predicted, it took only a few minutes, and in that time Korvel must have realized what was happening, because he climbed onto the bed and held Simone against him, his cheek resting against her short hair. Nick glanced at Gabriel, who shook his head.

And then the woman who had never lost a battle finally stopped fighting.

Chapter 21

O nly one ferry from the Scottish mainland sailed to Í Árd, and only when it was summoned by radio from the medieval villa that no one knew had been transported from Italy brick by brick to the supposedly uninhabited island. A month seldom passed without the ferryboat captain making at least one trip, but on this night his instructions were to stay away. And so he went to his favorite pub to have a drink with the lads and talk about anything but his work.

Within the center courtyard of the villa a hundred men stood in facing ranks, their battle armor polished like glass, their swords drawn and held aloft, the tips touching those across from them to form a steel canopy. Richard's black-and-gold standard had been raised, but another fluttered beside it, one Korvel had not seen since childhood, when his grandfather had carried it into battle.

Silver larkspur against a green field, the long-lost emblem of the house of Korvel. The symbol of everything he had once believed important, and noble, and good.

He walked through the ranks, holding Simone's body so that his steps did not jar her, the fluttering white silk of her skirts caressing his arm. When he reached the gardens in the courtyard's center, he saw the high pyre of carefully stacked wood. Someone, probably Richard's *tresora* Éliane, had placed hundreds of white blooms atop the wood. On this bed of roses he placed the body of the woman he had not saved, and as the flowers' fragrance enveloped them, he bowed his head to kiss her still, cold lips.

"If there is a heaven, I know you are there," he whispered to her as a circle of guards bearing torches marched in formation to surround the pyre. "Surely God recognizes an angel when he sees one. I did."

"Captain."

"I have served you for seven lifetimes, my lord." He didn't look at Richard. "You can give me a few moments with her."

"As you will." His master made a gesture, and the men drew back.

He turned back to Simone, resting his hand on the silk head rail covering her shorn hair. "I know I gave you my word that I would go on and live for us both. But you were wrong about me, love. When I have to be, I am a most convincing liar."

A drop of rain fell, landing to bead on the curve of her lip, and then another trickled down from her brow to the corner of her eye. Korvel reached to wipe them away, and only then did he feel the sting in his eyes and realize they were not rain at all.

He had not wept since his mortal life, and he brought her hand to his face so she could feel this last miracle.

"Korvel." The high lord's voice, which he could use as an instrument of pleasure or a weapon of pain, grew curiously gentle. "You must come away from there now."

Suddenly everything became simple. He stepped

down and took the torch from Stefan. "It seems that I will be breaking faith with you again, my lord. It will be for the last time. Forgive me."

Richard seized his wrist. "You are not thinking clearly. She would not want you to do this."

"For once the vampire king's right, Captain." Nicola walked up to the pyre. "I can guarantee you she wouldn't want this."

"You should understand better than anyone." Korvel glanced at Richard before he lowered his voice. "You know what it is to have no more reason to live."

"Maybe I did." She eyed Gabriel, who came to stand beside her. "But not anymore."

Looking at them, knowing they had everything that he had lost, proved too much for Korvel. "Let me go, my lady. I only want to be with her."

"Oh, for God's sake." As he turned to the pyre, Nicola plucked the torch from his hand and tossed it away. "I'm not letting you do this. Friends don't let friends set themselves on fire." She turned to Gabriel. "Can't you order him not to do this?"

"He has not yet made an oath to me."

"Details." She made a dismissive gesture. "You said you wanted to hang with us, Captain. I'm holding you to that." She cringed and held the sides of her head. "Oh, shit, not again."

Everyone in the courtyard went still, including Korvel, who didn't try to resist. *She's dead. You can kill me now, too.*

On the other side of the pyre a shadow shifted. *I never harmed her, warrior. It was your intrusion that caused this. But it is done, and she was not the last.*

Korvel saw Nicola walk up to the pyre and pull the head rail from Simone's body. *What are you doing?*

See with your heart instead of your eyes, Korvel, and perhaps you will find an answer.

Furious voices shouted from the ranks of the men as they regained control of their bodies. Gabriel went to Nicola, who was standing and staring at the pyre, while Richard strode around it, looking at the shadows.

"Silence," the high lord snapped, and his powerful voice rendered everyone mute. "I will know the cause of this." He eyed Korvel. "What was that thing in my head?"

"I cannot say, my lord." Korvel took the head rail from Nicola's hand and carried it back to Simone's body. "But I do wish you luck with it."

Nicola finally moved. "Captain, you heard him. Look at her with your heart."

Korvel didn't want to look at anything but her. In death she had the peace that she had never known in life. He brushed her hair back from her brow, lifting the head rail to drape it back in place. The fabric slipped from his fingers as he touched the top of her head and drew the hair back down over her brow.

The hair that she had cut off two days before had grown six inches.

The sound of Nicola arguing with his master made him look over at them.

"What has any of this to do with your ability?" Richard demanded.

"I can always tell how many humans and vampires are in one place. Dead or alive." She flicked a hand at Éliane. "I'm telling you, the only human on this island is your honey over there." She came over and climbed the pyre.

He caught her arm. "What are you doing?"

"Ruining the bonfire party." She bit into her forearm and then held the open wound to Simone's lips.

Korvel stared. "You can't revive her, Nick. She's dead."

"No, she's not." Nicola grinned and took away her arm as Simone's eyes opened. "Hey, girlfriend. Welcome back to the land of the never-dying."

Simone touched her mouth, and then looked all around her. "I'm alive?"

"Yes, and you're going to stay that way. For a very, very long time." As Simone sat up, Nicola put an arm around her and helped her down from the pyre. "Easy, sister. You're still weak."

Rose petals floated down onto Korvel's shoulders and chest, but he could not move, or blink, or breathe. "Simone?"

She nodded, pulling away from Nicola as she came to him, her steps unsteady but her gaze unwavering. "I could hear you, but I couldn't move." She touched her mouth. "I'm Kyn now. How can that be?"

"You're alive." His hands shook as he reached for her, pulling her against him, wrapping his arms around her. "That is all that has to be."

Richard joined them, studying Simone before he spoke to Nicola. "There was no spark of life left in her body when Korvel brought her to the island. We would have felt it. How did this happen?"

"Sorry, I'm the thief." Nicola looked past him. "You'll have to ask the doctor."

As if on cue, Alexandra Keller came into the garden. She carried a medical case and looked highly annoyed. "I hate Ireland. I hate planes. I had to haul a drunk ferryboat captain out of a pub to get here. He almost took me to Greenland." She finally saw whom Korvel had in his arms. "So this is how you keep your promises?"

"You were right, Doctor," Korvel said. "She died

of . . . the poisoning." He looked down at Simone. "But she has become Kyn."

"We need a room," Alexandra said to Richard. "And a lot less audience."

Korvel carried Simone inside the castle and to his chambers. Once there, Alexandra chased out everyone, including Richard.

"I know this girl is not Kyndred, Alexandra," the high lord warned. "I want to know what caused this to happen."

"Absolutely. I'll get right on that." She shut the door in his face and bolted it. "Nosy jackass."

Korvel glanced at her. "He can hear you through the door."

"Why do you think I said it?" The doctor came over to the bed where Korvel had placed Simone, and set her case on the lamp table beside it. "Since no one has bothered to ask, how are you feeling?"

"I don't know," Simone admitted. "A little tired. Hungry. Mostly confused."

"That's par for the course." Alexandra took out her stethoscope and used it to listen to her heart, then wrapped a blood pressure cuff around her right arm. "Korvel, how long did it take for her to die after I injected her?"

"Only a few minutes, just as you said." He couldn't stop looking at Simone. "Alexandra, what are you doing here?"

"Last night this voice got inside my head and said I had to come here." She pulled the stethoscope from her ears. "When I told it to go to hell, it took over my body. Next thing I know, I'm on a plane. How long has she been in transition?"

"She was not. She was dead."

"Her heart rate and BP say otherwise." She put an

electronic thermometer against Simone's ear and then checked the display. "Borderline hypothermic, but Kyn-normal." She removed a penlight from her coat. "Okay, sweetie, look at the annoying light for me. That's it."

Simone sat quietly through the examination, and the only time she flinched was when Alexandra produced a copper-tipped, open-ended syringe and some glass vials.

"I need to take a little blood now so I can use all the fancy equipment in my lab and see what's going on inside you. All right?" When Simone nodded, she began to draw the samples.

Korvel looked over as Simone's blood filled the first vial. "She handled both the scroll and the cross, Alexandra."

"I know." She exchanged vials.

He felt a surge of impatience. "They must have revived her."

"I thought every human who touched them died. Which reminds me," she said to Simone. "Were either of your parents Catholic, or maybe born in America?"

"I don't think so," Simone said. "My father was born in Garbia. Mother was a prostitute in Paris."

"At least you had a two-legged mother. Evidently mine was a Petri dish in some mad scientist's lab." She saw Simone's expression. "What's wrong?"

"It's not rudeness," Simone told Korvel. "She is only trying to help."

"He didn't say a word," Alexandra said, at the same time Korvel told her, "I didn't speak."

"You said the doctor should not speak so rudely to me. I heard you." She looked from Korvel to Alexandra. "Didn't you hear him?"

"She couldn't," Korvel said slowly. "I was thinking it."

"It could be part of the bond between you two," Alexandra said as she began packing up her case. "Sometimes Michael and I finish each other's sentences. It's probably best if you keep this to yourself," she added. "Bond stuff is private."

"You don't believe any of that," Simone said. "You also don't want the high lord to know about this." When the doctor didn't reply, she got to her feet. "Why?"

Alexandra ignored the question. "Okay, we've got telepathy. Captain, we have to get her out of here. I suggest now. I've got the Learjet waiting on the mainland; she can come back to America with me."

He nodded. "I am grateful for the generous offer, my lady. Would you give us a moment alone, please?"

She nodded, picked up her case, and left.

"Why must I leave now?" Simone asked. "I am one of you. You said I was."

"Come here, love." When she did, he swept her up and carried her to the large chair beside the hearth. "Alexandra's Kyn ability allows her to read the minds of some of the Kyn. Before she changed, no Darkyn ever had that talent." He took her hand in his. "But Alexandra's ability is also limited. She can only read the thoughts of killers, or those planning to kill. If you could read my mind and hers, then it seems you have the ability to read any Kyn mind."

"Why does that mean I have to leave you?"

"As Kyn you are now subject to Richard's rule. If he discovers the nature of your talent, he will command you to remain here so he can make use of it." He hesitated before he added, "There is someone who has the power to invade our minds and take control of our bodies. It has done this to the high lord tonight. He will not rest until he discovers who can do this—and once he learns of your ability, he will use you to find him."

"I'm not leaving you, and he can't use me." She got to her feet. "It's time to introduce the high lord to Helada."

"Absolutely not," he said flatly.

"I know what I'm doing." She held out her hand. "Trust me, please."

Korvel rose and took her by the shoulders. "You would have a good life in America. Alexandra would make sure of it."

She smiled up at him. "Not without my husband."

He tried to persuade her to change her mind as they walked from the room to Richard's study, but Simone assured him she knew what she was doing.

Richard sat by the fire reading a book, and nodded as Korvel bowed and Simone dropped into an elegant curtsey. "You are recovered?"

"Yes, my lord." She turned to Korvel. "Captain, would you perform the introductions?"

"My lord Tremayne, this is Simone Derien, sentinel sworn to the *tresoran* council, daughter of Derien of Château Niege, and the last surviving member of Cristophe Noir's mortal bloodline." When she gave him a pointed look, he reluctantly added, "She is also known as Helada."

The book fell to the floor before Richard seemed to recover his composure. "I always suspected that Helada was mortal."

"As I was, until today," she agreed. "Dr. Keller says I have made the change. So now Helada is truly immortal."

The high lord jumped to his feet. "The agreement was made with Cristophe's mortal family. You no longer belong to them. You are mine."

"I think the *tresoran* council will convince you otherwise." She looked at Korvel. "My family took an oath to serve the council under the rule of lineage. For as long as there are Deriens, faith can never be broken."

Richard uttered a low growl. "It was not meant to include mortals made Kyn."

"Neither does it exclude them, my lord," Simone said politely. "But perhaps we can renegotiate the terms."

The high lord moved away from them, going to stand before the windows that overlooked his gardens. "What do you want?"

"Freedom," she said simply.

"We are none of us free, my lady," Richard advised her. "Nor will I allow the two of you to run about the continent. We have more than enough rogues to contend with presently." His eyes shifted to Korvel. "This thing that spoke in our minds and controlled our limbs must be found. I will not tolerate such attacks. I expect you to lead the hunt."

Korvel considered telling him about the shadowy presence he had seen both in Jamaica and on the other side of Simone's funeral pyre. But if he revealed what he knew, Richard would never release him.

"I would not know where to look, and my hunting days are finished, my lord," he said at last. "Lord Gabriel has offered me a place in his household. I would like to accept it."

"Gabriel's household consists of exactly one razor-tongued shrew, who has never made oath to anyone or anything," the high lord said. "He refuses rule of Ireland, and so he has no territory, no stronghold, and no power."

"When we join him, I will transfer ownership to him of my father's properties, which are considerable," Simone suggested. "I will also increase his household to fifty-three. I should have mentioned I have my own garrison."

"Oh, of course you do." Richard turned around and regarded Korvel. "And you. You swore to spend your life in service to me. In the hour when I need you most, when I depend on your loyalty, you disobey my orders and ignore your duties. Where is my due, Captain?"

"Your due?" Korvel's hands curled into fists. "I made that oath as a mortal child, outcast and terrified. You preyed on my fears and took advantage of my despair."

"I see you recall the wretched condition in which you came to me," the high lord said. "A pity you have no gratitude for what I gave you in exchange for your service."

"What you gave me? You made me your prisoner," Korvel said. "My sentence, which should have lasted only a few dozen years, has continued for seven centuries and more. In all that time I have served you without question, my lord, even when I came to know what you did to me."

Richard uttered a laugh. "And what did I do to you, boy, but save you from starving in the hedgerows?"

"You knew what was happening to you when you returned from the Holy Land. You played God when you decided that I should not die a mortal death. You abused my faith in that oath until you almost destroyed my sanity and my soul. But I will give you your due this one last time." He drew his sword and thrust it into the floor between them. "My fate is yours. Release me or kill me."

Richard gazed down at the quivering hilt of the sword before he took hold of it and held it aloft. Several long seconds passed before he called out for his guard.

Simone took Korvel's hand as the two warriors came to flank him.

The high lord stepped forward. "You vowed by bond of blood to serve me and my house, and to obey me in all things. By disobedience and insolence you have broken that vow and released me from my obligations to you."

Korvel had thought the words would feel like blows, but instead he felt the chains inside him snapping, link by link.

Richard pulled back his hood and regarded the men on either side of Korvel. "Stefan, Howarth, I call on you as witnesses, and declare that this man has broken faith with me. He no longer holds position in my household or rank among the Kyn. His weapons and possessions will be confiscated, his privileges revoked."

It wasn't until the high lord inverted the blade and offered the hilt to Korvel that he felt the last chain, the one that had for so long imprisoned his soul, fall away.

"Korvel the bastard, I discharge you from my household. From this day forth, you no longer serve me as seneschal."

Epilogue

November 7, 2011
Somewhere in Provence

The vineyards surrounding the old château, which had once employed half the village, had not been worked for many years. All mourned the day the land had been bought from its elderly owners by a speculator, and when the property became an asset squabbled over during his subsequent lengthy bankruptcy, predictions of doom began to spread.

Ultimately the château and all the vineyards went to a bank in Paris, to be sold off again to the highest bidder. This, of course, would probably be some foreigner determined to renovate it into a profitable obscenity that would turn the village into another tourist trap. Dour bets were placed as to whether the new owners would convert the winery into a factory for cheap ceramics, a New Age cultists' retreat, or a backpacker hostel.

News of the sale reached the village, which initially rejoiced to learn a young couple had purchased it. To add to the excitement, it was rumored that they intended to keep it as a winery and start their own label. That joy crashed into renewed desolation when the owner was revealed to be an Englishman. Only when the Realtor also let it slip that he had a French wife did the locals decide that he must have some brains, and all was not lost.

En effet, he could have been married to an Englishwoman.

Simone lit the candle in the center of the old millstone table before she went to sit on the edge of the retaining wall. The music she had left playing in the house drifted out through the windows, coloring the frosty air with the wild, cascading sweetness of Debussy's First Arabesque. Tonight it brought her the same languid pleasure as the blue silk dress she wore. She could feel the frost like tiny crystals in the air, but the cold never bothered her now. Almost nothing did.

While the encroaching winter had stripped most of the leaves from the olives and the cypresses around the old château, and gleaned all of the fields in the valley to brown stubble, she could still smell the lavender in the air. It reminded her of the convent, which still remained deserted, and the sisters, all of whom had been relocated to a new sanctuary in Italy. Gabriel had inquired after them for her, and assured her that the council had them well protected.

Nicola had set up a secure computer system for Korvel, and Simone used it to contact each of her brothers. While she had used them like a threat against Richard, she had no intentions of further intruding on their lives, and tried to release them from the oath of loyalty they had been forced to make. She still couldn't quite believe they had all flatly refused, or that so many would soon be relocating to Provence to be near her and Korvel.

Alexandra Keller had called from America to tell

Simone about the strange green particles she had discovered in the samples of blood she had taken from her. "I intended to test them and confirm that they were fragments of these emeralds Richard wants, but when I took the sample out of the centrifuge they were gone. The pathogen responsible for making you Darkyn probably ate them. What I want to know is, how did they get into your bloodstream?"

"Pájaro struck me in the head with the cross," Simone told her. She recalled the tiny green glitter she had seen just before he'd hit her. "Perhaps it still had some power left in it."

"You're not going to tell me what you know about these emeralds, are you?" Alex said, and then answered herself with, "Good idea."

The little black dog came out of the woods first, racing up to the terrace to leap the wall and bounce around her, finally balancing on her hind legs as she pawed Simone's skirt. Her sharp, excited barks soon quieted to little grunts of pleasure as her mistress scratched behind her ears and across the white line of fur along her belly.

Simone gathered the puppy onto her lap as she watched the big man emerge from the shadows. His black woolen cloak flared as he removed it and hung it on a peg by the back door.

The puppy, already accustomed to the daily routine, jumped down and raced around her master's boots before she darted inside for her water bowl and the chew toy she had nearly gnawed in half.

Long flaxen hair fell in a curtain around Simone's face as Korvel bent to kiss the end of her nose. He smelled of earth and larkspur, and she brushed a bit of soil from his shoulder. "What have you been doing?"

"Walking the perimeter. Running after the dog. Inspecting the south vineyard. Wishing for a leash." He sat down beside her. "The soil is rich, and once spring comes and I've cleared the land, I think we can begin planting."

It had been only two weeks since they had moved into the château, and already it felt like a home. She had considered burning the summons sitting in the pocket of her apron, but that would not make it go away.

"This came while you were out." She handed it to him. "It's from Richard." As he crumpled it in his fist, she touched the back of his hand. "You should read it."

He unfolded and smoothed out the paper, scanning the brief message. " 'Rule of Ireland bestowed on the Kyn warrior who finds the Emeralds of Eternity.' How like him to turn foolishness into sport." He looked up at her. "Gabriel knows of this?"

She nodded. "Nick called soon after the courier left. She said that the summons made Gabriel laugh and that we shouldn't 'sweat it.' "

"Richard publicly insults him, and he finds it amusing." Korvel threw the paper across the terrace and watched the puppy race out, snatch it up, and carry it back into the house. "Now she will piddle on it."

"Better that than the rugs." She stood up and encircled his neck with her arms. "No one will come looking for me. Simone Derien died in Jamaica defending the cross. Now there is only Simone Cavelle, and this house in the hills, and the vineyards, and the dog that needs a leash." She sniffed at his shirt. "And her husband, who needs a bath, and his back scrubbed, and as many kisses as he wants."

He picked her up off her feet. "How much do you like this dress?"

Glossary

Aucune Sollicitation: No solicitation

Agenouillé-toi: Kneel down (command given to a horse)

Arrête: Stop, that's enough

Arts Africains: African art

Au revoir: Good-bye, until we meet again

Banlieues: Apartment buildings in metropolitan French cities built to provide housing for immigrants

Bonne chance: Good luck

Chérie: Darling

Cinq: Five

Clos Lucé: A manor house in Amboise where Leonardo da Vinci lived and worked at the invitation of the French king

Coucou: Hi, there (informal)

Couture: Dressmaking

Dix: Ten

Doucement: Easy (command given to a horse)

En effet: Indeed

En le chiffre noir: In the night code

Et alors: So what, big deal

Gendarmes: French police

Huit: Eight

Il n'y a pas de quoi: You're welcome (literally means "It was nothing" or "Nothing to thank me for")

L'attrait: The pheremonal body scent given off by Darkyn to lure and control humans (literally "the attraction")

Lapin: Rabbit

La Roseraie: The Rose Garden

La Théière Verte: The Green Teapot

Les anglais: The English

Les détectives: The detectives

Lève-toi: Rise (command given to a horse)

Ma belle, ma belle amie: My beautiful one

Ma petite amie: My girl (affectionate)

Ma sœur: My sister

Madame: Ma'am, Mrs.

Mademoiselle: Miss

Maman: Mother, Mama

Mais oui: Yes, of course, very much so

Maudite garce: Damned bitch

Merci: Thank you

Mon ami: My friend

Mon Dieu: My God

Mon frère: My brother

Monsieur: Sir, mister

Mourvèdre: The French name for a variety of dark blue, heavy-skinned grapes used to make red and rosé wine. Sometimes referred to as Balzac or Mataró.

Nautonnier: Navigator (Old French)

Neuf: Nine

Non: No

Oui: Yes

Propriété privée: Private property

Quarante: Forty

Quartier: Quarter, section

Quatorze: Fourteen

Reste: Stay (command given to a horse)

Salle des États: The location within the Musée du Louvre in Paris where Leonardo da Vinci's *Mona Lisa* is currently on display

Santon: A small, hand-painted clay figurine used to portray various characters in Nativity scenes

Seize: Sixteen

S'il vous plaît: Please

Sud: South

Trente: Thirty

Vous désirez: Can I help you?

Read on for a preview of

Nightbred
by Lynn Viehl

Available from Signet
in December 2012.

"So Richard offers rule of Ireland in exchange for some lost baubles. If I'd known that was the sole requirement, I'd never have crossed the pond." Lucan rolled up the summons Jamys Durand had given him and passed it to Burke. "I thank you for delivering it. Shall I have young Chris drive you back to the airport?"

Jamys hesitated. To remain in South Florida long enough to search for the Emeralds of Eternity, he would have to request permission for an extended visit. Lucan would want to know why, and if he told him the truth, it would probably result in a call to Thierry Durand. The moment Jamys's father discovered his son had joined the quest for the lost gems, he would order him back to North Carolina.

A warm hand touched the back of his. "With your permission, Suzerain, Lord Durand would like to stay for a few days," Christian Lang said. "He's been looking forward to spending some time with you and your lady and his friends among the household."

"Has he?" Lucan eyed the girl.

Jamys hid his surprise and inclined his head in agreement.

"Still having trouble getting the words out?" A glimmer of sympathy warmed the suzerain's silvery eyes. "Well, we've plenty of mortals around the place to help you with that. Chris, since you're already acquainted with Jamys, you can look after him while he's here." He rose from his chair. "Now, if you'll excuse me, I have to go collect my *sygkenis* before she spends the whole of the night filling out police forms in triplicate."

"My lord, perhaps you should text her first," Burke said as he followed Lucan out of the room.

At last Jamys was alone with Chris, and he turned his hand to catch hers as he projected his thoughts. *What have they done to you?*

"Done? Nothing." She lowered her voice before she added, "I'm sorry. I know I shouldn't have jumped in like that, but I got the feeling you didn't want to play twenty questions."

I don't mean that. He looked at her dark brown hair, which she wore in a sleek twist, and then all over her face, which had been made up with sheer, neutral cosmetics but no longer sported any piercings. The only jewelry she wore, in fact, was two blue pearl studs in her ears and a short, matching strand around her throat. *Why do you look like this?*

She glanced down at the front of her tailored navy blue suit. "This is what I wear to work." Her lips curved in an impersonal smile as she extracted her hand from his. "Would you like a tour of the stronghold? The suzerain has made quite a few changes since your last visit."

Jamys had no interest in going anywhere until Chris gave him some answers. Somehow during the three years they had been apart, Lucan and his *sygkenis* had turned the rebellious, fiercely loyal girl he had known into this polite, cool stranger. If he had not imprinted her features so deeply in his memory, he might not even have recognized her.

"If you'd rather have someone else assigned to you, I can ask Mr. Burke who's available," Chris was saying, this time without the smile. "You just have to let me know what sort of girl you'd like. There's a very pretty woman who runs our property management office downtown. She's a blonde. We also have a redhead who manages the restaurant Lucan just bought over on Las Olas—"

"No." He held up his hand to stop her. "You. I want you."

The words came out too rough, like the growl of an animal, but he had not used his voice to speak in so long, it was already beginning to fail him. He wanted to touch Chris again, and this time channel his thoughts into hers, to make her understand that he had come back in order to win her. Given the force of his emotions, however, doing so would also have triggered his talent, which made any mortal in his presence think or do or say anything Jamys wished.

He wanted Chris in every way he could have her, and under the influence of his talent, she would give herself to him completely. For as long as they were together, she would even believe it was her idea.

Nothing had ever tempted him more than the prospect of using his talent to command Chris's affection and passion. Back at his father's stronghold, he had often thought of it, and in the dark corners of his heart, he knew himself capable of it. He wanted her that much. But to turn this bright and beautiful girl into his personal puppet would have been a horrendous transgression—one that would render meaningless everything he felt for her.

If Chris came to him, it had to be without his coercion. He wouldn't have her any other way but willingly.

"You sound tired." Chris reached out to him, but when he stepped aside to prevent the physical contact, she snatched her hand back. "I'm sorry. I ... I should show you to your rooms now."

Chris had hidden from everyone her feelings for Jamys, but to cope with the loneliness she'd been forced to put her dreams and desires on ice. Now she wanted to throw herself at him, and cling to him, and tell him how hard it had been to train and wait and hope. She wanted him to know it was all for him. Everything.

And the moment she did that, he would gently set her aside, call for Burke and have the blonde from downtown or the redhead from the restaurant take her place.

She had to get out of the suite and away from him, now, before she made a complete ninny out of herself. What hadn't she told him about the rooms? "The blinds are on a timer, and close automatically thirty minutes before sunrise. They don't open again until thirty minutes after sunset." She squared her shoulders and walked over to show him the manual pulls hidden inside the end panels. "The windows on this floor are sealed, but the transoms open if you want some fresh air. The doors also lock automatically, so you'll need to carry this access card with you."

She reached into her jacket to retrieve the one she'd programmed for him. Pain made her hiss as the shard of broken glass in her pocket sliced across her fingertips.

"Excuse me." She kept her hand in her pocket and hurried into the adjoining bathroom.

Chris held her bleeding hand over the frost blue bowl of glass that served as the sink, and winced as cold water from the automatic tap washed over the open cuts. Because the Kyn healed spontaneously she hadn't thought to stock the suite with a first-aid kit; she'd have to wrap some tissue around her hand until she could get back downstairs.

"You're wounded."

The rough whisper of his voice across the bare back of her neck made her close her eyes briefly. Jamys knew she was hurt because he smelled the fresh blood; the Kyn were almost like sharks that way.

"I cut myself on a piece of glass I had in my pocket." She reached for the box of tissues, but Jamys had her bleeding hand in his and was examining the small wounds. "It's nothing."

His eyes shifted to hers, and she saw a thin ring of glowing amber encircling his pupils, which had begun to contract to thin vertical slivers. *Why did you wish to hide it from me? Did you think I would feed on you?*

The force of his thoughts pouring into her mind shocked her into honesty. "No. I was embarrassed because I was clumsy." From the look he gave her, it was clear that he didn't believe her. "I've been assigned to you, my lord, and I'm trained to take care of your needs. If you want the blood, I'll go get a glass."

Jamys kept his eyes on hers as he slowly lifted her injured hand to his mouth. His *dents acérées* flashed for a moment before he sank them into heel of his own hand.

Chris caught her breath as he raised his head. Two drops of blood beaded in the small puncture wounds that were already beginning to close. "What are you doing?"

Jamys guided one of her hurt fingers to his palm, and gently pressed the cut into the blood. Chris caught her breath as she felt the cool mingling of his blood with hers, and then her cut went numb. He repeated the act again with her other finger, and then used a tissue to blot the blood away.

Chris saw that both of her cuts had closed, just as fast as the punctures in his palm. "Jamys?"

You are not my food, Christian, nor are you my servant. He put his hand to the back of her head, holding it as he pressed a kiss to her brow. *You are my friend.*

"Friendship works for me." No, it didn't, but he wasn't asking for someone else. At least he still liked her. "Your eyes are doing the cat thing, though, and I know that means you haven't fed for a while. Or you want to have wild monkey sex. Or both." Had she actually said that out loud? God, she had. "I'll, um, go make a glass of bloodwine for you."

I have no desire to have sex with a wild monkey. Jamys removed the long comb holding her hair back and placed it on the counter. As the twist slumped against her nape, he worked his hand through it, releasing the wavy mass. *The last time I saw you, your hair was scarlet.*

"Mud brown is what I was born with." She knew with her hair down she looked about sixteen, too. "I stopped dyeing it after you left."

His finger stilled as he found the one hair pin she wore to keep her silver streak out of sight.

"That's not dyed, either," she admitted. "I started going gray in high school."

You should not conceal it. He spread the strands out. *It does not make you look older. It is beautiful.*

"I don't think anyone but Lady Gaga agrees with you." As he brought the silvery lock to his lips, Chris forgot to breathe. "You're kissing my hair."

It feels like gossamer. He smoothed it back and looked all over her face. *Your piercings are gone.*

"No one takes you seriously when you wear rings in your eyebrow, so I let them close up." Absently she touched a tiny scar on the curve of her lip, and then she understood why he hadn't recognized her at first. "You were expecting me to look the way I did three years ago?"

That is how you were in my memories. He touched each place where she had been pierced, and when he reached her lip, he ran his thumb back and forth over the small dimple. *Now you seem so different.*

"I'm not the same girl I was. I grew up. Everyone does, even if they're Kyn and they don't age. You've changed, too." She eyed the black hair spilling over his shoulders. "You've nailed the ponytail look, I think, but how did you get all this new muscle?"

Suddenly he looked tired and unhappy. *I have also been in training.*

What was wrong with him? Was she being too much of a pest? Was he sick of her already? "Is there anything else I can do for you?"

He turned his head as a three-tone chime sounded. *What is that?*

"Someone's at the door. Probably Burke." Chris sighed. "He worries."

She didn't find Burke waiting in hall; instead, one of the visiting Kyn stood outside the suite. As soon as Chris opened the door, the strong scent of almonds wafted over her, and she had to swallow a groan. It was the same troublemaker who had started the brawl in the armory.

Why is he on this floor? "May I help you, sir?"

"There ye are, Pearl Girl." His lips peeled back from his white teeth and fully emerged fangs. "The bald one said ye were occupied, but I suspected if I tracked ye, I'd find ye alone." He swiped at her wrist and then frowned when she moved out of reach. "Come, I would have ye before the night wanes away."

Have me? No Darkyn male had ever come after her demanding blood or sex, and for a second, she wanted to slap him. But Burke had warned her that European Kyn did things differently; evidently they expected to help themselves to the household humans. Lucan would have no problem with her refusing him, but he would expect her to do so without turning it into an international immortal incident.

"I'm sorry, sir, but I'm not available to serve you tonight." *Or for the rest of eternity, you pretentious ape.* "I'll be happy to call down to Mr. Burke—"

"I want no other." He gave her the once-over and breathed in. "Not been taken tonight, then? Be they blind in this stronghold? Never worry. I'll put ye to good use." He crossed the threshold and, when she backed away, leered at her. "No need to play shy, Pearl Girl. I know how it is with ye household wenches." He stopped advancing and frowned past her. "What is this?"

She glanced over her shoulder to see Jamys just behind her, his eyes glowing, his expression as lethal as the long copper blades in his fists. "This would be the reason I'm not available, sir."

New York Times bestselling author

LYNN VIEHL

Shadowlight
The first novel of the Kyndred

With just one touch, Jessa Bellamy can see anyone's darkest secrets, thanks to whoever tampered with her genes. What she doesn't know is that a biotech company has discovered her talent and intends to kill her and harvest her priceless DNA...

Gaven Matthias is forced to abduct Jessa himself so he can protect her, but Jessa has a hard time believing the one man whose secrets she can't read. As a monstrous assassin closes in and forces them to run, Jessa will have to find another way to discover if Matthias is her greatest ally—or her deadliest enemy.

"Lynn Viehl sure knows how to tell a hell of a story."
—Romance Reviews Today

Available wherever books are sold or at
penguin.com

S0067

New York Times bestselling author

LYNN VIEHL

The Novels of the Kyndred

Dreamveil

Rowan Dietrich grew up on the streets. Now she's out to start anew, find a job—and keep her identity as a Kyndred secret, as well as her ability to "dreamveil" herself into the object of others' desires. But Rowan isn't using her gift when world-class chef Jean-Marc Dansant is stricken by her beauty and strength. And when dark secrets from her past threaten her new life and love, she realizes she can't run forever...

Frostfire

As one of the genetically enhanced Kyndred, Lilah's mind-reading powers make her vulnerable to a mysterious biotech company willing to murder to acquire her superhuman DNA. But her true fear may come from her own Kyndred brethren...

Nightshine

As a psychic, Samuel Taske can see the future, but he never predicted that he'd fall for San Francisco paramedic Charlotte Marena, the woman he's been charged with protecting. GenHance—the biotech company willing to do anything to acquire superhuman DNA—is after them. And when Samuel discovers that his Takyn powers have abandoned him, Charlie and her secret nighttime telepathic ability are their only hope for survival...

Available wherever books are sold or at
penguin.com